# RENEGADE ANGEL

An **ASTRAL HEAT** ROMANCE 2

# LAURA NAVARRE

# CHAPTER ONE
## The Duel

As a notorious scourge-of-the-galaxy space pirate, Zorin had survived a lifetime of guys trying to kill him. He'd even survived having interstellar war declared on his ass by Dex Draven, First Indomitable of the Mogadon Empire.

The guy who was Zorin's ultimate nemesis, his mouthwatering obsession, and the galaxy's premier military power.

But after four-plus decades of nick-of-time near misses, it turned out what was gonna kill him was the girl. The girl he'd fallen for harder than an asteroid collision. The girl whose bed he'd laid his life on the line to compete for, against five hundred ambitious, aggressive, testosterone-fueled yahoos, in the galactic mating contest called the Tombola.

To be real specific, what would kill him—or at least paralyze him, pretty much permanently—was the nerve gun his opponent in the fighting pit was pointing at Zorin's chest.

And Dex Draven, in his role as referee and master emcee, was gonna see it happen. Maybe once he did, he'd finally find his way past that whole butchering-Dex's-psychopath-dad-in-cold-blood incident that had gotten Zorin exiled from Mogadon, back in his prior-to-being-a-pirate days. Back when Zorin was First Indomitable himself.

Maybe.

But Zorin didn't plan to stand here, dead in space like a stalled starship, and let it all go down. Not when his girl was counting on him to survive.

And counting on him to win.

Ten cubits away in the blood-spattered clay of the fighting pit, ringed by tiers of screaming spectators, his opponent grinned at him. The guy was half his size—hard-faced, sorrel-skinned, lean and wiry under the colorful robes and battle-scarf of a Kryllian bloodletter. Which was how the bastard had smuggled an illegal weapon into the pit for what was supposed to be strictly an unarmed throwdown.

A stricture that should've ruled out the microfiber steel net the Kryll had just flung over Zorin's sorry carcass to pin him down.

That net was complicating the heck out of Zorin's survival odds. *Well, shoot.*

Kaia of Kryll had been crystal clear from the get-go. Being tamely auctioned off to any joe in the show by her tyrannical dad was never part of her game plan. The fact that Zorin, out of all five hundred wannabe consorts in this galactic shindig, ended up being the guy who turned her crank?

He was one lucky sonofabitch.

And he wasn't gonna let his girl down. His rebel princess, his Tombola prize, his Prime Class cyber samurai.

Too bad all his struggles only tightened the net.

A guy could escape an unbreakable steel net in one of two ways. He could pick his way free with time. Or he could cut his way free with a blowtorch.

Zorin, right then and there, didn't even have a match.

"Come on, you big galoot," he muttered to himself. "Think it through."

Meanwhile, the Kryll was taking his sweet time lining up the kill shot with his contraband nerve gun. A gun that was outlawed across the galaxy due to that whole permanent paralysis issue.

Above him in the viewing box, Kaia was leaping to her booted feet—a breath away from drawing her cyber saber and flinging her furious body into the fray in his defense. In his periphery, Dex was charging into the pit, shouting rules and prohibitions despite the fact no one in this madhouse gave a single flaming shit. Because it turned out this hootenanny wasn't a ritual contest. Not anymore.

It was a hit job.

And the *only* reason that Kryll would be aiming a disqualifying nerve gun at Zorin's ugly hide was because someone had paid the guy to do it.

All around him in the arena's humid heat, his competitors were on their feet howling for his blood. Zorin's Syndax pirates—his best boys, brought aboard Dex's battleship to cover his six as they shot through space—were drawing their blasters and converging on the pit. Too bad for Zorin they were all moving way too slow.

The gamy scent of Mogadon pheromones flooded the air. That head-spinning hit of his own aggression gave him a biochemical kick in the pants, just the way Mogadon genetics intended. Adrenaline spiked his pulse and roughened his breath.

Danger streaking through his senses like a meteor shower, rage spurting through his veins like liquid nitrogen, he watched the Kryll's finger tighten on the trigger.

*Way* too close to miss.

Trapped in that goddamn net like a Solarian sardine, Zorin did pretty much the only thing he could.

He dove.

Directly into the Kryll with the nerve gun.

#

The nerve gun discharged—a shrill *bzzzzt* that pierced her eardrum like a drill. The combatants crashed to the dirt in a single thrashing knot.

"Let *go* of me, damn you!" Twenty cubits above the fighting pit in the viewing box, Kaia raged and writhed in her lifemate's grip like a harpooned eel. "I'll flipping kill you for this!"

"Not on your life," Ben Nero ground in her ear. "You're not going anywhere near that nerve gun. Let Dex deal with it."

"But he hates Zorin!"

"Give Dex some credit, Kaia. He'll handle it."

Chains and dreadlocks streaming, Syndax pirates were hurtling into the pit. But they couldn't fire without risking Zorin, their leader. Responding with precision to his steely orders, Dex's elite praetorian guard wheeled into motion, training stun rifles on the seething mob— barely holding off a full-scale riot. Only Dex's incandescent glare kept the agitated Syndax at bay. Someone was shouting for a blowtorch.

Over the chaos, the struggling knot of limbs and net erupted in a scream. A scream that cut short with jarring sharpness.

The entangled figures went fatally still.

Kaia, too, went slack, heaving for air in Nero's arms. He held her tight against his lean length, eyes glued on the scene in the fighting pit.

None of it remotely appropriate according to the Tombola ritual's sacred dictates. Not the nerve gun, not her ex-boyfriend's hands all over her, not her obvious favor for the Syndax pirate.

And she cared not a nanoparticle. Her entire being was riveted on the deadly drama like a rocket. Sure, she'd only just met Zorin when the contest launched. But she'd known from the start he was the only one of those five hundred candidates she wanted in her bed.

Because Dex and Nero, the only other guys she'd ever wanted, couldn't even bid. Dex Draven was her Tombola master, bound by a treaty with her father that Dex couldn't break, committed to deliver her fiercely resistant body to the winning candidate. And Ben Nero, her psychic lifemate and the galaxy's most powerful telepath, was oathsworn to guarantee it all went down the way her godlike father demanded.

Formidable and stern in his black uniform, Dex closed in on the combatants with a blowtorch, blue flame spitting from the nozzle. Swiftly he peeled back the steel net.

"I think…" Nero whispered. Clearly relying on his telepathic Valyrian senses to tell him what his eyes couldn't.

"You think *what*?"

Because Kaia, a half-Valyrian hybrid and unreliable telepath herself, was way too agitated to think or feel anything but sheer screaming panic.

"I'd say 'Nobody panic,'" Zorin announced dryly, untangling himself from the net. His Kryll opponent lay poleaxed at his feet. "But somehow I got a feeling it's a little late."

The bristling Syndax were first to react, jubilant fists shooting skyward, shouts of triumph ripping from a dozen throats. Dex was already in motion, seizing the contraband weapon and flipping back the Kryll's battle-scarf.

The would-be assassin lay sprawled at a nauseating angle, head violently wrenched to one side.

"Snapped like a wishbone," Kaia whispered, shaking with a violent surge of satisfaction. "He won't be saying a word. We'll have to interrogate his brothers to sniff out who hired them. They're Kryllian bloodletters, trained assassins—so they won't be easy informants. Promise me you'll do it yourself."

*Because no one breathing can lie to you.*

"If his brothers aren't long gone by now." Gently Nero released her and stepped back. "Those two probably had a getaway shuttle in the hangar bay on standby. Looks like Dex is battening down the hatches."

Dex was muttering into his wrist unit, nerve gun secure in his belt. His grim cobalt gaze sliced from the raucous Syndax and the agitated mob to Zorin's monumental frame looming over the dead Kryll. Jaw clenched with steely necessity, light flashing on platinum epaulets, Dex strode to his side and raised Zorin's mailed arm briefly overhead.

"The Syndax will advance," Dex clipped out. "The Kryllian brothers are disqualified."

The pirates roared in rowdy acclaim, echoed this time by the rest of the hoi polloi. Around Kaia, the rattle and flash of creds changed hands. Zorin had won himself more than a few allies with that impressive maneuver. Huddled in anxious pockets around the viewing stand, an array of less murderous candidates for her bed muttered and shifted in unease.

Fervently she wished Dex could disqualify them all.

From the pit, one fist raised high in victory, Zorin lifted his head and looked straight at Kaia—the rugged lines of his face etched with anticipation and triumph. Despite the physical distance that yawned between them, the smoking heat in his aquamarine eyes seared through her like an electrical charge. Beneath the bronze silk of her cybersuit, her breasts felt swollen and her knees felt weak.

Damn it to the moon and back. He'd just nearly *died*.

And in that raw moment of naked knowledge, when fragile life had never felt more vital, she knew on a visceral level exactly what he needed.

"Ready room," she whispered, shaping the thought with her lips. Somehow knowing he'd hear her, even though non-telepaths often couldn't. "I'll find you."

Zorin held her gaze while heat pooled and pulsed between her legs, making her slick and wet.

Even while Dex dropped his arm like Zorin was garbage and pivoted to confront his volatile viewers.

"The names of the two hundred finalists will be broadcast over interstellar news at midnight." Dex pitched his voice to carry above the ripple of anticipation. "The contest resumes for the finalists tomorrow.

Transport from this battleship for the rest of you departs for the nearest spaceport at oh-one-hundred. I'd firmly advise each of you *not* to be late."

"In a rush to get rid of them, isn't he?" Nero turned to find Kaia halfway to the stairs. "Gods of Solaris, Kaia, wait!"

"Try to keep up—if you must." Without slowing, she swung energetically over the rail and scrambled down the stairs. "Because I definitely don't need a babysitter."

"Why the hells are you always running away?" he muttered, glowering at avid suitors to keep them at bay as Kaia powered past. "Drives me insane to be always chasing you."

"Feel free to stop anytime." She edged sideways to slip between the scrum of Syndax bunched outside the ready room with knives and blasters bristling. "I meant what I said last night."

"I assure you, so did I."

The harum-scarum horde eased readily aside for Kaia, appreciation gleaming in their wolfish eyes. But they closed ranks tight before Nero.

"Not you, pretty boy," one tattooed titan said with a sneer. "Zorin only wants *her*."

As tall as the Syndax but far less wide, Nero smoothed back a sleek curtain of raven hair from his sculpted face. And eyed the obstruction with interest. "I'm the Valyrian Precursor. The galaxy's ranking telepath. Which means I can pull your brains through your ears with a passing thought. Out of curiosity, how precisely do you propose to stop me?"

"Good gods, Ben! Don't you think we've seen enough slaughter for one day?" Impatience simmered in Kaia's blood, laced with an agitation she seemed helpless to control. "Do you honestly think Zorin would let anything happen to me?"

"Comets! You know you're not supposed to be alone with the candidates. Dex has been more than clear—"

"Dex isn't my father. And neither are you, Ben Nero."

"Let me put it this way." Over the pirate's chrome-studded shoulder, Nero's violet eyes smoldered hot with promise. "If you're about to give that Syndax a congratulatory kiss, I definitely want to watch. Maybe he'll even appreciate a private demonstration from the galaxy's leading expert on how to blow your circuits."

An alchemical sizzle of heat seared through her. An instinctive response to the arrogant accolade she reluctantly acknowledged he'd more than earned after the way he scorched her synapses when they'd finally come together last night—all without violating her no-penetration edict.

The problem was, after abandoning her and letting her believe he was dead in the biowar for eight flipping *years*, she'd rather swallow her own tongue than admit the way Ben Nero still made her feel.

"Blast it, Ben! I assure you I have zero intent—" She eyed the titillated pirates soaking up every syllable and finished coolly, "Why don't you make yourself useful and interrogate those Kryll for me. Because I can't stand the sight of them."

Spinning away before he could lob another sexually incendiary innuendo, she shrugged the curtain aside and escaped into the ready room.

Zorin stood in solitude, etched against the battleship's viewport, towering frame and shoulders blotting out the stars. His craggy profile snapped toward her with an alacrity that told her she wasn't the only one with fight-or-flight adrenaline still sparking through her circuits.

Not to mention sexual stimulation bubbling in her blood.

Shyness was an impulse she'd outgrown years ago. Because shyness wasn't any help at all for a circus acrobat or a runaway samurai with a vengeful god on her tail.

Now a powerfully inconvenient surge of shyness reared up and hammered her feet to the floor. Tongue-tied, hot-faced, she could only stand and stare. Knowing if she said a word, she'd stammer like a Prime Class simpleton.

Confronted with her dumbstruck silence, Zorin's scarred brow hitched. He even nodded like she'd said something he understood.

"It's real now, isn't it?" His deep voice rumbled through the starlit shadows.

Her tight throat unlocked to release a careful breath. "What's real?"

"You and me." One corner of his mouth lifted in a wry smile. "This is new to me too. It's okay to be afraid."

"I'm not afraid," she shot back by instinct.

But that was a lie, wasn't it? She'd barricaded herself from every man she'd ever met behind an unbreachable battlement. That vow of abstinence she'd made before she was old enough to know what it meant, soldered in place by the crisis of Ben Nero's betrayal, had become the armor she hid behind to keep anyone from getting too close.

Ever.

Now she was going to venture out of that protective shell for him. The guy standing before her. The guy who'd just killed a man to clear his path to her bed.

The guy she still barely knew.

"I'm not afraid," she repeated, to make herself believe it. "You're the one. The one I'll fly away with on the *Relentless* five days from now. Together we'll end this whole monstrous farce."

"Cuz I'm the only guy with a snowball's chance in a sun storm of taking on Dex." His tone was easy, but his eyes were wary. "Dex with his fleet and his nukes and his badass arsenal. You figure I'm your best bet to stop that galactic germ war he's threatening."

"Yeah." She leaped headlong for that face-saving logic. "That's pretty much why. I'm half Valyrian. One biowar was more than enough."

*Enough to eradicate eighty-eight percent of the Valyrian race.*

*Even if the last war was his dad's fault, Maximus Draven's been dead for years. So the next one's all on Dex.*

Carefully she cleared her throat. "That's why I wanted you… at first. To stop Dex and prevent the war. But… it's not the only reason."

His eyes never left her face.

Like he was waiting for something he didn't want to miss.

Her tongue traced her dry lips. "Do you even realize you're the only candidate in this Tombola who's offered me *freedom*? As in—the only one. I've read five hundred bids over the past two days. And yours is the only one that doesn't turn my stomach."

"Well, it's an honest offer. I want you willing and eager or not at all." A subtle tension threaded his voice. "But I'm not the only choice you got, am I. You don't think Dex would hand you the Mogadon moons or anything else in the universe you ever wanted? Just to keep you with him?"

"Dex?" Her bubbling agitation erupted. An eruption far too long suppressed. "Why are you asking me about Dex? He's my Tombola master. You know he's not an option!"

"It's a fair ask, Kaia. The kid and me—we go way back. I was Dex's mentor back on Mogadon. I'm the one who taught him to fight. The one who taught him to kill." His steely eyes hardened. "And I can smell his mating scent on you all the way over here. Long story short? He doesn't act like a guy who's planning to let you go."

"It's not up to him. He can't bid!" Her volume spiraled until she was all but shouting. "And that's a choice he made all on his own."

"A choice he made before he met you."

"A choice he can't revoke." She planted hands on hips and scowled. "Even if he wanted to—" *even if I wanted him to* "—he can't! He signed a binding treaty with my father. An ironclad pact for Kryll's merchant fleet to supply his battlefront. In exchange for Dex's service as arbiter and enforcer of this whole farking contest. If Dex voids the contest now by claiming me himself, he'll lose his war, his command, and probably his life."

*Because my flipping father will declare a kill edict on his Indomitable head. And Kryll's faithful fanatics—men like those bloodletters—will carry it out.*

"That might be a risk Dex is willing to take." Before her obstinate stance, Zorin's hard face softened. "Look. I might not know you the way I'd like. But he's a compelling guy, sweetheart, and I think he's caught your eye."

An uncomfortable heat climbed in her face. A heat she knew in her heart there was no point denying. Because the scourge of the galaxy was nobody's fool. And every word he said was true.

Shifting on her feet, she glanced aside. "I don't get it. Why are you arguing against your own interests?"

"Cuz I'm not so sure it's in my interest taking a consort who wants me solely for my military prowess and because I won't make her wear chains in my bed. Not to mention a consort who's already half in love with somebody else. Like a lotta folks, I've had consorts before. Everyone wants it to last forever, but it hardly ever does. This time's the real deal. Trust me to know what it takes to make this work."

Unable to meet his level gaze, she paced the shadowy confines of the ready room. "You make a fair point. You really do. Even though I'm not in love with him." *Why is this so farking hard to say?* "Anyway, um, I haven't been totally straight with you. Those aren't the only reasons I—I wanted you."

"No?" As solid and settled as she was jittery and jumpy, he leaned one armored hip against the wall and crossed his bulging arms. Starlight brought out the silver in his sandy hair.

"You know it's not," she whispered. She couldn't look at him. *Angels and asteroids, is he really going to make me say it?* "I want you because… I just… want you."

In the history of confessions, this wasn't much of one. But the heat of making it scorched through her until she thought her cybersuit would burst into flames. Slowly her gaze lifted to find him.

An outlaw. A space pirate. A wolf in blast armor.

Too smart to trick. Too strong to overpower. And probably too old for her to boot.

But the thought of climbing out of her armor and stripping him out of his and giving him everything he wanted from her—access she'd never given another man, had in fact been saving all her life just for him—made her weak with wanting.

"It's true," she said, throaty with the fever burning in her blood. "You say you want a woman who's eager for your bed? Trust me when I tell you that's not going to be a problem."

He hooked his big hands in his utility belt and lowered his head to eye her. "You got Dex's smell all over you. But Ben Nero says you spend your nights in *his* bed. The way I see it, you maybe got a thing for all three of us. That's a pretty big chance for an old guy like me to take, Kaia."

"I know. It's mixed up. It's just—I'm trying to figure things out." Her eyes pleaded for understanding. "I feel the way I feel. That's why I'm choosing you. What more do you want me to tell you?"

"Tell me?" His rough rasp sent shivers shooting down her spine. "Not a goddamn thing. Why don't you shimmy on over here and show me?"

Kaia's heart thundered like a war drum and every synapse in her body thrummed in a symphony of nerves. Tingling with tension, she prowled across the expanse of ready room floor that was all that stood between her and this Syndax pirate she'd chosen to mate.

*Steady on, samurai. This isn't your mating night. There's zero reason to be nervous.*

*Even if he is watching you like he's finally letting himself imagine what you're going to look like naked.*

He'd kept himself so carefully in check since the moment they'd met. When she didn't know who he was, when he let her do all the talking, when she fell toes over tailpipe for this interstellar menace until nothing else mattered except finding some way to be his.

He was always letting her take the lead.

Just so she wouldn't run away.

He'd kept whatever he felt himself so thoroughly under wraps that the raw hunger animating his war-hardened face right now felt as intimate as the slide of a hand down her naked spine.

Tonight was different. Because tonight he'd almost died. He'd snapped a man's neck with his bare hands to clear his path to her bed. And those genetic Mogadon instincts that still drove him even in exile were driving him now to claim her.

The prize he'd killed for.

The woman his most primitive self now saw as his exclusive property to protect and possess.

That image alone, that bare whisper from her erratic psychic senses of the primal imperatives that drove him, made her breath hitch and her pulse pitch. Beneath her cybersuit, she was slick with her own passion, her clit a swollen nub that chafed against her cybersilk with every step.

He was done waiting.

He wanted her.

And her entire body ached to give him everything he wanted.

Her eyes slid slowly up his frame, all size and strength and raw physical power encased in the starmetal mesh of his armor. Battle-scarred space boots and thickly muscled thighs spread to claim the space around him, biceps bulging in the arms folded across his chest, broad shoulders blotting out the stars.

She wanted to drop to her knees and wrap her mouth around his cock. She wanted to climb him like a tree and wrap her legs around him and let him sink deep inside her the way no other man had ever done. She wanted him to ride her until she forgot her own name.

She wanted to feel him come inside her.

She wanted him to sire the son the prophecy said she had in her.

"Mars," he breathed, raw and ragged with wanting. "A guy could get used to the way you look at me. Better warn you I'm about six ticks away from tossing you over my shoulder and taking you back with me to the *Relentless*. And to hell with the auction. You're mine."

She added an extra sway to her hips and watched his eyes darken to navy. "That doesn't sound very civilized."

"I'm a space pirate, sweetheart. I don't do civilized all that well. Never have." One tawny brow hitched. "Neither do you, by the way."

"To everyone's dismay." She laughed, but it held a bitter edge.

"Not mine," he fired back, gruff with anticipation. "I know what I'm getting. And I wouldn't change a goddamn thing."

"Right back at you," she whispered, low in her throat.

Two cubits away, she tilted her head and looked up at him. He was way too tall for what she had in mind.

She put her back to the viewport and hopped lithely to the ledge, using her acrobat's strength to swing her bottom up to sit. He was still taller than she wanted.

But not by much.

Booted legs dangling, gaze never leaving his, she spread her knees wide in invitation and hooked a hand in his belt to pull him close.

A growl rose from his cavernous chest. He planted one big hand on either side of her hips and moved into her space. She ducked her head to study his hands, her slim fingers sliding over scarred knuckles and calloused skin, and heard the harsh husk of his breath.

Plenty of women would find him brutal. Even terrifying. All that size and unapologetic violence.

But not her.

She wanted it—wanted *him*—wanted the threat and the promise of everything he wanted with an intensity that made her entire body throb.

Leaving her hands over his—a silent plea for restraint she didn't know if he'd heed—she let her eyes rise over his mighty chest and muscled neck and the strong line of his jaw. The golden glitter of day's-end stubble tempted her to touch. And his eyes, locked on hers like heat-seeking missiles, were so intense she couldn't sustain his stare.

Keeping her hands where they were, she leaned in carefully and touched her lips to the rough bristle of his cheek. His sharp exhale rushed out. He'd been holding his breath. The sudden scent of steel and predator rose dark and hot from his skin.

The intoxicating essence of mating scent.

"I know I barely know you," she whispered in his ear. "But I really, really like you."

"Show me how much—" His voice broke as her tongue traced his ear. His hands tensed beneath her palms and a groan rumbled from his throat.

"You like this, don't you?" She licked the hot salty skin under his ear and felt his pulse jump. "And this?"

"Your mouth on me anywhere, answer's gonna be yes." He sounded strangled with the effort of restraint.

Tingling with the energy that leaped between them, she backed away just a little and leaned in to kiss his other cheek, stubble abrading her tender skin.

"I like your strength," she breathed in his ear, just to feel him shiver. "I like your restraint and I like your patience. I like when you're brutal and savage like you were in the pit. I like the way you feel safe and the way you feel dangerous—all at the same time."

She pulled back and leaned close, his lips a breath away. "But most of all, Zorin the pirate, I like the way you make me feel. Like there's no part of me you aren't going to own."

With a harsh sound, he leaned in and kissed her. Fusing them together with his mouth on hers, tongue meeting tongue, hot and fierce with need. Demanding the response she'd been born to give. He tasted like sex and violence held barely in check. And just the feel of his mouth on hers ignited the dormant volcano of craving deep inside and made her burn with an aching caldera of need.

*Gods, I need you. Need you inside me. You're going to be the one. And I don't think I can wait.*

She moaned and leaned into him, arms wrapping around his neck, hands threading through the short rough spikes of his hair. His hands closed over her thighs and dragged her hard against his bulk. Her legs wound around his hips and his armored cock nudged her clit.

"Please," she panted, rocking into his heat, hardly knowing what she was begging for. Just knowing she needed more than she was getting. "Please—I need—*more*. I need more of you."

"I'll conquer worlds and lay them at your feet. Every star system my army claims is another realm for you to rule." He leaned his brow against hers while they both fought for breath and her body begged him to ride her. "Just let me look at you. Let me at least do that much. I've been imagining you in my bed since the moment we met. I'm gonna lose my mind if I can't see the real you. *All* of you."

She closed her eyes against the molten metal of his stare and whispered, "Yes."

At that point, she would've said yes to anything if he was the one asking.

And she trusted him not to abuse the privilege.

His hands spanned her waist and eased up to find the tender fullness of her breasts. She arched her back to push into his touch, head falling back, stars swimming in her eyes. She heard the buzz of a zipper, felt her bodice release, shivered when the frigid cold of space through the viewport licked along her naked spine.

He muttered something rough and reverent in a language she didn't know.

Then his palms chafed her naked nipples. Twin jets of tingling pleasure shot through her. Straight to the pounding need between her thighs. The sudden musk of her own juices, hot and slick and pumping, mingled with the wolfish whiff of his mating scent.

He breathed her in deep and growled like the apex predator he was. His hands slid her cybersuit to her waist. Her wrists tangled in her sleeves' tight fabric, snared in her Valyrian torques. That paralyzing pleasure immobilized her—exposed and helpless as a harem slave. Hard fingers cradled her breasts and tweaked her nipples. He was different from Ben, his touch less polished and a lot more rough. His pace less thoroughbred and a lot more draft horse.

Her hips thrust against him with panting need. Desperate for the starmetal friction of his cock.

"Jumpin' Jupiter," he said hoarsely, "you like that, don't you? Being tied up while I work you."

"Seems so," she gasped, head falling back to give him more access. *Who'd have thought?* "Gods, Zorin. I never even… knew I wanted…"

"To be restrained? Sometimes what turns us on is what scares us. And you like it a little rough too, don'tcha?" His growl sent a shiver skidding down her spine that answered him without her having to say a word. "We can do this any way you want. You can't hurt me. And it makes me crazy that you smell like Dex. You're *mine*."

One solid arm slid around her back to close off her escape, but she only pressed harder into his heat. One deft pull of his hand, hard enough to sting, released the knot that held her hair. It slid down her back like a silk curtain. His mouth seared her breast, hard lips closing over one tingling nipple—the scrape of teeth over sensitized skin, the pulse of pleasure between her legs. She cried out and clamped her legs around him, booted heels digging urgently into the hard bulge of his ass.

That dark savage scent poured from his skin and made her head reel.

With an oath he lifted her, mouth finding hers in a scorching kiss—more certain, less restrained, more dominant now he knew how much she liked it—and staggered to the couch. Beneath her back, the sleek leather sank under their weight.

Gasping for oxygen, she forced her eyes open. "We can't, um, do everything. Not until the mating ritual…"

"Kaia." He straddled her hips without crushing her, one hand fisting in her hair, the other finding her breast. "Gimme some credit, will ya? I've been waiting for you my whole life. You're gonna be my consort and the mother of my sons. You'll rule the Syndax horde at my side. I'm not about to do this in the ready room of a fighting pit with a dozen of my boys listening in."

His voice deepened. "But damn if I'm not tempted."

The hard pinch of his fingers on her nipple rolled her hips and made her writhe. He caught her aching cry with a kiss that claimed her like a brand and made her even hotter.

One big hand freed her arms from her sleeves, then engulfed her wrists and pinned them overhead. Her eyes flew open to find his rough-hewn face looming over her, starlight gleaming silver in the spikes of his hair, eyes burning platinum with arousal, full mouth ruthless with intent. She tugged against his confining hand and his grip tightened.

And the hot rush of pleasure that rolled through her nearly made her climax on the spot.

"Angels of Anaxos," she panted, legs twining around his hips to pull him closer. "Zorin… I need…"

"Maybe this is what you need?"

Trapping her wide-eyed gaze with his, he eased a hand down her bare tummy under her open cybersuit to find the slick folds of her pussy.

And Kaia, who could count on one hand with fingers left over the number of guys she'd ever trusted enough to permit the privilege, let her thighs drift open and her body arch into his touch.

Feeling her arousal drench his fingers, his jaw clenched and his eyes darkened to lapis. Heat surged into her face. Suddenly way too conscious of just how much she wanted him—how close to the ragged edge of total surrender she was riding—she turned her hot cheek into the cool leather cushion.

"I'm right here, sweetheart," he said, thick with passion. "Look at me so I can see if you like this."

If he so much as grazed her clit, he was going to ring her bell. When he eased one careful finger into her slick heat instead, she clenched and pulsed around him.

A low savage cry rolled through her. Blind with need, her eyes found his and let him look straight into her soul.

"Gods, you're so wet for me, aren't you?" He eased back and her hips rose to meet him. With a groan, he slid deeper, hand cupping her soaked flesh, and she moaned in unison. "So wet and so tight and so darn perfect, I'm about a whisker away from losing my mother-loving mind. Guess the rumors were right. You're a virgin, ain't ya?"

"Story of my life. Does that… turn you off?" *Please, gods, don't let it turn him off.*

"Pretty much the opposite. I'm dying here, Kaia." He gasped out a laugh. Which sent a vibration through the careful rhythm of his thick finger inside her.

A vibration that pushed her hard over the edge.

With the force of a star imploding, a sonic wave of orgasm shot down her thighs and curled her toes. Her head fell back and comets streaked against her closed lids. Her mouth opened on a scream that he caught with a savage openmouthed kiss.

She cried out her climax into his mouth, barely caring if he managed to muffle the sound.

When her head cleared, her entire body was still rippling with gentle pulses of bliss. And he was still braced above her, sparing her his formidable weight, with the cataclysmic strain of sexual restraint engraved in his granite features and the galaxy's most monumental erection jutting between her thighs.

A flood of contrition scorched through her. "Ohmygods, I'm so sorry! I, um, wasn't actually planning on having that happen."

"Don't you dare apologize. I loved every bit of what just went down. Good to know I can rock your world, sweetheart. We're gonna need that."

With meticulous care, he disengaged and rolled off her replete and satiated body to sprawl on the floor beside her with a labored groan. "Shindig or no shindig, I'd take you to bed right now if I could. But scuttlebutt says you sleep in Draven's quarters."

His gaze swerved toward her. "It's true, ain't it?"

"He's very… protective," she managed to mumble, knowing the

admission only validated every dark suspicion he was already harboring about Dex.

*And Dex's fixation on me isn't exactly unrequited. Which I'm pretty sure you've also figured out.*

This Syndax she'd chosen wasn't a telepath and couldn't transmit, but he seemed to have no trouble at all receiving. At least from her.

His measured curse rang heavy with frustration.

"You and Dex, huh?" He scrubbed a big hand against the back of his neck. "What in tarnation am I gonna do about you and Dex?"

Without a flicker of warning, one electrifying option sizzled through her. A visual of what would happen if he took her to her quarters and Dex found him in her bed. A sudden searing image of Zorin's big hand in Dex's burnished hair, the rough consuming hunger of mouth on mouth, a flash of tongue meeting tongue as these two fiercely dominant men came together above her. In her runaway imagination, while the two of them went at it, her hand slid under her soaked panties to finger her swollen clit.

Asteroids. She could come just watching the two of them kiss.

"Neptune's knickers," Zorin said from the heart. "What a visual. Is *that* what you want?"

"I, uh, think I might… want both of you," she admitted in a whisper. "Both of you together."

Breathless not only because the mere thought had her perched again on the naked edge of climax—but because she was reeling under the sudden, searing, completely unexpected impact the image was having on Zorin.

"Gods of my father, Zorin. You want him too… don't you? You've wanted him forever. You can barely even remember a time when you didn't want him."

Grappling to get her head around that revelation, she suffered through his complicated silence.

"I can see having a telepath for a consort's gonna take some getting used to," he said wryly, bowing his head against her bare shoulder. "This is a lotta excitement for an old guy like me. Gimme a tick to catch my breath, will ya?"

*That's not a denial,* she thought, skin tingling. *You don't need to catch your breath. And you're not old.*

But she knew better than to press. The first rule of courtesy any telepath learned was never to intrude without an invite.

Even when she was suddenly tingling under the rush of a shining, unlikely, utterly novel notion. The notion of becoming the bridge that finally brought these two galactic rivals together.

*The way they were meant to be.*

Against her skin, Zorin pulled in a long inhale. When he raised his head, his face blazed with masculine satisfaction. "Now you smell like *me*. And I damn well intend to keep it that way. No matter what it does to Dex. If he doesn't intend to claim you himself, he needs to stay outta my way."

"I smell like both of you." The deep ripple of sexual pleasure that rolled through her nearly derailed her train of thought—but not quite. "I'm into both of you. And I think both of you need to talk."

"And I think that particular parley's gonna have to wait," he said lightly, letting her read nothing in his face. "Cuz if Dex ever found me making love to you in his bed, you better believe joining in would be the last thing on his mind. He'd probably declare interstellar war on the spot. Oh, wait, he's already done that."

"Or it might be just what the two of you need," she murmured, wiggling regretfully back into her cybersuit. Because as much fun as she was having with Zorin on that couch, he wasn't her consort yet and she knew they needed to stop.

He lounged on the floor beside her and watched her with aqua eyes whose lidded heat made her shiver.

"Meaning?" he rumbled.

"Meaning I heard what you told him about his father—and I believe you." She pushed up to sit. "You killed Max Draven all those years ago because someone had to. You went into exile so you wouldn't have to kill Dex. He was your student. You were his mentor. And I don't think the two of you should be enemies."

"I happen to agree. But Dex isn't exactly on the same page, is he? And even if someday we buried the hatchet, it doesn't follow like two plus two that we'd end up in the sack. Anyway, I gave up that sorta thing years ago."

She made a neutral noise.

*But Dex still turns you on.* She gave him her back and swept up her hair so he could join her on the couch and zip her up. *Even if you've just spent years convincing yourself he doesn't. The bare fantasy of you kissing him, and him kissing you back, was just about enough to spank your monkey.*

And the thought of him alone in his space-cold quarters on that rusting hulk with his hand wrapped around his cock and Dex's name on his lips was just about enough to make *her* come.

Again.

Suddenly, with the certainty she associated with her inherited and unpredictable dash of Valyrian foresight, she wanted to see the two of them together. Wanted it so bad she could taste it. And the thought of both of them looming over her, pushing her flat, one bucking into her mouth to hit the back of her throat with every thrust, while the other spread her wide and rode her hard and fast—

"Kaia, I'm begging for mercy here." Half laughing, Zorin eased up her zipper. "Dex and I are not about to fall swooning in each other's arms, believe me. We're at war, in case you haven't noticed. And the one and only time he and I got a little too cozy—at my initiative, by the way—the bastard up and shot me."

She absorbed the inflammatory memory playing through his mind of Zorin's legendary escape from Mogadon. Which certainly gave her oodles to think about. Including the fact that Dex might've shot his former mentor for kissing him—but that didn't mean Dex hadn't liked it.

In fact, maybe it meant the opposite.

Clearly reading the speculation scrolling across her face, Zorin chuffed out a wry chuckle. "Aw, come on. If he walked in here right now and I laid one on him the way you want, I guarantee he'd haul off and sock me in the face. And that's if I'm lucky."

*Would he?*

She wondered.

His hands squeezed her shoulders, then firmly put distance between them. "Now pay attention, sweetheart. I gotta mosey on back to the *Relentless* for some shut-eye. Before I do that, I got something for you."

"A Tombola gift?" A happy sense of anticipation bubbled through her. She scooted around on the couch to face him and bundled her wine-red hair in a twist. "Because you haven't given me anything yet."

"Just my heart on a plate with a carving knife." He eyed her efforts to tidy up. "Leave it down. It suits you. And right now I want every guy on this ship to know I've been all over you."

"If they did, there'd be a riot." Apparently Dex wasn't the only Mogadon male who got possessive with his woman. She pressed her thighs together to suppress another wicked pulse of need. "What did you bring me?"

"Like presents, do ya?" Grinning at her enthusiasm, he dug from his utility belt a flat steel box the size of an antique postage stamp. "Gotta remember that. So I can spoil you, sweetheart. You'll find I'm a pretty indulgent lover."

"I like the sound of that." With a delighted little bounce that made him grin, she accepted the box and snicked it open. Eagerly she leaned in to check out the flat glittering object, no bigger than her pinkie nail, on its bed of velvet.

"A cyber chip!" Her astonished eyes flew up in surprise.

"Figured it was a fitting gift for a cyber samurai." He leaned forward and tapped the cyberport at her temple. "Was I right?"

"It's perfect." She lifted the chip to study it with a professional eye. "This is gorgeous work. How's it programmed?"

He looked pleased by her appreciation. "Well, it's really just a prototype. Ginned up by a cyber wiz who followed me from Mogadon into exile. It's a transcription chip."

Her mouth fell open. "A *transcription* chip? I thought they were an urban myth."

"They were." His big shoulders lifted in a self-deprecating shrug. "Jules—my man Julius—managed to make it work. I'm no samurai, but I've used it myself. Believe me, if it wasn't safe, I wouldn't be letting you anywhere near it."

"Never mind if it's safe. It works!" Excitement sharpened her voice and spiked her pulse. "Where did you go with it?"

"Ever wonder how I powered from the Omega Sector the night Dex declared war—the night I ambushed his patrol in deep space— onto the *Relentless* six clicks later to coast into Mogadon airspace for your auction?"

"I didn't think you commanded that ambush yourself. It takes weeks at hyperspeed to fly that distance."

"Yep." He grinned. "With that transcription chip, I plugged into a full-body cyberport and ported from the Omega Sector to the *Relentless* in less than a click. You need a working port at each end, dead accurate coordinates programmed into the chip, a decent level of skill to navigate the cyberverse—and titanium balls. I'm not gonna lie about that. Cuz once you commit, you can't back out. The only way out is through."

"No kidding!" She stared at the chip in fascination. Totally jonesing to try it. "Everyone who's ever tried to transport their physical body through cyberspace from one geospatial location to another has flipping *died*. Or else disappeared permanently trying it."

"Except Jules and me. And pretty soon you, if you're game to give it a whirl. That chip's programmed to navigate to the cyberport on the *Relentless*—where I'm at. With your chops in the cyberverse, you can program it to go anywhere in the galaxy, long as you have working coordinates to a full-body cyberport at the other end."

Her brain raced to juggle the implications. "If you can mass-produce these chips—and if the tech holds up—it's a game changer. Whoever holds the galactic patent will earn billions!"

"Spoken like a true Kryll," he murmured. "Fact is, that patent's the main act in my Tombola bid for your Pops."

"Who'll definitely appreciate the value. He may be a god, but he's also a merchant. Just don't call him 'Pops' when you bid. He strongly prefers 'Your Holiness.'" For the first time since she'd landed in this whole mess, she dared to feel hopeful. "All we need to do now is make sure you make the final ten."

*Then hope like hell my father chooses you.*

"And you'll leave that to me," he said firmly, unfolding to tower over her with his colossal height. "This entire gig's a bomb rigged to blow. You're supposed to be neutral, sweetheart. And after what just went down in the pit, you better believe every joe in the show knows I'm your guy. That's despite watching gorgeous Ben Nero with his hands all over you. By now, every poor schmuck on this ship either wants to fight him or fuck him."

"That's Ben for you," she murmured, studying the chip cradled in her hands. "He specializes in inspiring that effect. I keep telling him we're done. To go back to his telepath breeding program and his pedigreed stable."

"With the way he looks at you? And the way you look at him every boot-scootin' time he touches you? Doesn't look like you're done to me—not even close. And I guarantee you he's not buying it."

He held up a patient hand to fend off her flustered protests. "Not to mention whatever the heck's going down between him and Dex. Then there's the First Indomitable himself going hardcore Mogadon and threatening to rip the head off anyone who touches you with his bare hands. Long story short? Your shindig has this entire ship on edge. And two thousand Mogadon with twitchy trigger fingers packed on this nuclear-armed battle bus… well, it's enough to make a Syndax war dog like me a little twitchy myself."

Infected by the warning that threaded through his words, Kaia pushed to her feet and started to pace. "I know this Tombola isn't going the way it should. Dex took a knife for me today, and you almost died yourself. Obviously, I know it's dangerous. What do you think we should do?"

Zorin checked the blaster at his hip. "Play the game, samurai. Play it out like a champion to the last blasted move. That's what Dex is doing—shipping these wannabes off his ship by the boatload before they spark a mutiny. And preferably before he gets spaced by some political rival who's even more ruthless than he is."

Violently she shivered and chafed her arms to ward off the deep-space chill that tiptoed down her spine. She didn't like thinking about just how much danger Dex was putting himself in.

And she liked even less hearing Zorin treat the same danger so casually.

*Once he cared about Dex so much he fled into exile to protect him. Maybe I'd even say he loved him. Surely all that emotion doesn't just disappear?*

Feeling Zorin's thoughtful gaze, she shot him a pensive look. "What happens then?"

"Easy-peasy. When we're down to the last ten yahoos, that's when you tell Pops I'm your guy." One side of his mouth tipped up in a rueful smile. "Then we let the strength of my bid and my natural charm do the rest."

His plan was simple and solid. It made eminent tactical sense. Except for the lurking sense of dread she couldn't seem to shake that his easy-peasy plan wouldn't go down the way they both wanted.

# CHAPTER TWO
## The Ambush

Ben Nero stood in the sterile confines of the high-security holding cell in the *Inevitable*'s brig and thought about how easy it was to kill a man.

Even trained assassins like the two Kryllian bloodletters who lay sprawled at his feet in a pool of their own vomit and the still-steaming dregs of the mining acid that laced their drinking water.

*The Mogadon spy strikes again?*

*Or is this something altogether different?*

"We'll perform a forensic autopsy, of course, although I fear we may learn nothing." The apologetic murmur of the attending physician plucked at his attention. "The cause of death is readily apparent. It's the culprit himself who remains a mystery. Would you care to examine the cell more closely before these two are transported to the morgue?"

"What the hells for, man?" Nero tore his appalled gaze from the acid-scoured remains of the killers' bared teeth—because the chemical reaction had eaten through their lips—and eyed the slender blond physician hovering politely near his sleeve. "I'm a telepath, not a police detective. Whoever spaced these two knew it was the only way to keep me out of their heads."

"Commander Draven won't be pleased to find the investigation he's ordered into the assassination attempt against the Syndax has come to such an abrupt end." Eyes lowered, the physician directed a squad of prefects into the cell to cart out the corpses.

*If he were any less honorable himself, Commander Draven would be the prime suspect. Between his father's murder and the way this Tombola's headed, no one on this ship has better motive for wanting Zorin dead.*

*But it wouldn't be Dex's style to hire someone else to kill him. He'd rather kill the guy himself.*

*And when Dex finds out I let Zorin go off alone with Kaia to do he-knows-perfectly-well-what while I mucked around down here, he's going to want to kill me too.*

"Would you care for a bit of something bracing, Precursor?" The physician was still waiting, quietly attentive, at his elbow. "Perhaps a dram of Mogadon whiskey? Death can be unsettling, and these men met a particularly nasty one."

Reluctant to hurl himself back into the fray until he sorted out his head, Nero trailed the slightly built Mogadon into the sterile, antiseptic confines of a painfully tidy office. While the fellow bustled efficiently about, producing whiskey and glasses from a supply cabinet, Nero finally got a look at the identity badge pinned to his lab coat.

"Dr. Cato?" Surprised, he searched the other man's mild-mannered features and the kind blue eyes under his burnished hair. "Pontius Cato? You're Dex's—"

"Chief scientist," the other supplied smoothly. "As well as the technical director of his biological research program. That's the relationship we both acknowledge."

"Comets, man! If that's the way you want to play it. I've heard a lot about you, going way back."

Under the guise of accepting his whiskey, Nero slid an appraising eye over the other's quiet elegance. If Pontius Cato was what Dex told him way back when, then he—Nero—was eager to know the guy better.

Nero draped himself over an office chair and turned his glass between gloved fingers. "Have you been following the Tombola?"

"Rather closely, since I'm one of the candidates." Cato tucked himself comfortably behind the functional desk and sipped his whiskey. "To be entirely honest, I'd meant to withdraw. I can't compete with the big spenders, and the maharani herself wasn't particularly taken with me… to put it mildly… when we met."

"She hasn't been particularly taken with anyone except Zorin," Nero murmured.

*And Dex. And me—hellbent though she is to deny it. But Dex and I can't bid.*

"Him she likes a lot," he finished aloud. "You said you meant to withdraw. Did you?"

"Commander Draven asked me to keep bidding." Cato lifted one slim shoulder in a diffident shrug. "And what Commander Draven wants, he typically gets. I'm reliably informed I'll make the final two hundred."

"Lucky you." Nero hitched a leg over the arm of his chair and swung his booted foot. He supposed Pontius Cato was a good-looking guy if you liked the icy, aristocratic blue-eyed blond look.

The Draven look.

Nero was certainly a fan.

Without thinking much about it, Nero gave him the slow smoldering once-over that typically reeled in anyone of any gender who caught his eye. If he couldn't have Dex in his bed—an outcome Dex remained actively determined to resist, despite recent developments—then Nero might as well have Dex's—

"You really ought to save your energy, Precursor." Over a cautious sip of whiskey, Cato gave him a diffident smile. "All that formidable sexual appeal is entirely wasted upon me. Scientific endeavor is my mistress, and she's quite a demanding lover."

Nero wasn't particularly into the guy. He liked his men bigger, harder, and one hell of a lot more alpha. Not that any guy in the galaxy could force the Valyrian Precursor to submit to his demands in bed, but Nero liked it a lot when they tried. Dex's chief scientist seemed far too submissive himself for the particular games Nero liked to play with his men.

Still, Nero was as human as the next guy. He didn't enjoy rejection. And between Dex and Kaia—and now even this mild-mannered medic—he was getting rather a lot of it on the *Inevitable*.

And it flipped him off.

Especially from this guy, with his unique connection to Dex.

Nero drew in a slow breath of the whiskey's smoke-and-caramel bite and held the keen gaze that reminded him so vividly of the guy he really wanted in his bed.

Deliberately he lowered his telepathic barriers and sent without saying a word, *Ever tried it with someone like me, Cato? Because you can't know the facts until you've examined all the data.*

With his abilities, there was no humanoid in the galaxy—telepath or no—whose mind he couldn't breach. But Pontius Cato was a blank white wall, a perfect cypher, a hissing screen of static that blotted out the workings of the lively brain beneath. And the man showed no indication he'd even picked up the thought Nero had planted in his brain.

Nero hid his frown behind his glass. A glass whose contents he had zero intention of sipping after seeing the way the mining acid in their H2O had eaten away those Kryll faces.

And thinking about the Kryll brought him sharply back to thinking about Kaia.

He'd left her with Zorin—someone he actually did trust to protect her—at least from everyone except Zorin himself. But considering the still-unrevealed Mogadon spy in their midst, the unknown identity of whoever had paid those Kryll to kill Zorin, and the Swarm assassins lying in wait for their chance to murder the prime maharani the way they'd murdered her twin, Nero suddenly realized he had better things to do with his time than seduce a kind-faced scholar just because he happened to look like Dex.

"Thanks for the whiskey." He set down his glass without tasting the contents, flowed to his feet and swept the surprised Cato a perfunctory bow. "Send those autopsy results to Dex's quarters, will you? That's where I'll be tonight."

*Even if I have to sleep on the floor,* he added silently as he took his leave.

Outside the commander's quarters he found everything in order, well warded by four of Dex's uniformed praetorian watchdogs. All armed to the eyeballs and bristling with vigilance after the day's numerous lethal disturbances.

He sorted deftly through their thoughts—a moment of glancing contact that needed no more than a breath—then locked eyes with the earnest young redhead whose rampant fantasies about Nero himself were more wistful than predatory.

"Hi." He flashed the kid a smile just charming enough to fan the flame of all those innocent fancies. "I'm looking for the maharani and the commander."

"Commander Draven's on the bridge… my lord," the redhead scrambled to reply, groping for a title Nero didn't mind a bit. "But the maharani's inside."

"And not to be disturbed." This from the big brute with the sneer. The one who held Nero in scathing contempt, but would pay a month's salary for an hour alone with him—so long as none of his war buddies found out. "Commander's orders, *my lord.*"

"Good man," Nero lied easily, exerting a tendril of telepathic pressure on all that pheromone-fueled hostility. "But the commander's orders don't apply to me."

"Right." The brute frowned and shook his head. "I forgot about that."

Nero gave them all a little mental nudge and aimed another smile at the kid, who hastened to punch in the access code on the wall panel. The portal sissed open and Nero slipped past, sliding a sidelong look at the brute.

Normally this sort of dalliance with the rank and file would be rather beneath his notice.

Tonight that promise of carnal aggression caught his eye.

Given two hundred Mogadon suitors pumping out pheromones in a confined space, the way Kaia had blown every circuit in his body last night but still wouldn't let him inside her, and the prolonged sexual torture of living in such close and largely platonic proximity to Dex, Nero was subsisting in such a state of permanent arousal he could practically see steam rising from his skin.

Under these particular circumstances, the prospect of a rough-and-tumble interlude spent in his bed with a muscle-bound brute whose ruthless attentions were driven by unrelenting hostility and an unstoppable cock held a certain unsavory appeal…

As the door *shussed* behind him, Nero's eyes lifted and his mouth fell open.

Amid the impersonal confines of Dex's ruthlessly functional living room, all cold shining nanosteel and purposeful slate polymer, Kaia was framed in the panoramic viewport that dominated the far wall.

To be precise, she was balanced on her hands on the narrow ledge that ran beneath the window, slender legs spread in a perfect split against the dazzling blue spray of the Cascade Nebula, burgundy ponytail brushing the sill between her hands.

As Nero stood gaping, her head swiveled to find him. Gracefully she folded into a cartwheel on the ledge and dismounted with an effortless double flip.

She landed lightly on her bare feet and straightened, tawny skin rosy with exertion, damp tendrils clinging to her face.

"Hi, Ben," she said breathlessly. "Learn anything?"

*That you only get more compelling with every day that passes*, he wanted to say. *That thinking about a life without you in it makes me die a little every night. That if you and Dex and I don't figure out this thing between us pretty damn quick, I'm going to self-destruct.*

"Sorry to interrupt your workout," he said aloud.

"I don't mind." She lifted her silken ponytail away from her neck. The motion pressed the lush swell of her breasts against the stretchy silver fabric of her high-necked cybersuit. It also showcased the sinewy strength of her exposed shoulders and the lean lines of her sleek hips.

Nero felt like he needed a stiff drink and a cold shower just looking at her.

"I seem to have energy overload all of a sudden," she admitted with a laugh. "I must've been working out for two clicks in here. I think it's Tombola nerves."

Eyeing the healthy glow in her face, the lavender light in her eyes, the vivid claret of her hair, Nero felt his skin begin to tingle. A tremor of awareness raced down his spine and a tornado of psychic energy sucked the air from his lungs. He focused on Kaia and looked *inward*, telepathic senses sweeping light as fingertips along her sexual channels.

"What are you doing?" She shivered, but looked more intrigued than alarmed. "Scanning me? It… sort of… tickles."

"Gods and demons, Kaia," he breathed, heart hammering so hard it made his ribs vibrate. "What have you done?"

"What do you mean?" She tilted her head with a curious look.

"I mean—" He moved right into her personal space, but even with the gauntlets, he was afraid to touch her. Gods, she smelled like Zorin. "What. Exactly. Have you and that Syndax. Just. *Done*."

"Me and Zorin?" Quizzically she peered up at him. "Nothing—I mean, nothing major. Just… you know… foreplay?"

Nero didn't even need the enhancement of his telepathic senses or the breathless hitch when she said the word to understand precisely what had transpired.

"I should never have left the two of you alone." He clenched his fists against a sudden swell of urgency. In his breeches, his cock hardened to chromium. "He must have one hell of a touch. That punking space pirate just flipped your switch."

She eyed him rather coolly. "Well, I'll admit he rang my bell if that's what you mean. Not that it's any of your—"

"I mean that you're *fertile*!" he burst out. "Whatever the flip you just did with that farking Syndax sent your nubile Valyrian body the signal it's been waiting for. All you need to do now is ovulate and procreate. And you'll conceive."

"Is there a neon sign flashing on my forehead?" She looked honestly bewildered. "How can you possibly even know that?"

"Because I've sired forty-three offspring for the breeding program, that's how! Those couplings are conducted for one purpose—procreation. You think I haven't figured out how to pinpoint to the farking nanosecond when a woman's fertile?"

*"Forty-three—?"*

Somewhere in his head the danger light was flashing. But every erg of bandwidth was consumed with the primal surge of need pounding through his shaft.

*You should have seen this coming, Nero. For the past eight years you've programmed yourself to sire offspring on command. And she's your lifemate. You should have realized how hard it would hit you once she's fertile—*

"Listen." It took all he had to summon words and arrange them in sentences, when *all* he wanted now was to rip off his breeches and tear off her cybersuit and finally—finally—bury himself deep inside her and ride her until they both exploded.

*Use your words, man. She needs to understand what's happening. She's a virgin. You'll be her first time. You can't just drag her to Dex's bed and start riding her—oh hells—I NEED—*

"Listen. Angel." He dragged in oxygen and fought for coherence. "You've been sexed up for days now, and we both know it. We just didn't realize how close you were. Now that you're fertile, all we need for you to ovulate is a good strong climax. If we start now, we can conceive within days. Comets, I can't believe I've been so clueless."

"That's one word for it," she said slowly. Her eyes narrowed. "What exactly do you mean by *we*?"

He reached for her, but she slid deftly aside.

An evasion that drove him absolutely insane.

"Kaia, you're my lifemate," he said hoarsely. "I'd kill for you. I'd die for you. You and I—we're meant to be. I know you'll have to have offspring with that blasted Syndax if he's the consort you insist on taking."

He locked onto her wary gaze and spoke straight from the heart. "But your first son—the prophecy son—he's mine."

#

Kaia stared into the hot purple smolder of Ben Nero's eyes and knew she was in serious trouble.

Maybe the worst trouble she'd been in through this whole flipping nightmare.

Every time she was with him—every single time—that promise she'd made her mom a lifetime ago was in mortal danger of being broken. It had always been Nero's respect for her boundaries—never her own self-restraint—that let her sashay away from their encounters with every sexual craving in her body more than met…

And her virginity still intact.

What she was seeing in Nero's eyes and reading in his mind right now told her more clearly than a printed placard that this safety net had been stripped away. He was her lifemate—an unbreakable bond that was part genetic, part psychic, and overwhelmingly sexual.

Not to mention the most beautiful man in the galaxy even without the lifebond.

Then and now, she couldn't even look at him without her knees going weak. Without her whole body cramping in a delirium of desire. Without that tide of aching need surging through her, screaming to be claimed by him in every possible way. A drive stronger and more potent than an electromagnetic pulse.

His tongue in her mouth. Her hand on his cock. Her channel slick and eager to ease his way inside her. His low command in her ear telling her when to climax.

Reading the dark purpose that hardened his face, feeling the raging need that pounded through his blood, viewing the rigid heat that pressed against his pants, she swallowed hard and measured the distance between them.

Six cubits wasn't nearly enough.

Six parsecs wouldn't be nearly enough.

If he touched her now, she was lost.

"Take it easy." She raised a cautious hand in a plea for restraint. "Nothing here has changed. I've chosen Zorin. Which makes him the father of my son."

"You're not listening." Low and husky with need, his voice rolled through her. "Everything's changed. Our bond now is a hundred times stronger than it was before. Don't tell me I'm the only one who feels—"

"Don't make this about me or our lifebond. It isn't!" A desperate fury clenched her fists at her sides. "It's about that flipping prophecy."

He nailed her with a burning look. "That prophecy only raises the stakes. Now you need the strongest consort you can find. You know that man is me."

"Consort?" Helpless wrath churned through her. "You're Dex's neutral second for the farking contest. You can't bid!"

"No one in the galaxy is strong enough to stop me." His eyes flickered with the eerie orchid glow of psi fire. "This Tombola's over and done. I'm not some confused kid anymore. I'm the Valyrian Precursor, and I have the Senate of Psychics in my pocket. Once we conceive, they'll have no choice but to accept you."

At that mention of the Senate—the ruling body of her mother's people, though a half-Kryll hybrid had never merited their attention—a bitter curl of anger flooded her mouth with bile.

"So your grand plan is for us to pitch up on their racially discriminatory doorstep with an angry god on our heels and a death warrant on our heads and throw ourselves and our hybrid son on their dubious mercy?" She folded her arms across her chest. *"That's* your plan?"

She wasn't even sure he was listening. He was watching her body with a naked hunger that shot straight to that urgent pulse between her legs. She'd never seen him this close to the jagged edge of losing it.

When he spoke, his voice was thick with sexual instinct he could barely control.

"If you don't like that plan, here's another one. Stop fooling around with that pirate. Stop working against those Valyrian candidates for your bed. And take the one I tell you."

"Do you really think it's that easy?" If she weren't already so angry she could barely speak, she would have laughed. "Let's assume for the sake of argument I had any intention of saluting your diktat and saying 'Yes, sir.' You think Zorin would just shrug and walk away?"

"He's an opportunist with a war to win. He'll cut his losses and run—"

"Before tonight, he might have. *If* I said I didn't want him. Now he knows I do. His mating scent's all over me. You try to take what he sees as his, and you'll punch every Mogadon button he has."

"He's going to have bigger problems than me, Kaia." Seething with tangible impatience for the roadblocks she kept throwing in his way, Nero prowled toward her. "With the Tombola over and the ceasefire lifted, Dex will go after Zorin with every nuclear-armed battleship in his fleet. The Syndax and the Mogadon are still at war. That pirate will be far too busy fighting for his life to worry about us."

Nero at his best could pick an argument apart with the discernment and patience of a master politician.

This was Nero at his worst. Thinking not with his brain, but with the raging need between his legs.

She backed away.

Away from the orgy couch and the dangerous lure of Dex's bedroom. Instead she angled for the steel island that barricaded the living space from the galley.

"I've chosen him, Ben. Not you."

Intent and ruthless as a hunting panther, he stalked her. Closing the distance between them with every step. His voice like silk and his words like velvet.

"It was always going to be me, angel. After last night, you know it's true."

A searing memory reared up before her. Nero bound to the ductwork of the Blind Tiger like a wrathful demon. Herself sobbing with pleasure at his cock between her legs the moment he lost himself and came all over her.

She licked her bone-dry lips and lied. "Last night meant nothing—"

"You'll choose a Valyrian," he ground out, "and I'll see to it he steps aside for me. Or else you can take us both. You know I won't mind another man in our bed."

None of the Valyrian candidates possessed Nero's unearthly beauty, but they all shared some shadow of his devastating appeal. Just the thought of two Neros in her bed made it hard to breathe.

Still she mustered the fortitude to say, "No."

*No* to everything. *No* was her word with him, and somehow she had to keep saying it.

"Then it'll just be me." His voice thickened. "Either way, Kaia, we'll be together. I'll protect you from the Swarm and the Patriarch and the whole flipping universe. And I'll protect our son."

He was close enough to touch. Close enough to hear the ragged rasp of his breath. He was clinging to control by his fingernails—and losing it.

One finger at a time.

Cautiously she skirted the island and put that barrier between them. Across its shining surface, she planted both hands to confront him.

"Here's the thing. I don't trust you. I don't trust you not to walk." Eight years of anger dialed up her volume decibel by decibel until she was almost shouting. "You walked out on me. You walked out on Dex. You apparently walked out on *forty-three children*—"

A lifetime of buried hurt lashed out at him. He went white beneath the impact.

But he just kept coming.

"All those women ever want is my DNA. Sticking around's never part of the program. Every one of them has a designated consort. A man handpicked for the role and sworn to treat my offspring as his. In fact, men fight for the privilege."

She was way too appalled to hide it. "And that's supposed to make it okay? That another man's willing to step in and protect all those children you've sired?"

Her mouth was dry as space dust. A pitcher and glass stood nearby. With trembling fingers, she raised the glass to her lips and gulped down a slug of icy water. "How do I know you won't do the same to me—and our son?"

Face hard with purpose, he gripped the counter in gloved hands and pushed the words through gritted teeth. "I know I hurt you before. I get it. I've hated myself for doing it. I'll have to earn your trust, angel—and I will. Starting right here. Right now. In Dex's bed."

The slow smolder of his gaze slid over her. "No more talking. I want you to strip."

*Oh gods, yes.*

Sweat dampened her palms and broke out on her brow. "We're not doing this, Ben. I mean it! I don't trust you. Which means I don't want you anywhere near my bed."

"You can lie to yourself. But not to me." Lithe as a cat, he sprang to the counter and crawled sinuously toward her. "You're already aroused. I can feel it. I'm going to ride you so hard you can't walk. By the time I'm finished, you're going to beg me to climax inside you."

"No," she whispered.

Even though her entire body was throbbing with the blind imperative to say *yes*. If she let him touch her, she had zero doubt he'd bring every one of those dark fantasies flaming to life.

A cubit away, he crouched over her. His voice sank to a whisper. "I'm the one. You know it. The father of your son."

The dizzying incense of musk and sandalwood lapped at her senses. "I don't trust you."

"I'm the only man living you can trust." Eyes never leaving hers, he peeled off one glove with his teeth. "You can trust me, Kaia. I swear it."

His bare hand grazed her chin. The searing heat of his touch scorched through her.

"I said no. I'm still saying no." Yet somehow she couldn't pull away.

He sensed the conflict that tore her in two.

His eyes blazed with triumph. "Your stubborn samurai head's saying no. But every cell in your body is saying yes."

Holding her immobile with that potent featherlight touch, he leaned in. The sweet scent of cloves mingled with warm breath. Beneath her feet, the floor shifted in a surge of desire strong as an earthquake.

"Trust me," he whispered, voice frayed with yearning. "*Please* trust me."

Her lips formed the word *no*, but she'd lost all will to voice it. Fumbling blindly for a resolve she no longer possessed—had never possessed where Ben Nero was concerned—her hand bumped against the pitcher.

"Kaia," he whispered, silken lips brushing hers. "I've waited for you a lifetime. And I've never stopped loving you."

If he kissed her, she was lost.

Pulling her up on tiptoe with the barely there pressure of his hand beneath her chin, he leaned in to seal the deal.

With the lightning swiftness of sheer desperation, she dashed the pitcher's contents over his head. Icy water poured over him. Stinging droplets splattered her face and arms as water coursed everywhere.

Nero jerked back with a curse, breaking the paralyzing contact between them. His flailing arm caught the pitcher and sent it flying. It hit the floor and shattered with a shocking *ker-smash.*

Sputtering, he flung back a mane of drenched hair. "Gods and demons, Kaia, what the hells—?"

"I keep telling you no," she shouted back, "but your brain's buried too deep in your breeches to listen."

"Because I know you don't mean it! I'm a punking *telepath*—"

The entry portal snapped open in an inferno of white light. Dex strode in, eyes blazing with arctic ice, bootheels hitting the floor like hammers.

"What in seven bloody *hells* is going on in here?" he demanded. "Half the ship can hear the two of you carrying on."

Abashed, Kaia and Nero spun to face him. Kaia trembling with wrath in a pool of spilled water and shattered glass. Nero still crouched, drenched and furious, on the island.

"Stay away, Dex," Nero growled on the bare edge of savagery. "I'm warning you."

"The devil I will. Kaia's standing barefoot in a sea of broken glass."

Spearing Nero with an irate glare, Dex strode across the room, glass crunching beneath his boots. Effortlessly he swung Kaia into his arms. Completely undone by the wrenching effort of saying no to Ben Nero, she wrapped her arms around Dex's powerful neck and went weak with relief.

The scent of strength and arousal enveloped her—the concentrated essence of perfectly contained power that always meant Dex to her.

"Thank you," she whispered. "Sorry about the pitcher."

Gruffly Dex addressed Nero's crouched and wary frame. "I'll ask again. And this time I fully expect an answer. What. In blazes. Are you doing?"

Nero's eyes slid from Dex's wrathful face to Kaia's trembling body nestled in his protective grip. Anguish twisted his face, framed in ropes of dripping midnight hair.

"Forget it." Lithely Ben sprang down and put the island between them. He raked his hair roughly back.

Kaia saw his hands shaking and her heart twisted. "Ben," she breathed. "I'm so sorry—"

"I said forget it!" Shaking himself free of excess water, he powered for the door.

"Bloody hell, man." Dex scowled at his retreating back. Wrapped in her arms, his body vibrated with frustration. "We'll never solve a damn thing among the three of us if you run away every infernal time there's an issue."

Six steps from the door, Nero snorted and swung to face them. "Oh, now you want to talk about our issues? You think *I* run away? It makes me space-sick to think how fast and how far you'd run if the two of us ever did what we both damn well want to."

To that, Dex could say nothing. Channeled by the physical contact between them, she felt the surge of hopeless longing that swelled his chest.

And the knot of desperate denial that fisted his gut.

Faced with his stubborn silence, Nero pushed out a bitter laugh. "If you ever decide you want to talk about *that*, space cadet, you know where to find me."

He stormed out, leaving shattered glass and shattered hearts in his wake.

A wisp of memory floated through her head. Zorin's cryptic remark the day they'd met. *"You're all pretty young, Kaia. What you three kids are trying to do—it almost never works."*

She closed her eyes against the sudden sting of tears.

In the echoing silence, Dex pushed out a heavy breath. His slow tread carried them to the couch. When he sank into it, she gathered herself wearily to slide free. But his commanding arms tightened and settled her firmly in his lap.

"Stay here for a tick," he murmured. "You're trembling. I want to know why."

She made a heartsick sound. "It's hardly appropriate. The two of us here like this."

"Do I look like I give a damn? I'm not the etiquette police."

She sighed and subsided, burrowing cold feet between the cushions, tucking her face against the muscled swell of his shoulder. The crisp fabric of his jacket felt warm against her skin. His capable hand wound her ponytail gently through his fingers.

Surrounded by his quiet strength, she felt her trembling gradually ease.

"Sometimes, Dex Draven, you can be a very nice man," she whispered.

"Don't tell anyone." Humor lurked in his voice. "It's a scandalous trait for a First Indomitable. Now tell me what's wrong with Ben."

"He's lost his flipping mind, that's what's wrong," she groaned. "He's determined to sire my mythical son. I think he's going to bid."

His wry chuckle caught her by surprise. "Rather a lot of that going about."

"At least we're rid of the first three hundred," she muttered. "We are rid of them, aren't we?"

"Boarding their shuttles as we speak." He squeezed the back of her neck, and she barely bit back a moan of pleasure. "Under suitably heavy guard. I've pulled my praetorians off escort duty to whisk your lovelorn suitors off this ship. I'll be your bodyguard tonight."

The deep rasp of his voice scraped against her senses. Reminding her of all the reasons why lying in her Tombola master's arms like they were lovers was a really bad idea.

She closed her eyes. "You really should talk to Ben. He's upset. He's hurting. And I can't—I can't go near him right now."

He cleared his throat. "I'll talk to him later. We've the final two hundred to run through tomorrow. Most of them will be upping their bids—"

"Not about the auction." She pulled in a steadying breath and lifted her head to meet his brilliant blue gaze. The harsh lines of his face were chiseled granite. But where she'd once seen coldness, she now saw strength. In his ruthless control, she found boundless security.

"Dex," she whispered through an aching throat. "Ben's in love with you. You know that, don't you?"

*He's in love with you. And I think I might be too.*

*And given this space opera-slash-war-slash-nightmare we're caught in the middle of, it's scaring the punk out of me.*

A shudder swept through his muscled frame. He clenched his jaw and stared fiercely through the viewport.

"He's not in love with anyone. I'm a diversion for Ben Nero," he bit out. "I'm an entertaining challenge. I'm that rare oddity who doesn't fall swooning into his well-trafficked bed the moment he crooks his finger."

"You know that's not true. Stop trying to trivialize this." Her eyes narrowed. "But if it were true, it would bother you. Because it's not a casual thing for you either."

He heaved a heavy sigh. "It's not any sort of thing for me, Kaia. It can't be. I'm First Indomitable of the Mogadon Empire. If I did… what he wants… chances are I wouldn't be for long."

"I don't get it! Mogadon men take male lovers. They *do*. I saw plenty of them at the orgy—"

"Not men of my rank. It's always been a private matter. An unspoken arrangement. But my father made it an absolute taboo. For a military man in particular—men who saw friends and comrades convicted and crucified for same-sex unions under the interdict— there's a powerful stigma."

*Your father was a monster. And that's what this is really about, isn't it? Max Draven's been dead for years. But he's still destroying lives.*

None of which she had any intention of saying out loud given all the father-related baggage Dex was carting around. But with that weird sensitivity that had sprung up from nowhere between them, Dex pushed out a breath that acknowledged he'd heard her.

"My father specialized in that. Destroying lives."

*Then Zorin did you a solid by killing him. He views it as an act of patriotism. He sacrificed his own future for his people—and for you.*

"First Ben. Then my father. Now that bloody Syndax." Gently he massaged the nape of her neck. With a shiver of pleasure, she pressed into his touch. "You're not a particularly easy conversational partner tonight, are you, darling?"

But he said it without heat. And his casual endearment sent her heart into a total tailspin.

"Guess there's a reason I'm a samurai and not a diplomat." She lifted her head to look up at him, hoping like crazy her whole heart wasn't showing in her face. "Does it bother you—talking about your father?"

His gaze stayed fixed on the viewport, where a slow-moving queue of transport shuttles streamed slowly past, bound for the nearest spaceport. Probably counting them to confirm every one of the failed three hundred was off his ship for good.

Because Dex was nothing if not thorough.

Overlooking the general exodus, the battle-scarred hulk of the Syndax ship *Relentless* brooded against the endless night.

"He's been dead for years," Dex said at last. "His draconian edicts on military morals long since overturned. But I still can't give Ben what he needs. Even if…" He pulled in a breath and finished in a whisper, "Even if I'd like to."

A whisper that came closer than anything she'd ever heard him say to acknowledging the tangled knot of guilt and love and fiercely stifled desire that dominated his feelings for Ben Nero.

Recalling the anguish that ravaged her lifemate's face when he went tearing out, her heart clenched in a fist of pain.

"He's in love with you," she repeated gently. "He's been in love with you forever. And the two of you need to talk, no matter what you decide. Keeping it bottled up inside is killing both of you. Promise me you'll talk to him."

"I fail to grasp how talking to him about that particular topic will serve any useful function whatsoever." He shifted in his seat. "However—since it's you asking, and since I'm particularly keen to get into your good graces before I broach a sensitive topic of my own— then yes. I'll speak to him."

"Thank you." She leaned in, planning to kiss his cheek. Because guys liked that sort of thing when they did you favors. Even military leaders who ruled half the known galaxy.

Quick as an indrawn breath, his head turned and their lips met.

You'd think she'd be getting used to kissing him by now. Because he definitely seemed to like doing it. But she was realizing a girl just didn't get used to kissing Dex Draven.

The hard heat of his lips, the electric shock of his tongue, the way he growled in her mouth and the way she moaned in response and the way they both shivered—every potent sensation sparked explosions of breathless craving that went off like fireworks between her thighs. She wound her arms around his neck and gave him everything.

Everything he demanded.

His strong hands closed around her waist to lift her. Knowing by instinct what he wanted—because satisfying the same pounding need was what she wanted—she straddled his hips to let the elemental jolt of his cock hit her sweet spot. Right through the thin silk of her cybersuit. He pulled her into him and a breathless sound spilled out.

"All right?" he murmured, hands closing around her derrière to ease her up against him. "Gods, Kaia. You smell like Zorin. I swear I can't bloody stand it."

"I smell like both of you. And I *want*—"

He rocked into her core, and a rush of slick heat dampened her panties. Her teeth sank into her lower lip and her head fell back.

In the back of her mind, the caution light was flashing. Because Dex Draven was every subatomic particle as dangerous to her vow of celibacy as Ben Nero.

Trying to think even when she didn't want to, she managed to gasp, "Is this… why you wanted to be… on my good side?"

He uttered a startled laugh and stilled. Gently he cradled her face between his palms. She opened her eyes to find his laser-hot stare searing into her and savage possession written all over his face.

"I relish the fact that I can make you climax. And I fully intend to keep doing it, darling." There was that endearment again, and he was going to seriously mess with her head if he kept using it. "But that isn't quite the topic I have in mind."

She eyed him with caution. "Will I like the topic you have in mind?"

"I honestly have no idea," he said wryly, lifting his wrist to check the time. "But I certainly hope you might. The unwelcome three hundred should be well away by now. How about we discuss our sensitive topic over a late-night dinner?"

"Dinner—as in, the two of us?" She hesitated. "Just you, me, and nine hundred on-duty Mogadon in the crew cantina?"

"Just the two of us. I thought we'd dine in."

*That sounds suspiciously like a date, Commander.*

He grinned and said nothing. For no logical reason whatsoever, she felt herself blushing.

"I'm, uh, not exactly a gourmet cook," she warned.

"Fortunately for you, I grill a wicked steak." Exerting only a fraction of his strength, he swung her to her feet. "You can pour the wine."

He shrugged out of his jacket and holster, leaving his blaster on the couch. As he prowled toward the galley, she struggled to squash a sneaking sense of disappointment. Apparently he'd never had any intention of blowing all her fuses after all.

Dutifully she reminded herself of all the reasons it was truly for the best he'd stopped. An intimate late-night dinner with her Tombola master would be scandalous enough. Especially with the whole ship already buzzing and half her suitors convinced they were lovers.

Somehow she had to stay out of his bed.

Especially now she was fertile.

Standing in the galley, Dex lifted his wrist unit. "Marcus, I'm in for the night. See to it I'm not disturbed. Just give me a status after the interstellar broadcast."

When the expected acknowledgment didn't follow, his brow furrowed in a frown. "Marcus? Titus? Does anyone copy?"

"Battery dead?" Kaia offered, starting across the room. "Or a software glitch? Want me to take a look?"

Without answering, he switched on the wall unit. "Marcus? Titus? Bridge, do you copy?"

Faced with nothing but silence, his eyes flashed electric with a pulse of alarm. His gaze shot to her, standing exposed halfway across the room. Through that humming channel of connection between them, she felt his skin crackle with the buzzing zing of combat. Something he thought of as his battle sense.

His blond head snapped toward the exit. "Kaia—it's an assassination squad. *Get down—*"

The explosion ripped the door open with an ear-popping *ka-boom*! A purple flare of psychic energy raced around the lintel and charred the floor as it blasted through. Her vision cleared with alarming slowness.

Only to find a tall raven-cloaked figure sweeping toward her, psi fire sparking from his fingers.

Kaia's heart stuttered, stumbled, and stopped.

Her soul split with the knowledge of absolute betrayal. She cried out a single word that tore straight through her heart and shredded it to ribbons.

*"Ben!"*

# CHAPTER THREE
## The Pivot

The instant her vision cleared, Kaia realized the intruder wasn't Ben.

Not at all.

*Thank you, gods. If he betrayed Dex, I couldn't have stood it. Survived it.*

No, Dex's would-be killer wasn't her lifemate. But he was another telepath. One of her suitors, not much more than a kid—albeit one with lethal powers. Not to mention the wall of armed and armored Mogadon muscle pouring in on his heels.

Her frozen world lurched back into motion.

"Maharani!" the telepath cried. "Stand back. This doesn't involve you."

"Like punking hell it doesn't!"

At the edge of her vision, Dex dove from the death trap of the narrow, no-way-out galley for the cover of the steel island. Kaia pelted for the same cover, three running steps launching into a tumbling run. Halfway home, the high-pitched pulse of blaster fire chased after her, all but singeing her heels.

"Not her!" the telepath cried. Some sort of scuffle erupted in a flash of violet fire.

She had zero time and zero patience for that kind of space trash.

She flipped into a cartwheel, caught the counter with a handstand, and vaulted into a triple somersault that sent her hurtling over the island.

Dex swept glass roughly from her path and pulled her down beside him. Near the door, men were cursing in the blinding glare of ultraviolet strife. While she dragged in air, brain scrambling for options, he flung open the island's storage compartment and emerged with a short-range taser barely larger than her hand.

An irritant. A distraction. A non-lethal crowd-control weapon.

Not a blaster. Not even close. Because he'd left his blaster holstered on the couch.

On the other end of twenty cubits of open floor.

Around the corner, he fired a quick crackling burst that hit home with a *zzzat*. Near the door, a Mogadon curse erupted.

"Just so we're clear," Dex shouted. "This is an act of high treason. Throw down your weapons and surrender. I'll see you're given a fair shot in the fighting pit."

"Gee," Kaia whispered. "Talk about an offer they can't resist. Couldn't you sweeten the deal?"

"We'll give you the same terms, Draven!" a rough voice sneered. "You and your pretty boy telepath. Give up and come out. You're trapped like a rat in a drainpipe!"

Dex countered with another crackling current of electric fire that ripped a pained yell from his target. Kaia was no tactician, but even she knew one guy with a temporarily immobilizing taser couldn't hold off an army of brutes with blasters.

Even if that guy was Dex Draven.

"Damnation!" he muttered. "I need that blaster."

Kaia risked a quick glance around the island, glimpsed two Mogadon heavies down and trembling with taser shock—

And nearly had her head taken off with a blue burst of blaster fire.

"Stop firing at the maharani!" the telepath yelped. "Give her a chance to come out."

"Only six of them," she whispered. "It's not a mutiny. We can take them. I just wish I had my cyber saber."

"*We* aren't 'taking' anyone. Much less with a bloody saber. And *you* are staying right here," Dex growled sotto voce, squeezing off another dangerously accurate round of electric annoyance.

Someone yelped in outraged agony. The rest scrambled for cover from his deadly aim and holed up behind the couch.

"Don't be such a cliché! I'm a Prime Class samurai, remember?" She touched his rock-hard shoulder—steady as a planet even in crisis—and felt an unexpected flicker of comfort.

This wasn't a man who had any intention of dying.

He shot her a steely look and unclenched his jaw to speak. "Whatever we do needs to be done quickly. Those men I tasered won't be down long. Once those bastards finish bickering, they'll storm this island from both ends."

"Not if we move out first."

Determination flashed in his eyes like lightning. "What do you propose, samurai?"

"Diversion." Heart pounding with nerves and adrenaline, she straightened to a runner's crouch. "I'll draw their fire. You bolt for that blaster."

"Hold on one bloody tick! The day I let you paint a target on your back—"

"No time to put this to a planetary vote." She shifted her weight and dragged in a breath. "Give me a sec, then grab that blaster and hit 'em."

Without waiting for an assent she didn't think she'd get, Kaia erupted from the island at a dead run, screaming for effect like a Mogadon rock banshee. She got off four strides before the first blaster pulse. Already she was launching into a triple flip that gave her distance and a burst of speed.

She'd finished her last rotation and was pulling her legs under her to stick the landing when blue fire seared across her upper arm.

Her world went white with pain.

The floor rushed up to meet her. She connected in a tangle of limbs with bone-jarring impact.

Her arm exploded with hot anguish. Her gut clenched in an agonized scream. Barely able to navigate through a sea of tears, she slithered into the galley and got her back to the wall. She braced herself against it and tried to clear her head.

Around the corner, the room lit up with a blinding barrage of blaster fire. Men were shouting threats and curses. Someone was howling like a wounded jackal—a visceral response she could fully appreciate but refused to allow herself.

She would've paid real money for a good yell from Dex to let her know he was still breathing. But apparently he wasn't the yelling kind.

At least not in battle.

She curled her knees to her chest and clutched her burned arm. Blaster fire had cauterized the wound, so blood loss wasn't an issue. But the sickening hammer of pain that pounded her damaged nerves would send her straight to Shock City if she wasn't careful. Already blackness was eating away at the edges of her universe.

"Hold it together, angel," she panted through gritted teeth. "Don't you *dare* black out."

She forced herself to release her throbbing arm and reconnoiter for a weapon. A fumbled search with her good hand through a drawer revealed steak knives and a cleaver. Grimly she palmed the cleaver and scooted around to face the entry, leaving bloody streaks on Dex's shiny floor. It turned out running barefoot through a sea of broken glass hadn't exactly been therapeutic for her feet. Now her soles were shredded.

So much adrenaline was pumping through her system she hadn't even felt the damage.

Until she saw the blood.

Gods knew she wouldn't be good for much if Dex needed help with that kill squad. She wasn't even sure she could stand. But she was pretty flipping certain of one fact.

She wasn't giving up without the mother of all battles.

*If they kill him—gods of my father, if they kill him—*

Her vision was narrowing to a tunnel of darkness. The clamor of combat receded, like she was zooming away from the action at hyperspeed, even though she was trying like blazes to stay present. If only the nanosteel floor weren't so flipping cold. A deathly chill seeped through her, rattling her teeth and leaching her warmth.

*Have to stay tight. Stand up, samurai! Dex needs you on your feet.*

She was trying to gather her bloody feet under her, still clutching the cleaver—all without jarring the screaming inferno of her arm— when a shadow burst into view.

"Pluto's coldest *hell,* Kaia!"

Burnished hair falling into blazing eyes, Dex crouched before her. Fresh blood splattered his arms and painted his hands, but she didn't think it was his. At least one of his enemies out there had died not by blaster fire, but up close and personal under the First Indomitable's fatal hands. His face was chiseled cordite, unyielding and lethal with Mogadon violence.

His warm hand cradled her face, fingers finding the pulse that fluttered way too fast beneath her jaw. She fought to focus her blurry eyes.

"Just—get me up," she got out through chattering teeth. "I can still f-f-fight."

"You blessed, beautiful, impossible girl, you're not fighting anyone." Tenderly he smoothed back her sweat-damp hair. "All five of those treasonous Mogadon are dead. And you can believe they felt it. I beat seven shades of shit out of them."

She was no lightweight, but his grim tone made her shiver.

"What about the t-t-telepath?"

"The young fool took to his heels, but we'll apprehend him straightaway. My praetorians are locking this ship down tighter than a deep-space airlock."

Deftly he relieved her of the cleaver she was still clutching. His hands moved swiftly over her body to assess the damage. His blond brows drew together in a ferocious scowl and she thought fuzzily that he was as beautiful as Nero.

Beautiful in a harder, more brutal, more physically lethal way.

But still definitely beautiful.

"Sorry I was slow," she mumbled. "They shouldn't have been able to… touch me."

"Slow?" Something clenched in his face.

A tremor moved through his hands, finally shaking his unshakable calm. "You moved faster than a Mogadon trooper at peak performance. That was a bloody suicide sprint. I swear to Ceres you're the bravest, strongest, smartest, most bloody-minded loyal woman I've ever known."

A powerful undercurrent of emotion roughened his voice. An echo of the violent riptide of anger and fear and desperate relief she sensed churning through his head.

*It feels… almost… like he…*

"Let's get you up, samurai." Carefully he gathered her in his arms and lifted her. "Fortunately, I've a safe room absolutely no one knows about. Fully stocked with med supplies, fluids, cot, blankets—everything you're going to need to get through the next few clicks. I'll ask Ben to stay with you."

"Better not." If only she could clear her head. Or at least her vision. She was cruising about two ticks away from a blackout. "Not him. Take me to Zorin."

Already halfway through his living quarters and moving with relentless purpose, Dex pushed out a snort.

"The devil I will. All this blasted tinderbox needs right now is the inflammatory presence of that infernal Syndax to blow us all sky high."

"I want him," she whimpered. Which was just punking pathetic. She was on the edge of blurting out *why* she wanted him, why she couldn't have Ben—this unforeseen crisis of her sudden fertility—

But instinct held her back.

An instinct whose rationale her short-circuiting brain couldn't even articulate.

Instead she finished feebly, "It can't... can't be Ben right now. It can't."

Still carrying her without effort, Dex swept into his bedroom.

"Kaia, this plan isn't open to negotiation. I need to lock down this ship and deal out discipline in an immediate and spectacularly public fashion or I'll be dealing with a full-fledged gods-damned mutiny." Cradling her against his body, he punched a button. A wall panel she hadn't even seen slid silently open. "When it comes to your protection, Ben Nero is the only man I trust."

Overwhelmed by emotion she lacked the wherewithal to articulate, she batted weakly at his hands. Weak as a flipping kitten.

"I can walk! Let me go..."

The darkness was rushing in. But his husky whisper followed her into the night.

"I'm never letting you go now, darling. And that's one promise I fully intend to keep. I'm afraid you'll just have to get used to me."

#

"I want a military tribunal convened at oh-nine-hundred to try these men for integrity violations, dereliction of duty, and high treason. As this vessel's commanding officer, I'll head that panel myself."

Standing in his ready room with hands clasped behind his back, Dex eyed the three praetorians arrayed before him. All dishonorably disarmed under heavy guard, demeanors running the gamut from shame to defiance. While he couldn't yet prove they'd been involved in planning the attack on his life, they'd sure as hell been complicit in the execution.

They'd accepted hefty bribes to disable his comm links. Then ensured the duty officer wasn't monitoring the vid feed outside his quarters.

All of which had been nearly sufficient to finish him off.

If not for Kaia.

And the incontrovertible truth that the creeping rot in shipboard discipline, thanks to this bloody Tombola, had seeped from isolated pockets of the rank and file to infect his elite guard was going to be absolute murder on morale.

He harbored utterly no doubt what needed to be done. He needed to nip this infestation of treason in the bud.

Especially with Kaia's safety at stake.

"You want I should double the guard on your digs, boss?" At his side, his *optio*'s gaze stayed steady and vigilant on his face. A good man, that one.

"Four men as usual, Marcus." Concerned though he was about the volatile shipboard situation, he'd no intention of making a public display. "Don't deploy the praetorians. They've enough to manage enforcing the security curfew. Get me four enlisted men from the brig who've been sentenced to the fighting pit. For procedural violations, not incompetence or dereliction. Tell them if they satisfy me— meaning if they keep me breathing—I'll commute their sentence."

That had been Kaia's idea, back when she first discerned how little he trusted the men who were sworn to defend him.

A natural suspicion on his part, since his eventual killer would almost certainly rise from their ranks.

The notion of enlisting condemned prisoners to defend him—and pardoning them if he lived—was unconventional. Even iconoclastic. Like most of Kaia's notions.

Still, it had stuck in his head.

"You telling me you want convicted felons guarding your Indomitable ass?" Despite the surprise he clearly felt over the unorthodox arrangement, Marcus's canny gaze turned thoughtful.

"I am," Dex said crisply. "Make it happen."

"Guess it's your funeral, ain't it?" Gruffly his *optio* issued orders to the guards, who promptly herded their prisoners off to the brig. "What about those two hundred suitors?"

*Plague take those two hundred suitors. I'd like to jettison them out the nearest airlock.*

But Dex was still scrambling to manage the delicate matter of the Patriarch—Kaia's infernal father—and their equally delicate alliance.

"Curfew until oh-nine-hundred. Then it's back to the races. I'll hear new bids in my ready room. And I want those Valyrians kept under armed escort twenty-four/seven—except for the Precursor." Dex pivoted away and strode for the door.

"Oh, and Marcus?" He stopped sharp. "See to it the maharani and I aren't disturbed. For any reason."

The ghost of a grin lurked in Marcus's grizzled beard. "I hear you, boss. You can count on me."

"I know that, man." Dex spared him a grin of his own and got the hell out of there before something else went wrong that needed his attention.

He'd been seething with impatience to get back to Kaia since the moment he left her alone with Nero. Which wasn't to say he didn't trust Nero.

When it came to Kaia, the only man he trusted was Nero.

But he was having the devil of a time getting the sight of her—lying burned and bloodied on his galley floor, but still spitting with fight—expunged from the hellish cycle of play/rewind/repeat on permanent blooming broadcast in his brain.

He needed to know she was safe.

And the violent intensity with which he needed it—needed *her*—just about knocked him on his backside.

He disabled the lethal electrical barrier he'd set on his quarters to reinforce his damaged door with a biometric scan and reset it behind him. His five would-be killers lay sprawled in their blood where he'd left them. A distinctly unsavory mess some unfortunate prefect would shortly be tasked to tidy up.

The portal to his bedroom was likewise locked and trip-wired. No one had triggered it since he'd left.

Which meant the hidden door to the safe room remained hidden. He tried with limited success to slow his pace so he wouldn't scare the piss out of anyone bursting in.

The door hissed open on the cozy cell, its intimate confines softly lit in amber. Kaia's huddled figure lay sleeping on the cot, slim and helpless as a child under the silver heat retention blanket, burgundy hair a tangled banner across the pillow. The neat square of a silicon bandage covered her injured arm. One slender foot, likewise bandaged, poked from beneath the blanket.

Nero sat on the floor beside her, knees drawn up and back to the wall, dark head lifting alertly from folded arms. His wary gaze swept over Dex.

Despite looking gaunt and haggard as all seven hells, hair a tangled mane of ebony silk around his pale face, Nero would have blasted any other man who pitched up on their doorstep clear into the next century.

"Jupiter, man, you look like hell." Dex pitched his voice low so he wouldn't wake her. But concern for both of them roughened his words.

A concern he couldn't deny.

"Sorry to disappoint." Nero sounded more than a little ragged himself. "Keeping Kaia horizontal and resting while you rooted out treason and mutiny out there with no backup wasn't exactly easy. I had to hit her with a double dose of that sedative from the med kit."

Dex grunted his appreciation of that considerable achievement. He'd known Nero was the only man for the job. "How is she otherwise?"

Nero raked back his hair with a weary hand. "By some miracle, the lacerations on her feet are minor. I patched her up with silicon and a shot of antimicrobials. Cleaned out that blaster burn—which is a lot less minor—and pumped her full of pain meds. Eventually she'll want a real medic for a skin graft. Right now, she's high as an orbiting satellite.

"The key thing's to keep her warm. Whether that's what *she* wants or not."

Dex closed his eyes against a surge of staggering relief. He'd known she was resilient. Known Nero would open his own veins if it meant saving her life—just the way Dex would himself.

But he was only starting to know what it all meant.

Pulling his head together, he cast an approving eye over the setup. He knew a bit of trauma medicine—enough to appreciate competence when he saw it. He didn't often think of Nero that way, but the Precursor was Valyria's war leader. At some point, he must have studied trauma medicine himself.

"I did." Nero sighed. "And before you complain, I'm not in your head. You're projecting all over the damn place."

"Sorry. I'm not exactly accustomed to living with telepaths." Dex suffered an uncomfortable stab of guilt. "And I wasn't about to complain. You've done a bloody good job."

"Glad you approve." Nero let his head fall back against the wall and closed his eyes.

He looked wrecked, and Dex felt an uncharacteristic surge of protectiveness for the guy that nearly knocked him over. Gods knew this Tombola had been murder on them both. He himself was all but dead.

He supposed it would do no harm, just for a breath, to succumb to the weariness that dragged at his limbs like a full-pressure spacesuit. There wasn't much room in the cubby, and none at all on the cot.

But, really, there was only one place on this ship he wanted to be.

He walked over to Nero and said gruffly, "Scoot over."

One purple eye opened to slant him a narrow look.

Dex supposed it had been a while since anyone told the Valyrian Precursor to scoot anywhere. But Nero slid obligingly closer to the cot. Dex put his back to the wall and slid down beside him.

A tight fit, but he made it work.

Even if it left his thigh and shoulder pressed against Nero's and his head full of the dark spice of musk and sandalwood.

Even a hint of his own mating scent.

If he'd been any less wrecked himself, the fact that Nero was walking around smelling like Dex in a mating frenzy would have worried him. In his current state of depletion, his primary reaction was a fuzzy sense of satisfaction.

*There isn't a man or woman on this ship who hasn't been eyeing him and wondering. Including that blasted pirate. Zorin's been all over him. Well, they can all just stay the hell away.*

"For gods' sake, Dex. I've barely even spoken to Zorin," Nero murmured, eyes still closed. "Know the identity of the Valyrian who attacked you?"

Dex let his own eyes drift closed. "I didn't get a good look. Rather a lot going on at the moment."

"I don't doubt it. Still, if you glanced at him once, I can find the guy. The Valyrian contingent isn't very large, and I know them all by sight." Nero's voice was atypically diffident. "If that's what you want."

Without raising his head from the steadying wall, Dex turned to eye him. "You know it's what I want. Why wouldn't I?"

Nero's own head turned toward him and his eyes opened. And the sight of all that breathtaking beauty less than a cubit away, disheveled like he'd just stumbled out of bed, filled Dex with a violent impulse to drag him close and do every blasted thing he'd ever fantasized about doing to Ben Nero.

Those eyes he'd never forget stayed steady on his face. "In order to do that, I'm going to need to look in your head. And you're going to need to let me."

Dex swallowed hard and tried to impose some sort of discipline on the carnal riot in his cranium. If this was what Nero needed to do in order to find the fool who'd done his level best to get Kaia killed, then he—Dex—was going to give it to him.

No matter what else Nero saw in there.

"Fine." He tried to keep his voice level. "Tell me what you need me to do."

"Just relax." A hint of a smile flitted across Nero's lips. "And try to breathe."

"Right." Dex pulled in a breath and worked to loosen up.

"Ready?" Light as breath, Nero's hand settled against the hard plane of his cheek. Again that flicker of a smile came and went. "You need to shave."

Dex reminded himself to breathe. But his voice was still breathless. "Does it bother you?"

"Nothing about you bothers me." Nero's gaze went distant. "Now relax."

The orchid glow of psi fire pooled in his eyes and the delicate breath of psychic energy stirred on Dex's skin. Nero was a thing of beauty, an exotic wonder, the illusive dream of a mythical Olympus Dex had never had any prayer of scaling.

The tug of longing in his gut, the burn of yearning in his chest, the ache of wanting in his groin, all familiar by now as his own name…

He made a resolute effort to hide none of it.

A deft touch, both familiar and strange, rifled through his thoughts light as fingers shuffling a deck of cards. Searching, skilled, gentle. Yet precise and lethal as a surgeon's scalpel.

He knew from the old days horsing around at the ashram—not to mention a few of those steamy visuals Kaia kept projecting—that Nero could be savage.

When Nero was gentle, the way he was now, it just about killed him.

"Ah." Nero's gaze narrowed, purple light shifting the shadows around them. "Got you."

*You've always had me,* Dex told him without saying a word. *Good gods, Ben. Do you even have the first bloody notion how incredible you are?*

The psychic glow faded and Nero's eyes went wary. His hand fell away from Dex.

"Doesn't make any difference, does it?" But he looked more sorrowful than angry.

"But—"

"It doesn't matter, Dex. Truly. I know who attacked you. I'm going to bring him in."

"Hold on a tick. Damn it to blazes—"

But Nero was uncoiling to his feet. Dex scrambled up with him. Wanting to touch him, warn him, tell him to *wait.* Just wanting to be with him.

Wanting to be with him all night.

"No way, Dex." Nero's guarded gaze held him off. Even if only barely. "We're not doing this. Not right now. You're not yourself. And I'm tired of letting you treat my heart like a punching bag. I'm way too beat up to handle any more rejection."

*"Ben."* He felt like his own heart was beating outside his chest. Because letting Ben Nero into his head while feeling the way he did would do that to any man. "One of these days, you're going to have to stop running."

"Good night, Dex." Too swift to capture, Nero swooped in and brushed Dex's cheek with his lips. "Take care of our girl."

Then he was gone, a whisper of fur and musk floating in the air like a ghost. Dex stood staring at the closed door between them, his skin still tingling and his chest still tight from that heartbreakingly sweet, electric kiss.

*Take care of our girl.*

Our *girl.*

*Because that's what she is.*

Something was shifting between them—between him and Nero. An unspoken recognition that whatever happened in five days when this Tombola ended, the three of them wouldn't be drifting off into separate orbits like random asteroids after a meteor strike.

Now they were all fixed in orbit around the same flaming sun. Anchored together by a gravitational pull far too powerful for any of them to break.

Powerful enough that Dex was starting to think he'd been going about this whole Tombola business entirely wrong. His entire plan—to the extent he'd *had* a plan since he ascertained what the devil he wanted, which hadn't really been until Kaia flung herself headlong into mortal peril to save his clueless ass—had been focused with laser-like precision on claiming her exclusively for himself.

Now, at the edge of thought, a potent new possibility was tugging at his sleeve for attention. Instead of it being the two of them who walked away together from this galactic death fest…

Maybe—just maybe—it was meant to be the three of them.

# CHAPTER FOUR
## The Secret

Kaia rolled over with a moan.

She was dreaming. Another of the vivid, intensely arousing dreams she vaguely attributed to the combination of her sudden and profoundly dangerous fertility and the potent double sedative Nero had shot her up with.

At least, she assumed this *had* to be a dream.

Because there was just no other way to explain the searing sight of Zorin—massive, muscled, splendidly naked and violently aroused—pushing Dex to his knees.

A Dex who was also magnificently naked, sinew rippling across back and shoulders and flexing his truly spectacular ass under leagues of sun-bronzed skin.

A sight made all the more electrifying by the pirate's big hand fisted in Dex's burnished hair.

And Dex's mouth wrapped around the pirate's cock.

"Jumpin' Jupiter," Zorin groaned. "You're making me crazy. First time doing this?"

"Consider yourself lucky," Dex growled in response.

Kaia couldn't look away from the thick glistening length of Zorin's cock. Mind-blowingly oversized just like the rest of him. An unforgettable image at any time—but never more so than now, slick with saliva, sliding in and out of Dex's mouth in tempo with Zorin's quickening, increasingly urgent thrusts.

"Lucky, my ass," Zorin rasped through gritted teeth, his rugged face clenched with the effort of restraint. "Kid, after eight years' exile in the armpit of nowhere, you owe this to the old guy."

"I'm not a kid." Dex's hands slid up Zorin's thighs and gripped his ass to anchor him. "And you're not old."

"Prove it," Zorin got out between breaths. "Prove it for both of us—stars, yeah, like that—oh baby—"

His speech dissolved into gasped curses and hoarse cries, head tipped back in an agony of pleasure, both hands gripping Dex's head to hold him in place while he bucked into his mouth.

That image alone was just about enough to push Kaia's oversexed body over the edge.

Even without Nero's husky whisper in her ear and the silken ends of his hair tickling her naked back as he bent her forward over the bed and fitted his cock against her soaked and aching channel.

"Are you watching?" he whispered, warm breath brushing her ear.

She moaned in agreement, far too focused on the feel of his erection between her thighs to structure the sound into words.

"Pay attention, angel." His finger dipped inside her and smoothed her own copious juices up the crease of her derrière. She moaned again and arched her back to encourage him. "This is how you're going to do it."

"Do what?" She panted. "Comets, Ben, I *need* you."

"This is how you're going to save us." His wet finger traced her tight rear pucker and eased inside. The slight burn of penetration—someplace she'd never even dreamed of being penetrated—pushed her even closer to the edge. Desperate for relief, she slipped a hand between her legs to find the engorged bud of her clit.

"Pay attention." His tongue traced her ear and his teeth nipped her lobe. A whimper slipped out between her lips and her hips rotated against his finger. "This is how you'll bring peace to the galaxy. How you'll keep the Syndax and the Mogadon away from each other's throats. How you'll bring us all home. Just like this. You and Dex and Zorin and me."

His finger eased deeper, stretching her, working her, probing her, prepping her. And what with the pressure and the burn and the fullness of violation she wasn't sure at first she liked, she knew she'd lose her mind if he didn't stop… no, she'd lose it if he *stopped*…

"Oh gods Ben please no I can't no it's too much—!"

"You're ready for me now, aren't you, angel? You like this. Don't you?"

"Yes!" she sobbed.

"Good." His voice roughened. "So do I."

The electric slide of his cock, slick with his precum and her own juices, sheathed him deep in her eager ass. An act of penetration they'd both been waiting a lifetime to consummate.

Even if it wasn't going down exactly the way she'd imagined.

Her cry of shocked pleasure echoed his savage grunt.

A pleasure made even more intense by knowing Zorin was watching them through burning eyes while Dex worked him over.

"Mars and Mercury, the three of you," Zorin groaned, both hands gripping Dex's blond head in a silent command not to stop. "You're gonna make me come so hard. Dex… baby… you're gonna make me come in your mouth. If that's not what you want—fair warning."

Dex moaned around his cock to urge him on.

Nero anchored Kaia in place with a rough hand on her hip and rode her hard and fast, with the same careless dominance that always flipped her switch.

He'd always known her. Known her right down to the molecular level. Known what would turn her on even better than she knew herself.

"Oh, Dex—oh baby—holy *gods*—"

Zorin's guttural shout of climax echoed Dex's muffled groan. Dex wrapped a hand around his own cock and a single rough stroke finished him off, ropes of thick seed spurting over his hand.

Watching the commander of half the known galaxy get off on another guy coming in his mouth, Kaia shuddered all over with a deep shock of pleasure. Her rear channel softened and stretched to let Nero all the way in, ripples of arousal gripping his cock. Her pussy clenched and released in aching need as she rubbed her desperate clit, found her rhythm and thrust against the friction.

Nero gripped her hips to hold her still and pistoned into her with the steady rhythm that drove her mad, keeping her fixed in place so he could set the pace. Finding a rhythm that pleased him. Expecting her to take him.

Knowing just what would push her over the edge.

Penetrated and possessed in a way she'd never imagined, she arched her back, raised her bottom and rocked into him, her rhythmic pleas urging him on. The most mind-erasing orgasm she'd ever known rolled through her like an avalanche.

His cock spasmed inside her, spurting his spunk so deep she knew she'd never be free of him. The night rang with his hoarse shout of triumph.

Right before Zorin leaned in to claim him with a scorching kiss—

Kaia woke with a gasp, thighs slick beneath her silky pajamas, body shaking with seismic aftershocks. She lay panting on her side in the dim confines of Dex's bedroom, watching the cosmic sparkle of stars draft past the viewport. Through the floor, the *Inevitable*'s propulsion reactor hummed and pulsed.

And she lay with Dex's warm solid weight sprawled over her. With her back tucked tight against his naked chest. With his fierce arms wrapped around her ribs. Without a wisp of open air between them.

From his face buried in her hair to his ferocious erection wedged against her bottom.

"Gods," he groaned into her nape. "That was one hell of a dream."

Which led her to wonder if she'd been projecting *her* dream.

Or if he'd been projecting his.

Just the thought of Dex getting off on dreams about Zorin— dreams where he submitted sexually to the man he considered his ultimate nemesis—made her shudder with an earthquake of primal need.

She squirmed in his arms, relieved to find that her Tombola master was at least wearing sleeping trousers. Even if they were lying in each other's arms in his bed. That potent knowledge of his prohibited nearness, combined with the bracing musk of his mating scent, made her head swim with danger.

Because, climax or no climax, she was still turned on as twelve hells.

And so was he.

It was all she could manage to remember why she couldn't just roll over and wrap both hands around his—

"How's the arm?" he murmured, lips brushing her naked shoulder.

The stretchy fabric of her sleeveless sleep shirt was an annoyance between them she longed to be rid of. But that wouldn't be happening.

*He's your Tombola master. What you're jonesing to do with him is blasphemy. Try not to forget it.*

"I'm, um, better. Less searing agony and more dull burn." Carefully she touched the sleek square of her silicon bandage. "Ben did a primo job patching me up. How're the ribs?"

"Sewn up by the medic as instructed. Nanostitches. They'll be gone in a week." His gentle hand brushed her hair back so he could nuzzle her bare neck. A shiver of tingling pleasure raced through her. "Warm enough?"

"Mmmmm." That wasn't much of an answer, but it was all she could manage. Helpless as an infant to prevent it, she pushed her bottom into him. His instant response was the hitch of his breath.

And the insistent jut of his shaft against her backside.

Which only got her thinking about what Nero had been doing in her dream. And how shockingly much she'd *liked*—

"Kaia." Dex's voice in her ear was strained. "If you want me to exercise any restraint whatsoever tonight, I'm going to need the same from you. I'm a whisker away from losing it."

Here was her cue to say again what she'd been saying for days like a robot—to Nero, to Dex, to Zorin, but most of all to herself— about her vow and her consort and her mother. Even though she *really* didn't want to.

Not anymore.

Maybe it was all that sedative and analgesic Nero had shot her up with.

Or maybe she was starting to wonder if she'd just had a prophetic dream herself.

When she said nothing, letting the whisper of her rapid breath push back against the silence, Dex pulled in a harsh inhale. Against her back, the solid thunder of his heartbeat quickened. On her waist, his hand tightened. Above her pants, his battle-hardened touch chafed her bare skin.

And just that fleeting hint of hunger in his grip sparked a jolt of excitement down her spine.

"Gods, Dex," she breathed, aching with a longing for him she couldn't hide.

A beat of silence stretched between them. A silence pregnant with his question and her reply. Slowly his hand eased beneath her shirt, smoothed over the tight ripple of her ribs, and closed around the naked curve of her breast. A hoarse groan rasped through him. Her nipple rose taut against his hand and her shuddery gasp slipped out.

"I was supposed to wait," she said on a scrap of breath. *Wait like I promised my mom.* "For my consort."

"Darling." His voice dropped two octaves and shot goose bumps all the way down her spine. "The only consort you're taking is me."

Her heart gave a powerful leap against his hand and swelled with a shocking surge of certainty. The certainty of knowing those were the words she'd been waiting a lifetime to hear.

A certainty goosed with a potent jolt of Valyrian foresight. Her own foresight, and the sudden explosive insight of her mother's prophecy.

"We—we can't," she whispered. "It can't be the two of us."

*It's you and me and Zorin. And I think it might even be Ben. It's the four of us.*

*But I'm not sure the four of us are a future Dex is ready to accept.*

Still tingling with that psychic shock of foresight, she barely swallowed back the incendiary truth she burned to reveal. Finally she glimpsed what she needed to do—somehow—both to survive this Tombola with her soul intact and save the galaxy from apocalypse.

Breathless with excitement, she trained her brain to the practical. "Let's say I agreed. How exactly would we do this?"

"I've the start of a plan, albeit a desperate one," he said dryly. "Not to mention one that requires a modicum of trust—on both our parts. I launched certain elements into play after I nearly died in the pit. This was the conversation we were supposed to be having, incidentally, over that intimate dinner. The main question now is…"

His fingers found the hard nub of her nipple. "Do you want me?"

A current of raw yearning streaked from her nipple to the wet ache between her legs. Helpless against it, she arched into his touch.

"Wanting you isn't the issue!" she gasped. "It was never the issue. The issue is—you're Mogadon. I'm Valyrian—"

"Kaia, we're made for each other. We've both known it since the moment we met. Tell me I'm wrong."

He pinched her tingling nipple and she moaned in response, hips rolling in a rhythm she couldn't control. The dark spice of his mating scent poured over her.

"What would it take?" he breathed in her ear. "For you to choose me?"

"You'd never agree," she said on a breathless laugh. Of that, she was all but certain.

"Try me."

The smoking visuals from her dream raced against her closed lids.

"Ben," she gasped, running on pure-octane foresight. "I'm furious with him. I really am. But… he's my lifemate."

"Done." His primal growl matched the savage thrust of his cock against her bottom—a rhythm neither one of them could resist. "I'll take both of you. I *will*. And the whole farking Empire will just have to live with it. I damn well decided that much tonight. But Ben has to agree—and, as he currently despises me for an act of ethnic genocide I tried to prevent but couldn't, that outcome is far from a forgone conclusion. What else?"

"No more biowars," she said without thinking.

Because the time for thinking was done.

"I'm going to part with a state secret. An act that, in case you're wondering, is a security infraction and a felony offense." He pulled her closer, pushing up her shirt to bare her breasts. Knowing fingers cupped her fullness, weighing her in his hands. When she pushed into his touch, he found her taut nipples and worked them in unison.

She thought she'd lose her sanity.

Mindless with wanting, she writhed against him. "I can keep a secret. Tell me."

"I was never going to use novicide against the Syndax," he muttered. "That was my accursed father's weapon. I can't abide the stuff—only keep mine for deterrence. To ensure it's never used against me. And I'm trusting you with my life and the security of the Empire by telling you."

It never even occurred to her to wonder if he was lying. Her sense of his personal integrity had never squared with her knowledge of his arsenal of nasties.

Which meant she believed him.

"And Zorin," she finished in a rush. "He's part of this. You know he is. You know we both—"

"Absolutely not." He pinched her nipples hard. Hard enough to make her moan. A fresh rush of heat slicked her thighs. "Don't finish that thought. I don't care what the devil you just dreamed. *Not him.*"

She pulled in her breath to argue. With a rumble of warning, he slid his palm down the taut plane of her tummy and eased under her pajamas.

"You're wet for me," he whispered in her ear. "I can smell it. Aren't you?"

Her brain jettisoned every syllable of reason.

And all she could do was pant.

His calloused fingers dipped beneath the silky scrap of panties for the very first time to find her slick heat. Bare as an egg because that worked best with a cybersuit.

"Gods of Olympus," he groaned on a long exhale. Her entire body tingled as she breathed in another hit of the come-get-me pheromones that spiked his mating scent. His clever fingers slid down her slit, glided through her hot cream, spread her wide and swirled her own wetness over her clit.

A lightning bolt of need shot straight through her. She rose into his touch, eyes falling closed, her shuddering pants loud in the deep-space silence.

She thanked all Ninety-Nine Gods in the Kryll pantheon he knew just what she needed, holding her spread and exposed to his touch, circling her swollen clit until she thrust against him, her thighs wide and trembling with tension.

Blind to everything except her own violent need.

"Please," she gasped, hand closing over his to deepen the pressure. "Oh, gods of my father, Dex, *please*."

"I want to see you beg for my cock. I want to feel you ride my hand. I want to hear you cry my name. And when I decide you want it badly enough—when you convince me you're ready—I'm going to make you climax until you plead for mercy."

Trapped between the solid strength of his chest behind her and the rhythmic friction of his hand in front, arms tight around her, fingers unsparing as he played her, she knew he was more than capable of carrying out his threat.

She could think of nothing, see nothing, feel nothing but him.

Dex Draven.

Master of half the known galaxy.

With all that contained power and ruthless will and boundless patience bent on the single-minded mission of making her shatter into a trillion tiny pieces.

"Beg me for it, darling." While he worked her clit, one finger slid into her tight heat. "Gods, you're so hot for me. So ready for me. So perfect for me. Beg me."

He wanted her to beg? So she begged. While she thrust into his hand and clenched around his finger and they shot through space at hyperspeed and stars swam in her eyes.

"Dex, please, I need—if you're the one, I need…"

"I am the one." His voice went guttural with passion. "There's nothing I won't give you. Tell me what you need."

Finally she gasped out the words she'd never said to a living soul.

"I need you inside me. You—I mean—your—" She swallowed hard. "Your cock. I need you right now."

The room crackled with a volt of electric silence. A silence laced with their labored breath.

Then he was dragging off her pants and she was pulling at his. Distant starfire transmitted just enough energy over light-years of empty space to reveal him—the guy who'd finally stormed her castle— powerfully built as a Mogadon battleship, flat planes of muscle flexing in his chest and bulging in his biceps under skin seared bronze by the Mogadon sun.

All that strength so perfectly contained under his buttoned-tight uniform. He was bigger than she'd thought.

In every way.

A supple column of abdominal muscle pulled her gaze down to a spectacle that stunned her like a blaster bolt. Dex Draven, ferociously aroused and ready for her, thick cock ridged and swollen and dripping, was a sight to steal any girl's breath.

As she watched under lowered lids, mouth open and hands itching to touch him, he wrapped a fist around his cock and gave a few leisurely strokes that spread glistening moisture down his length and made fresh precum gather at his slit.

Her chest vibrated with a groan of longing.

He knelt over her, blond hair falling over eyes that blazed like cobalt suns, the hard planes of his face predatory with possession. His gaze devoured her—naked now herself except for the stretchy shirt rucked tight above her bare breasts. Taking that off would disturb her bandage.

Besides, she thought he liked the sight of her in disarray, clothes pushed carelessly aside to bare her for his pleasure.

That combustible notion propelled her past her last hesitation. Teeth sinking into her lower lip, she slid her hands over her breasts and undulated her acrobat's body.

"Are you just going to sit there and watch?" she whispered.

A visible shudder rippled through his sinewed frame. In an eyeblink he crouched over her, crawling up her body with a lion's stalking menace, tongue painting a trail of heat up her belly, cock a column of fire between her thighs.

"Kaia," he rasped against her skin. "Tell me the truth. It's your first time, isn't it?"

"Just… the penetration part."

She couldn't pretend it didn't scare the space out of her. Trusting this—trusting him—trusting anyone. He wasn't even her consort. They hadn't dealt with the Patriarch. They hadn't even dealt with Zorin, and they *were* definitely dealing with him, and Zorin had been half in love with Dex forever, and now she knew Dex wanted him too—

"Stop thinking about that blasted Syndax." He raised his tawny head to nail her with a burning stare. "I'm the only man in this bed. I'll make it good for you. I swear I'll make it so good."

She slid her hands over the smooth skin stretched tight over his shoulders and down the powerful column of his back and wrapped her fingers around the succulent bulge of his ass. His cock probed the slick folds of her heat. A moan rippled from her throat and she writhed beneath him.

"It's already good for me," she whispered. "The way things are with me right now, you can't do this wrong."

She traced dry lips with her tongue and watched his eyes ignite. "You wanted me to beg for your cock? Dex, please, I'm begging you—"

His mouth claimed hers with an openmouthed moan before she'd even gotten the words out, tongue meeting tongue in a sizzling stroke of possession. In tandem, he eased two fingers into her aching channel. And her brain just about short-circuited. He worked her in a rhythm that had her thrusting against his fingers, her hands clutching his derrière to drag him close.

"Dex," she panted, "I can't—can't wait—"

"Yes, you can. You made me wait," he groaned into her mouth. "You made me lose my mind waiting. Gods, Kaia, you're so tight. Do you have the first blooming notion how amazing you're going to feel wrapped around my cock?"

When he added a third finger, her body went supernova. She bucked against him like he was already riding her, breasts bouncing beneath his fiercely dominating stare, her own desperate cries shrill and shameless.

"Don't pretend—it doesn't get you off," she gasped. "You're Mogadon—aren't you? I thought—you relished—the hunt."

And just to keep him from getting too complacent, she did what she'd been dying to do ever since she saw him naked.

She wrapped her hand around the hot hard column of his cock.

Gripping him was like gripping a live electric cable. His body jerked and his shaft jumped. He was taut and smooth and slick, already as wet for her as she was for him. She swiped a finger across his slit and spread moisture down his length, jacking him slow and steady, loving the way he thrust into her fist.

She knew she couldn't play with him the way she did with Nero. Who was atoning for years of suffering. Nero had let her dominate him—at least, he had *once*—and she'd always sensed what Nero needed from his men was domination.

Dex was a different beast. He dominated everyone he'd ever met. He was the literal alpha male of the entire Mogadon race.

And if the Empire's alpha male ever did submit to the Syndax leader? The two of them together were going to be thermonuclear.

"Not happening," Dex growled at the thought, even while his breath hitched and he thrust hard and fast and savage into her hand. Getting off on what they were both thinking.

Dex on his knees with his mouth full of cock.

And she was really… *really*… losing it…

With a curse he pushed her flat, pinned her beneath his weight, nudged her thighs roughly apart with his knee.

On the naked edge of climax, she clawed at his back and sank her teeth into his shoulder.

"You asked for this," he groaned. "You and your filthy fantasies about me and that damn pirate. I'm telling you. It's. Not. Happening."

Still, his consuming obsession to claim her was entwined with the incendiary notion of Zorin getting off in his mouth. Even when his rigid cock prodded her slick channel and thrust slow and deep, claiming her with tender violence. The elemental, unprecedented shock of penetration slammed through her.

As though the three of them… even the four of them… were already in bed together.

And thinking of the three of them—maybe even the four of them together—being claimed and used and ridden by all three of them… maybe even all three of them *at once*…

That landslide of powerful visuals, coupled with all that mind-blowing physical sensation, wrenched from her throat a sharp cry.

"Sorry," he muttered. "Hurting you?"

"It's nothing," she panted. "Samurai, remember?"

"Damnation, this isn't one of your hair-raising illegal cyber runs. I *am* hurting you—"

"Only if you stop," she gasped, frantic hands clutching him close. "Don't you dare stop."

He cradled her face between his hands and caught her cries in deep, hungry kisses as he rocked into her. Tremors of building crisis rocked her and made her mindless.

"Kaia—gods—darling," he grunted, savage with need. "You feel unreal. This time—I'm not—going to last."

*Neither am I,* she thought. Beyond speech. Beyond thought. Beyond anything. *Love this… Love your cock inside me… I love—*

"Let me feel you come for me," he growled. "Right now."

Her orgasm shattered and broke her. Her pussy gripped him and milked him in tight rippling spasms that pushed him hard over the edge. He convulsed with a raw shout of elation.

Gouts of liquid heat spurted inside her.

She must have shot into the stratosphere like a supersonic missile. Because when her vision cleared, Dex was crouched over her, peering into her face with worried eyes.

"Was I too rough?" he rasped. "Talk to me."

"Actually, um, I loved it." Body aching with satiated pleasure—a pleasure she was still astonished and gratified he could make her feel— she summoned a sleepy smile and patted the golden stubble of his cheek. "I loved all of it. And I love it when you're rough. Which can't be a total news flash, can it, space cadet? When you sent me skyrocketing through the ceiling, I wasn't exactly subtle."

A fiercely masculine pleasure surfaced in his face. "You were positively incandescent. So gorgeous it hurt to look at you. Knowing you chose me, knowing I'm your first? Darling, you couldn't possibly have made me happier."

Yet his eyes were still anxious as he cupped her chin and searched her gaze. "But your injuries…?"

"As I keep reminding you, I'm a Prime Class samurai. I'm fine. More than fine. I'm perfect."

She pulled in a deep breath. And felt the familiar straitjacket of Tombola nerves close around her and squeeze until she could barely breathe.

*Well… maybe not perfect.*

Pulse jumping against her skin, she rolled to her uninjured side to study his pagan profile against the star-streaked night. "What I want to know is—now that we've done this—now that we can't go back—what comes next. With the Tombola."

"That gods-cursed Tombola. We keep playing your father's gods-cursed game, that's what," he said grimly, eyes hooded and brooding. "We play it through to the bitter end. Tomorrow you'll rest and you'll heal and I'll run the show. Entertain the new bids. We'll down-select the final hundred, shove more of the bastards off my ship…"

He kept talking, and she kept trying like blazes to focus. But sleep was rising to roll over her in a sonic wave.

With a sigh, Dex pulled her into his arms and tucked her tight against his chest. She snuggled into his strength with a contented murmur. She hadn't been sure he was the kind of guy who'd like to hold her while they slept. But, yeah, he seemed to like it plenty…

"We need to talk to Ben. And Zorin. They'll help," she mumbled. "It's the four of us, Dex. It *has* to be the four of us."

"We'll talk about the four of us later." His flinty tone left no room for debate. His hand cradled her head and his chin rested on her crown.

Just this once, she was too done in to argue.

She turned her face into the warm column of his neck and let her lids drift shut.

"You're fertile. You didn't tell me. But somehow… I *knew*. And Ben was losing it tonight because he knows too, doesn't he?" His whisper, raw with yearning, chased her into sleep. "Yet you still chose me. That's a choice I won't forget."

He barely breathed the rest, and she wasn't sure she heard him.

"Give me a son. Your son and mine. I swear I'll lay the whole Mogadon Empire at your feet. And at his."

#

"Absolutely not." Dex infused his voice with all the steely sternness of a First Indomitable's command. "Getting you into my bed required the guile of a serpent, the patience of a saint, and the discipline of a god. Not to mention the resilience to survive no fewer than three assassination attempts. The very least you can do is stay there and rest for a few clicks before you send us lurching into our next interplanetary crisis."

Snuggled up against the headboard of his bed, flushed and rumpled from sleep, her tight little body swimming in one of Dex's shirts while she sipped her morning *chaco*, Kaia wrinkled her nose at him.

"No need to go full-bore Mogadon. I said I'll stay here and wait for your medic."

Her lilac gaze wandered over him as he fastened the shining buttons of his dress uniform and buckled his ceremonial saber around his waist.

She was giving him the definite sense she liked what she saw. Which was nearly enough encouragement to persuade him to forgo the morning's distasteful necessities entirely and crawl back into her bed.

Contemplating that appealing prospect, his unruly cock stirred with interest.

But he had that damn tribunal to lead. An investigation into the conspiracy to oversee. Punishment for the latest attempt on his life to inflict.

Besides, Kaia needed time to recover from their recent encounter, whether she wanted time or not. Last night he'd been her first.

And he'd been ruthless.

Just the way she wanted him.

In that fashion and in so many others, he and his future consort were spectacularly well suited.

Eyeing his predatory grin as he loomed over her, she colored up— which delighted him—and buried her face in her mug.

"The least you can do is give me a sit rep," she urged. "What's happening out there?"

Deftly he buttoned his cuffs. "We're ninety-six clicks out from Quorum Central Starbase, where we'll rendezvous with your father, broadcast the victor over interstellar news, and complete the ritual. Which means we're precisely on schedule. By the time we dock, we'll have rid ourselves of four hundred ninety of your woefully disappointed suitors. To that end, Nero and I will be hearing bids all day."

He checked the time on his wrist unit. "And at some point during these interminable proceedings, I'll need to find some damn privacy to woo the man. Based on how skittishly he was behaving last night, I fully expect to find him reluctant."

Amid the day's tightly scheduled program of otherwise unwelcome obligations, the prospect of wooing Ben Nero—especially a reluctant Nero who made him work for it—made his entire body tingle with electric tension.

Because he wasn't nearly as blasé about breaking a lifelong taboo as he'd managed to make it sound.

And the thought of seducing his boyhood best friend—his secret obsession for half his lifetime—the thought of easing and teasing the guy past both their reservations and peeling off the sleek silks and lush furs of the Valyrian Precursor's barbarian finery and… oh gods, if he only dared… bending him forward over his bed and finally, finally knowing how it felt to work his aching length one breath at a time into Ben Nero's tight heat—

Gruffly Dex cleared his throat and ran a finger under his collar.

Damn if he wasn't sweating.

"All of which means," he finished gruffly, "there's zero reason for you to get out of that bed."

"What if I'd like to watch?" she murmured, husky with passion.

Saturn, he wanted that.

It took every particle of practicality he possessed to say no.

"Kaia. I've kept the man at arm's length for ten years. I very much suspect a heaping portion of humble pie is the featured entree on my luncheon menu. The least you can give me is privacy while I beg him for forgiveness."

She sipped her *chaco* and eyed his resolute bearing with a thoughtful expression that—knowing her the way he now did—made him decidedly twitchy.

*Take it easy. She's wearing your clothes. Sleeping in your bed. Bearing your child, all the gods willing. And no matter what you're off doing all day with Nero, you've scented her so thoroughly any Mogadon male who gets within twenty cubits of her—including her remaining suitors—is going to know you came until you couldn't see straight buried inside her last night. Every Mogadon on this ship will know precisely what that means.*

*She's mine.*

*And they'll back the hell off.*

All of which afforded him the most profound satisfaction.

He almost wished that infernal Syndax were here with them right now for a private tutorial on how thoroughly Dex had claimed his woman. In fact, the thought of sliding between her legs while Zorin watched… showing him just what it took to get her off and just how much she liked it… was so bloody tempting he was getting hard just thinking about it.

Although why in the seven devils it made him hard to fantasize about getting naked in front of his Syndax rival was a root-cause analysis he didn't care to conduct.

Kaia and Nero between them were going to be more than enough to command all his sexual attention for a lifetime.

No matter what the hell kind of dream he'd inexplicably had last night about Zorin.

Following his thoughts in that uncanny way she had, his future consort flashed him a grin that brimmed with sensual mischief.

"All right. If that's what you want, I won't object," she murmured. "I'll even stay here and rest and let you do your, uh, wooing of Ben without me. On one condition." Her delicate face hardened with purpose. "You let me talk to Zorin about all this."

"No," he shot back.

"Yes." Her voice rang with resolve. "He's part of this, Dex. Then you let me talk to *all* of you—all three of you."

"Kaia—"

"And you *listen*. Because it's going to take all four of us working together to survive this Tombola without triggering my father and his kill edict."

The chime of his wrist unit spared him the need to reply. Although he knew his reprieve to be temporary at best.

"Report," he clipped out.

"I beg you'll excuse the intrusion, Commander. I've the cleanup crew outside to tote those bodies off to the morgue. Along with Dr. Cato, sir."

"Ah." Dex allowed himself a crisp nod of satisfaction. "Very well, Titus. Give me two ticks. Then send them all in."

"Cato? What's he doing here?" Distaste flickering across her expressive face, Kaia placed her mug on the nightstand and started crawling out of bed.

"No, you don't." Dex planted a booted foot firmly on the mattress to block her exit. "You're staying right the hell here." *Where you belong.* "Cato's here at my request. He's a close ally. Very nearly the only truly reliable Mogadon ally I've got. Not to mention you need a medic and he's the best in the fleet—and the only one I trust."

"To examine me?" She looked appalled at the notion. Shooting to her knees, she faced him down with a scowl.

And the sight of her kneeling between his legs wearing nothing but her silky black panties and his shirt grazing her slim golden thighs provided the most profound distraction.

"Gods of the nine realms, *why?*" She braced her hands on her hips. "He runs your biowar program."

"He's a glorified administrator. Because, as you'll recall, we aren't actually deploying the novicide." Unable to prevent himself, he wound his hand in the burgundy silk of her hair.

Her mutinous mouth tightened. "And he's a failed suitor. Spectacularly so."

"Not quite." Dex waded into these dangerous waters with meticulous care. "I've advanced him to the final two hundred. And I plan to keep advancing him."

Violet lightning flashed in her eyes. Reminding him quite fetchingly of Nero in a temper. "I don't think so, Dex Draven."

"I'd like you to hear me out." He lifted her hair to his lips and breathed in the deeply satisfying scent of jasmine and ozone spiced with his own dark musk. "Cato's in on the plan." *To the extent that I have a plan.* "In fact, he's an indispensable component of the plan."

"Don't you think *I* should be in on the plan?"

Dex held on to his patience. "I'm trying to tell you. I intend to boost his bid. I'll put the entire Empire treasury behind him if I must. I'll boost him until he wins—"

Angrily she shook herself free. "Like punking *hell* you will—"

"At which point," Dex finished firmly, because firmness was the key to handling Kaia in a temper, "we'll trigger the substitution clause in his Tombola contract. And he'll step aside for me."

"That's taking one flying leap of a chance!" Wrathful color climbed in her face. "That clause is a relic. It's hardly ever used. And Cato's a mass murderer in a lab coat. Which means you trust him with our future *why?*"

"Darling, you're not being fair." Dex sighed. "To him. And the reason I trust him is because he's my brother."

#

"Why in the seven hells didn't you tell me you're Dex's brother?"

Despite promising herself she'd stay calm about this morning's news bomb—at least while Pontius Cato doctored her lacerated feet—Kaia couldn't help sitting bolt upright in Dex's bed while she fired off the question that bothered her the most.

Tidy hands busy with the polymer dressing on her soles, the slender blond medic shot her a cautious blue glance. She was kicking herself now for not seeing the family resemblance.

But the doc camouflaged it pretty much flawlessly behind that unassuming bedside manner.

"Don't be offended," he said mildly. "We're only half brothers—and I nothing more than another of my father's numerous bastards. One of a devil's dozen Max Draven left scattered about the galaxy. To say most of us are virtual strangers would scarcely be an overstatement."

"You're telling me Dex has a dozen brothers?" She gaped. "I mean… half brothers? Are they more like him or like you?"

"As I've said, I barely know most of them." Cato hesitated. "Except for Caligula, of course. Everyone knows Caligula. He's rather… the anti-Dex. In every conceivable way."

"You don't say?" Intrigued as blazes at the thought of a dozen Dravens, Kaia marshaled her mind to the matter and eyed him with suspicion. "And don't try to distract me. I'm asking about Dex and *you*."

"There is no 'us.' We weren't raised together, and even that nebulous relationship was rarely one our father cared to acknowledge."

"Why's that?"

Cato sketched a diffident shrug. "To Maximus Draven, I was the most profound disappointment. My scholarly interests were deemed to be… decidedly unmanly. Dex was the golden boy—the idol my father assured me I should strive to emulate. Is it any wonder I resolved early in life to succeed by my own merits rather than my family connections?"

As he finished up down below and shifted his attention to her arm, Kaia wiggled her toes experimentally. The new dressings were designed to cushion her feet when she walked. But she didn't think she'd be landing triple flips anytime soon.

"And yet," she pointed out, "you chose to apply your scientific brainpower to developing deadly bioweapons. Which was your father's obsession. Didn't he finally appreciate you for that?"

Cato looked blank, as though he'd never drawn that connection.

Finally he said, "He was in no position to notice. I was still at university when Zorin killed him."

She wished she could read the guy. Or that Ben with his Precursor superpowers was here to do it. But she didn't need to see inside Pontius Cato's head to decipher his bottom line.

Max Draven had left both his sons—and probably all of them—a legacy of emotional wreckage.

"With that kind of upbringing," she said softly, "I'm amazed you don't hate Dex."

"I've never seen the point. Our father was a monster, but Dex was always decent." He shot her a wry look. "Besides, one day he'll rule the entire galaxy instead of only half of it. I am at heart a pragmatist."

"So you're *friends* now, you and Dex?" She cocked a skeptical brow but scooted closer to give him better access. "He doesn't trust easily—but he clearly trusts you."

"That's because I'm thoroughly compliant," he said lightly, peeling back her bandage. "A survival trait one learns early under a Draven dictatorship."

But he softened the observation with one of the rueful smiles that had disarmed her the first time they met.

"You're wondering if you can trust me to walk away once I win." His slim fingers probed carefully at the edges of the blaster burn. "As I mentioned when we met, I'm faithfully wedded to my work. In fact, my dear, I may be the only healthy Mogadon male on this battleship who isn't currently harboring nocturnal fantasies that feature you as the star attraction. This despite the fact that Dex has all but issued a planetary edict telling the entire Mogadon population 'hands off.'"

Hissing with pain as he prodded gently, Kaia tried again to read him—with no more success getting into his enigmatic head than if he'd been a robot. Still, she'd developed pretty accurate antennae when it came to detecting masculine interest.

At this Tombola, that too was a flipping survival trait.

And that instinct was telling her every word Pontius Cato said about his nonexistent attraction to her was true.

Clearly perceiving her discomfort, he slathered on a numbing ointment. She released her breath in a sigh of relief.

"Better?" His blond brows lifted. "Excellent. This polymer dressing is antimicrobial, air-permeable and water-resistant. In other words, it should suffice to protect your injury splendidly for up to several days. I'll dispatch a clinician shortly to collect a DNA sample so we can synthesize your skin graft. Dex has issued strict instructions to have you patched up in time for your mating."

Just the thought of mating Dex Draven in four days' time had her hot. In fact, given a good four days to work with, she firmly intended to be mating all *three* of her men.

And the thought of having all three of them in the same bed—every one of them fiercely competitive and fiercely determined to sire her son—was positively explosive.

"Thanks for hooking me up," she said softly. "You'd really have no problem making a career of patient care since—" Suddenly recalling what she wasn't supposed to know, she covered her hesitation with a cough. "—since my auction seems to have delayed your biowar."

"Why, to the contrary." Cato smoothed her adhesive bandage and gathered his med kit. "I've received orders to lay down novicide on the Syndax outpost at Quorum Central Starbase. Our Chemical Corps is forward deploying to complete that mission as we speak."

Kaia's world lurched sideways and the floor dropped from her gut. *"What?"*

"Of course that information is embargoed," he continued calmly. "And exceptionally sensitive. But since you're shortly to become Dex's consort, you'll inevitably be privy to his warfighting strategy."

Her belly roiled with shock and dread. Her heart crowded uncomfortably into her throat. Kaia gathered unsteady legs beneath her and tottered to her bandaged feet.

Because somehow she knew she needed to be standing to face this.

"Cato—what the flip are you telling me?"

Belatedly it seemed to dawn on Pontius Cato that his patient was rather more agitated than standard medical treatment would warrant.

"Surely this comes as no surprise, my dear." He tilted his head with a quizzical air. "You must be entirely acquainted with Dex's hatred for the Syndax leader."

"But Zorin is *here*. And Dex—he *wouldn't*—"

"Our Zephyrs will be stealthed, and the Syndax we infect at Quorum won't become symptomatic straightaway. However, they will be highly infectious. Rendering the contamination of Zorin's *Relentless,* his crew, and the Syndax leader himself a mathematical certainty."

Upright or flat, she couldn't seem to wrap her head around what he was telling her. Maybe Cato simply hadn't gotten the message. Maybe somehow he'd garbled it. Maybe Dex hadn't had time to convey it.

Even if that wasn't what her instincts were screaming.

"But he—he's going to cancel those plans," she stammered. "If they even exist."

*He said he'd never use it. The novicide.*

"To the contrary, Dex confirmed the launch order this morning." Cato paused. "I'll allow you do appear a bit startled."

*That's the understatement of the millennium. Especially since I was starting to think I'm in love with him.*

All of which left her with perishingly few palatable options. Beyond blind denial.

Which had never worked well for her.

"It would violate the ceasefire," she said inanely.

To which he said nothing. But his eyes were so sympathetic, he broke her heart anyway.

"Cato. I don't—I don't believe you."

And her voice when she said it was so lost and desperate it didn't even sound like hers.

"Well, you certainly needn't take my words on faith." Cato unfolded to his feet and slipped quietly toward the door. "In fact, I'd encourage you not to. All the data required to validate my assertion are readily available in the *Inevitable*'s hangar bay. The novicide is being loaded onto the Zephyrs for dissemination as we speak. If you wish to know the truth, why not investigate the matter for yourself?"

He was halfway to the door when she pushed past her shock and switched on her brain. "Wait a tick, Cato—wait. Why are you even telling me this, when you knew how I'd react? Some kind of sibling rivalry? Can't stand to see your golden boy brother get the girl?"

Cato placed a gentle hand on the door panel and slid her a level stare.

"I'm a physician, Kaia. Which means I'm not exactly eager to see innocent billions perish in the next Draven biowar. The reason I'm telling you, specifically, is because I know you share the sentiment. And because I'm daring to hope you'll help me stop him."

#

Something was up with Dex.

Nero knew it as clearly as if Dex's defense attaché had just handed Nero a briefing memo. All they'd been doing all morning was sit in the sternly functional confines of Dex's ready room hearing Tombola bids from an unrelenting barrage of Kaia's insufferable suitors.

But every time Dex looked at Nero, color crept up the First Indomitable's neck.

Normally Nero would be scheming to get him alone. Just to explore what other physiological responses his intimate presence might stimulate.

Because Dex was definitely into him.

He'd have to be headblind not to know exactly how much Dex was into him. Not after Dex threw open the gates to the castle last night and let Nero hunt through his head for the face of the telepath who'd attacked him.

An idiot kid who was still—annoyingly—at large. And had quite possibly fled the ship.

But he'd meant every syllable he told Dex last night. Thanks to his psychotic father, the guy was carting around in his cranium a whole battery of sexual hang-ups he was never getting past. After that peek in Dex's head, Nero was now an expert witness on the minefield of same-sex Mogadon prejudice embedded in Dex's psyche.

Not that Dex had ever kept his upbringing secret. Nero simply hadn't understood how deeply those corrosive roots had invaded.

All of which meant Nero needed to accept the irrevocable reality of Dex's limitations and finally—*finally*—move on with his life. He was done letting his boyhood best friend cut his teeth on Nero's lacerated heart—

*Shock. Grief. Rage. Betrayal.*

Without a pebble of warning, an avalanche of devastation crashed over him. A blast wave of emotion from his lifemate. Emotion so strong it would've rendered a lesser telepath catatonic.

Suddenly Nero found himself on his feet and running for the door.

"Bloody hell, Ben." Dex thrust to his feet, cutting short the tiresome bluster of Kaia's nineteenth suitor of the day, rudely interrupted mid-bid. "What the devil—?"

"It's Kaia." Barely stopping himself from running blindly into the hall, Nero spun toward Dex, cloak swirling in his wake. "Where is she?"

Dex didn't waste time asking questions. He clipped into his wrist unit, "Marcus, where's the maharani?"

After an agonizing wait, the faint reply came back. "Hangar bay. Doing a spot of maintenance on that sweet little K-class cruiser—"

"The *Interstellar Angel*." Nero's heart nearly stopped.

He wasn't prescient—that wasn't his gift—but he didn't need telepathy to know something was way the hell wrong.

"Dex! Don't let her near that ship!"

Without waiting for Dex to start issuing orders, Nero bolted through the portal and tore down the corridor like the seven devils were hunting him. Dex's booted footfalls pounded at his heels in pursuit.

Nero ran with his heart in his gullet.

Because it didn't take a particle of prescience to know they'd arrive too late.

# CHAPTER FIVE
## The Transcript

*Just pretend everything's normal.*

*Even though nothing will ever be normal again.*

Eyes swimming with tears of shock and betrayal, Kaia strode with furious purpose through the harshly lit industrial clamor of the *Inevitable's* hangar bay. Making a beeline from the three Zephyrs whose underbelly spray tanks were sucking up slurry from the truck blazoned with its biohazard warning. Where a pair of grim-faced techs in hazmat suits and respirators just kept manning the pumps as the fighters absorbed their lethal payload.

*He lied to me.*

*I slept with him. I trusted him. I even thought I loved him.*

*And that farking son of a bitch lied to me.*

But she couldn't think about Dex now. She couldn't. Not unless she wanted to lose it right here on the tarmac. Because once she started crying, she didn't think she'd stop.

And she had way too much mission to accomplish right now to allow herself that luxury.

Across the hangar bay, the *Interstellar Angel* had never looked better. Kaia had already fired her up through the psi tech in her lightning bolt earring. Told the watchdogs Dex had tailing her she was running routine maintenance.

Which no one had any cause to doubt.

After all, she'd been a model prisoner ever since they lit out from Mogadon. She was sleeping with their alpha and the whole ship knew it.

She'd been given free rein.

And no one got past the magnetoelectric lock on the *Inevitable's* outer blast doors to punch a cruiser free from the belly of the beast without layers of security code and hard-copy permits she didn't have.

But that wasn't how she was leaving.

She kept her stride quick and confident. Added a little sway to her hips in her sleek black cybersuit for the benefit of her viewing audience. While she touched her earring and murmured to her ship.

"Okay, *Angel*. Fire up the full-body cyberport."

As she walked past a hundred pairs of curious eyes, she slipped from her utility belt the cyber chip she'd gotten as a gift from Zorin and pressed it discreetly into the jack at her temple.

For a breath, the world around her went gray and filmy. The metallic tang of the cyberverse turned her tongue to rust.

"Stars and planets," she breathed.

That transcription chip was one potent piece of tech.

Which it flipping well needed to be, since she was about to entrust it with her life. A chip programmed to probe a half-baked theory that was more urban myth than hard science. A chip that had been tested on a real human exactly twice. A chip she was smart enough to fear.

Because that transcription chip was dangerous.

*Steady on, samurai. Zorin used it. He trusted it.*

*And if you can't trust him, you really are punked.*

The *Angel* yawned before her, hatch down to frame her cockpit's flashing violet lights. In her shadowy belly, the cyberport hummed, the twin columns of her master cables hanging at the ready.

Her heart was pounding. Her chest was tight. Her mouth was parchment.

*You can do this, angel. Just sashay into that cyberport and grab those jumper cables. The chip will do the rest...*

*I hope.*

"Kaia!" The bark of Dex's bellow, shredded with fear and taut with fury, riveted the entire hangar bay in its boots. "Stop!"

*Step it up. It's showtime.*

Kaia shifted to a run. Every stride sent agony shafting through her soles. The impact hammered her damaged feet.

"Stop that woman!" Dex roared. "Bloody *now*!"

She ducked her head and sliced a look sideways to find Dex and Nero pelting toward her—thirty cubits away but closing fast. From the opposite quadrant, her watchdogs barreled toward her, electrified by sheer terror of their infuriated alpha.

"Kaia, for gods' love, *wait*!"

That was her lifemate, voice infused with psychic dread. Terrified for her without knowing why. He couldn't make sense of the mess in her head.

For Nero, she might have waited.

Except she knew she'd never be allowed to leave the *Inevitable* if she did.

And she needed to warn Zorin before Dex unleashed his apocalyptic weapon.

Before he launched another biowar that would slaughter billions.

Her pursuing lovers were barely five cubits from the *Angel*, Dex surging into the lead, when she pounded past them up the ramp. She caught a single searing flash of their faces that would be burned on her brain forever—if she survived this crazy stunt—stark with urgency and blazing with determination.

"Comets, Dex!" Nero gasped. "She's got something. Don't you dare let her near that cyberport!"

Raw fear and deadly purpose invading his face, Dex drew his blaster.

Kaia launched through the air and dove into the cyberport—body airborne, arms stretched, fingers straining.

*Please please please—*

As she catapulted past, her desperate hands closed around the dangling cables and gripped tight.

Lightning slammed through her with the howling force of a hundred hurricanes.

Her whole world went white.

#

Dex fired his blaster barely a beat too late.

The bolt slammed into the *Angel*'s power source and fried it to toast. The console's flashing lights and sensors went black. Smoke billowed from the battery and the scent of burning wire stung his throat like acid.

But Dex didn't give one demonical damn.

He was staring at the empty cyberport. Staring at the jumper cables still swinging gently from their impact with Kaia's flying form.

But not staring at Kaia.

Because Kaia herself was… simply… *gone*.

"Gods and demons," Nero whispered at his side.

Dex sliced him a sharp look and found him white-faced and stricken. Frozen with a look of helpless terror he'd never seen on Ben Nero. Dex found he really didn't like seeing it there now.

His heart was slamming against his chest. He had to clear his throat twice before he could speak. "Ben—where—is she?"

"Nowhere. She's nowhere. I can't feel her."

Dex staggered and groped for something… anything… to steady him on his feet before he fell. When his vision cleared, he was clutching fistfuls of Ben's tunic in a desperate grip.

With Ben grasping Dex's shoulders like he was in imminent danger of falling himself.

They stared each other down. Held each other up. Kept each other sane.

Just barely.

While Dex struggled without success to order Ben's words into reason.

He tried again, syllables scraping painfully from his locked throat. "Where. *Is.* She."

"That's what I'm trying to tell you." Nero's face was haunted and his eyes black with shock. "Dex—she's just—*gone*."

#

Kaia couldn't breathe.

Because she didn't have lungs.

She was only a notion, a spark, a memory. Hurtling through space at a supersonic pace that stripped away blood and bone and skin and sinew and every scrap of psyche. She didn't have a body. Yet her entire being felt flayed and dipped in acid.

She was nothing. She was nowhere. She was terror. She was agony.

She tried counting backward from *ten… nine… eight…*

The vast expanse of sky was burning. A sheet of solid flame raced across the starry arc of the cyberverse faster than the blast wave of a hydrogen bomb. The roof of the universe was disintegrating. Splintering into flaming fragments that fell around her in a fiery rain.

Burning her to ash. She was agony.

*Six… five… four…*

She couldn't breathe. She couldn't breathe. Her heart was bursting in her nonexistent chest. Sky falling… walls burning… worlds colliding…

*Three… two… ONE…*

Something black and terrible rushed toward her and slammed into her with bone-breaking force.

Pain exploded through her limbs. Because she *had* limbs, lungs, body. Albeit a wretched body that felt scourged and scoured with salt. She was hunched on hands and knees over a metal grate, palms stinging and knees throbbing.

Somewhere, a woman was screaming.

When she dragged an excruciating breath past her raw throat to fill her starving lungs, the scream choked into silence.

That's when she realized the scream was hers.

"Moons of Jupiter, lady!" a gruff voice implored. "Please stop screaming. Where the punk did you come from?"

Blindly her head lifted. Through a curtain of wind-whipped hair and swinging cables, she made out the confines of an unfamiliar cyberport, cobbled together with last-gen tech. Loops of old graffiti sprayed over walls of bolted titanium, puddles of chemical condensation shimmering under grated floors, rows of overhead lights guttering in corroded sockets. Clogging her nostrils, the industrial reek of rust and motor oil hung thick.

Six cubits away, two tattooed titans in knotted dreadlocks with scuffed fighting leathers and shitkicker boots were scowling down at her.

Space pirates.

*Syndax.*

"Blow me," one of them rasped. "That's Zorin's girl."

Kaia closed her eyes and panted.

"Go get the big guy, Hotshot," the other rumbled. "Stop staring and beat feet. Now, you space trash!"

The hurried clunk of boots on metal clanged against the walls.

Something warm was dripping from her nose. Kaia fumbled a hand to swipe at the drip and found her fingers covered in blood.

"Please, lady, whatever you do—no more screaming," the

remaining Syndax pleaded. "My nerves can't take it. But you got yerself one heck of a nosebleed. Lemme get you a rag or something."

"Stay back," she scraped out, in a throat flayed raw from screaming.

"You're the boss, lady."

Not that she was in any shape to enforce it.

Pinching the bridge of her nose with shaky fingers, she straightened her aching body. Tried to get her legs under her. Tried to get her wits about her.

She saw nothing in her new digs to hearten her. In fact, she'd seen less unsavory ghettos on a mining asteroid. The pitiless cold of deep space seeped through the rusted walls and set her shivering until her teeth rattled. Belatedly, it occurred to her to wonder if betting all her creds on Zorin's play—a space pirate she'd known exactly two days— had really been her best move.

*A little late for regret, angel.*

The heavy thud of boots on metal brought her hand flying out to hold the world at bay, one knee braced under her, body splayed on the grating for balance.

With her hair in her eyes, she couldn't see squat.

"Kaia?" The familiar rasp of Zorin's voice slid through her. She closed her eyes in relief. "What the bewhosis is going on over there on the *Inevitable*? You look like someone dragged you backward through hell by the ankles."

"Sorry to barge in… without an invite." She struggled to get her feet under her. "I, uh, think your transcription chip needs a little work… before it's ready for prime time."

"Thanks for the user feedback." Humor warred with worry in his tone as the big Syndax hunkered over her. "Looks like you had a rough ride. Something happen at the other end?"

"Yeah, you could say that." She focused on just breathing. "I think Dex just blasted the hell out of my cyberport. He really wasn't on board with me lighting out of there."

"Goddamn lucky the kid didn't kill you with that stunt."

The lights must be guttering again, because the world was going dark. She squinted up at Zorin—shock and concern written all over his rugged features under spikes of sandy hair. Gods, he looked good to her.

Brow furrowing, he caught her struggling form and swung her

capably into his arms. And even that bare hint of the monumental strength contained in his colossal body made her weak.

Comets, this fertility thing was going to kill her. She'd already cast aside years of caution and tumbled into Dex's bed like a flipping fool.

And damn if she wasn't about to do the same flipping thing with Zorin.

"I can walk on my own." Actually she wasn't sure she could, but she deemed it prudent to pretend.

"Not on your life, sweetheart."

He cradled her against the broad slab of his armored chest, deep voice rumbling against her ear. The steel-and-wolf tang of his mating scent filled her head. And it was all she could manage not to swoon like the heroine in an antique novel and drown in his velvet darkness.

"I got you," he breathed. "I'm gonna take care of you, the way I should've insisted on right from the get-go. You're safe here on the *Relentless* with me."

"Zorin," she whispered through an aching throat. "I need to talk to you."

He shifted into motion with a predator's grace. The graffiti-sprayed walls blurred around her as his measured stride propelled them down that alarming-looking corridor.

"I'm all ears, sweetheart." His voice hardened to starmetal. "But I'm gonna have a few goddamn things to say to Dex Draven. I leave you in his hands for safekeeping—at his insistence—and you turn up here half-dead—"

"No." She gripped his face in her hands, strong jaw rough with silvery stubble beneath her palms. With the bump of his long-ago broken nose and the scar that split his tawny brow and the lines that bracketed his full mouth, he was brutal and beautiful.

He reassured her and he frightened her.

She fought to clear her head.

"Listen—Zorin—it's a trap! That's what I came here to tell you. Dex—he's sending Zephyrs to your docking station—on Quorum Central Starbase."

His aqua eyes locked on hers like heat-seeking missiles. Beneath her fingers, his face went hard and wary.

"You mean he's attacking?" His words were level, but his eyes were deadly. "He's violating the ceasefire?"

"They're stealth ships," she said miserably. "Armed with novicide. No one will even know they've been there. Zorin, you have to evacuate that base before—your docking crew, they'll be infected—and you wouldn't… wouldn't know…"

Ugh. She was losing it. Losing all ability to assemble words into sentences. Tears of frustration flooding her eyes, she dropped her hands and swiped at her face.

"Now you take it easy." His big hand cupped her dizzy head and eased her back against his shoulder. "I'll take it from here. By gods, you got more courage and more loyalty in your little finger than a Mogadon legion, don'tcha? You proved yourself to me and all the Syndax today. You better believe I won't forget it. And neither will my boys and gals. They're yours now, Kaia. They'll worship you."

She didn't need to be worshipped. And she couldn't take it easy.

Not until she knew what he intended to do.

"Zorin—you and Dex—"

"Kaia." His bulging arms cradled her gently as a litter of kittens. But his voice was grim enough to split rock. "You leave this with me. I know how to deal with Dex."

"Don't kill him." She was crying now for real, and knowing it was pathetic wasn't the same as stopping it. "Promise me you won't kill him. My father—the Tombola—Dex—I love him, Zorin, I love him, I was stupid and I slept with him and I love him. And Ben's on that ship. Gods of my father, promise me—promise me you *won't*—"

"Easy now." Warm lips brushed her cold forehead. "Sure wish your first rodeo coulda been with me. But I'm not gonna fire up my nukes and blow his sorry ass out of the sky for that. Leastways, not right this second. Any joe who takes out the *Inevitable* and those two hundred wannabes is gonna have the whole honking galaxy sending out the lynch mob. You can bet your blaster it won't be me who fires the first shot."

She swallowed down the sobs that burned her throat and pulled in a shaky breath. Too wiped out to express what she felt. That paralyzing surge of relief.

"Thank you," she whispered. Sweet and simple.

*Thank you for listening. And thank you for not blowing up over Dex and me. I knew there's a reason I trust you.*

"Hey, Hotshot." He aimed this directive at the two titans clumping at his heels. "Get me the head honcho on our docking station at Quorum. Tick Tock, I want probes nailed on Draven's missile tubes and torpedo bays. And scout ships deployed on our flanks. If that bastard even twitches—or if he tries to park stealth ships in our backyard—I wanna know about it *yesterday*, you feel me?"

"You got it, chief."

The two titans went charging off, space boots clanking against the grating. Zorin ducked his head to meet Kaia's worried gaze.

"I promise I'll talk to him first," he repeated, in a voice like soldered steel. "I'll even do it in person. And Dex better count himself all kinds of lucky he's got you pleading for his life."

Which left Kaia wondering if her actions had really delayed the outbreak of war between the Syndax and the Mogadon the way she'd hoped.

Or if she'd just made that war inevitable.

# CHAPTER SIX

## The Imposter

By the time Zorin strode into Dex's ready room—which still felt like Zorin's ready room, damn it—with four of his best boys to cover his six, he'd pretty much gotten a handle on that whole murderous rage thing he'd been fighting like holy heck to keep a lid on since Kaia turned up desperate and half-dead on his doorstep.

But whether Dex walked away from this long-overdue come-to-Jupiter convo still alive and kicking?

That was totally up to Dex.

He found the Mogadon lion pacing the confines of his den. All burnished hair and flashing epaulets and handsome enough to break hearts like always, blaster and saber strapped over his formal threads. Restless and deadly as the chained griffon of Mogadon myth.

Gleaming with silk and the dark glitter of gemstones, Ben Nero stood vigilant at the viewport, gauntlets stripped and hands lethal, his elegant frame charged with a dangerous stillness.

Both of them wired for violence.

Dex pivoted sharply to face him, lines of strain chiseled in his hard face, blue flames burning in his icy eyes. "How is she?"

"Like I told you on the horn—she's resting. And she's safe." Zorin signaled his boys to hang tight and let the door whoosh closed between them. "We're all damn lucky you didn't kill her with that knuckleheaded stunt. You know that, don'tcha?"

"And whose fault is that?" Dex said tightly. Working like the dickens to keep his cool, with mixed results. "What the devil were you thinking—giving her that cyber chip in the first place? With her reckless courage, her impulsive nature, you had *no bloody business—*"

"Easy, Dex," the telepath murmured, cloak whispering around his slim frame. "He knows who she is. We all do. But we didn't all know what she had."

"My point precisely." Dex strode forward to confront Zorin. Got right in his grille. Close enough to get a good whiff of the guy's mating scent.

The same scent he'd left all over Kaia.

Zorin would know that scent half a parsec away.

Even though the fact he'd become intimately familiar with Dex Draven's mating scent was something he was trying like hell not to dwell on. Along with the inconvenient discovery that having Kaia smell like both of them gave him that damn erotic kick.

"I'm sending Nero with a shuttle to that bucket of bolts you call a ship," Dex clipped out. "I want my Tombola ward back on board the *Inevitable* ten bloody ticks ago."

"Not happening." Zorin kept his voice level, which wasn't exactly easy with Dex pumping out enough pheromones to fuel a bloodbath— or an orgy. "I run a tight ship. One heck of a lot tighter than the three-ring circus you got going on over here. How many times has Kaia almost bought it with you running the show?"

"My protection has proven to be more than sufficient!" Dex clenched his fists and glared. "Until *you* gave her that farking chip—"

"Come on, kid." Zorin kept his hands where Dex could see them and away from his blaster. "How many more near misses do you need to face the truth? This whole hootenanny's about to blow up in all our faces. You know you can't keep her safe."

"There's not a guy in the galaxy who can pull that off." Nero slipped deftly between their bristling bodies. "That includes the two of you. Keeping Kaia safe and this Tombola afloat is going to take all three of us. That's what she believes. Which means the two of you need to find some way to bury the hatchet and make this thing work."

"Yeah," Zorin said softly. "About that *hatchet*. I got a few conditions of my own. Starting with a goddamn honest explanation for why I got docking crew in hazmat suits on battle alert over on Quorum waiting to get sprayed with novicide, *Dex*."

Bristling with aggression, Dex leaned in.

Which couldn't help but raise his own Mogadon hackles.

"This isn't a negotiation," Dex bit out. "I want Kaia back onboard this ship and that's a bloody order—"

"Gods of Solaris! You Mogadon males." An unlikely current of humor surfaced in Nero's voice. He laid a hand on Dex's chest and one on Zorin's to keep them apart. His languid purple gaze slid to Zorin. "Can't the two of you just play nice?"

And right there, in the middle of a showdown that could easily end in war, Zorin felt the light pressure of that potent touch shoot straight through his starmetal armor like a neutron torpedo.

Turned out he didn't mind having gorgeous Ben Nero's hands on his body.

Not even a little bit.

Even if that breaking news was pretty flipping inconvenient.

As his gaze locked on Nero's, the telepath's eyes darkened and his pupils dilated. The exotic scent of sandalwood swam in his head. Molten heat coiled in Zorin's cock.

He cleared his throat and tried a little thought experiment.

*Maybe you better let Dex and me duke this one out alone,* he suggested, all without saying a word. *You're kinda, well, a distraction. For both of us.*

Which was putting it mildly. Thanks to their head-to-head combat over Kaia, Dex already viewed Zorin as a sexual rival. Last thing the kid needed to see now was Zorin putting the moves on Nero.

Nero studied him with interest. *Is that something you think you might be doing? Putting the moves on me?*

One corner of Zorin's mouth curled up.

*We got our hands pretty full here, gorgeous. And I haven't had a boyfriend in years, so I'm pretty damn rusty when it comes to all that. But once this intergalactic shitfest's in our rearview mirror? I wouldn't rule it out.*

Nero's long lashes fell over his violet eyes. He gave Zorin's big body the sort of smoldering once-over that could keep a guy up at night—

"All right," Dex said gruffly. And he didn't look like he minded having Ben Nero's hands on his body either. "I'll allow that you have a legitimate grievance. But I'll say again what I said when you hailed. I never ordered any attack on your station. However…" A muscle flexed in his jaw. "I have been able to verify that three of my Zephyrs did indeed launch—without my knowledge or authorization—two clicks ago."

"You don't say?"

Despite the wall of distrust looming between them, Zorin was surprised as all get-out to hear Dex admit anyone scratched their ass on this war wagon without his authorization.

"They're stealthed, so they won't break cover to answer our hails." Making a visible effort to loosen the tension knotting his shoulders, Dex frowned and glanced away. "They logged a flight path to Quorum Central Starbase before they went dark. Moreover, it appears my brother Cato has flown off with them."

Pain tightened his blond brows. The pain of betrayal.

A pain that was plenty familiar to them both.

"Although his purpose remains unclear," Dex forged on grimly, "it's fair to conclude at this point those launch orders came from Cato. As did that biological payload—an experimental strain of some kind. I'd advise your docking crew to evacuate before those Zephyrs arrive."

Zorin had every reason in the world not to trust him. But for some damn reason, he believed the kid.

Maybe because Valyria's strongest telepath was standing right next to him. And as the scion of a race devastated by biological warfare, Nero wouldn't still be standing there—wouldn't have Dex's back the way he obviously still did—if Dex had just launched another germ war.

And if Dex was lying, Nero would know.

"My docking crew's trained and equipped to handle this. Long as they get a heads-up before impact, like we got from Kaia." Zorin frowned, trying to remember Dex's kid brother from the old days. The best he could conjure up was a fuzzy visual of a skinny blond bookworm in spectacles who'd dogged Dex's every step. "Cato. Isn't he the guy who just ratted you out to Kaia? The guy who set her off this morning?"

"That's the one," Nero said softly. "And, curiously, he's the only human I've ever met whose head I can't get into."

"Assuming he's human at all," Zorin muttered.

Although really, it couldn't be. The wild-ass suspicion that was tugging his sleeve for attention was way too far-fetched to believe.

"What the devil does that mean?" Dex demanded. "Cato may have just betrayed me—which, if true, constitutes an act of treason I can scarcely afford to ignore. But, traitor or no, the fact remains he's still my brother."

"Dex." Nero's eyes were locked on Zorin, deftly plucking thoughts right from his noggin. *Stars, that's gonna take some getting used to.* "Someone on this battleship paid those Kryllian bloodletters to murder Zorin. Someone with enough access to snuff the killers themselves in your brig before I could interrogate them. Now those men on duty at the blast doors swear on their lives *you* gave the order to launch those Zephyrs. That you gave the order in person."

"What precisely are you saying?" Dex demanded.

"That's what I saw in their heads." Nero swung toward him. "And it's what I saw on the vid feed from the hangar bay. Even though I know that's impossible. Because you were with me hearing Tombola bids the whole time."

Dex pushed out a frustrated breath and resumed his pacing. "Now you're telling me there's an imposter on my ship?"

"An imposter… and a shapeshifter." Zorin grunted, feeling the pieces fall into place. "Neptune's knickers."

"The only shapeshifter I've ever heard of is Proteus. The leader of the farking Swarm." Dex shot him a glacial look. "Your blood-sworn ally, I believe."

Zorin snorted. "Proteus is no ally of mine. Oh, I'll admit I gave it a think. My guys and gals fought side by side with the Swarm to kick some gangster butt over on Chiron. But I didn't like what they did with the survivors after my gang softened 'em up. Told Proteus our deal was off."

"That's not what I heard." Dex spun to fix him with an accusatory finger. "That's half the infernal reason I just declared war on you— that, and your incessant provocations on my flank."

"Heck, I admit I've been jerking your chain." Zorin eased a hip against Dex's desk and took a load off. "Why don't you put yourself in my space boots for a tick? I've been eking out a living in self-imposed exile at the ass-end of nowhere for the past eight years—when I could've been ruling the Alpha Sector as First Indomitable."

He hesitated, but figured he might as well come all the way clean.

The way his girl wanted.

"And the whole reason I made that call was to avoid having to slaughter your ass in the fighting pit. Cuz I had a soft spot for ya, kid." Zorin hitched one shoulder in a shrug. "Still do. Now you're wearing the crown I handed you. And doing a bang-up job, aside from your paranoid fixation on me. I wouldn't be human if I didn't resent you for it a little."

Dex studied him through narrowed eyes. Zorin couldn't tell whether he was finally getting through to the guy or not.

But at least he was finally listening.

Nero uttered an elegant snort. "This is what happens when for eight years the two of you don't talk. You're going to need to start talking now if we want to get Kaia and her kid sister through this Tombola without the Swarm wiping all of us out or the Patriarch launching a holy crusade for our heads. Speaking of which…"

Nero shifted gracefully into motion and strolled for the door. "We need to cull another hundred candidates from the bidding pool by midnight. I'm going to hear the rest of the bids before those suitors start a riot."

"Ben," Dex started, then cut off whatever protest the guy was planning to make. He shot a shuttered look at Zorin, then finished quietly, "This Syndax and I aren't the only ones who need to talk. I'll need some time alone with you as well."

And why that anodyne suggestion turned Ben Nero aloof and wary as a cornered cat, Zorin didn't have the slightest.

"You know where to find me." At the door, Nero paused to glance over his shoulder, smoothing back a curtain of sleek black hair.

"Be nice," he repeated softly. "The two of you might have been at war. But you're allies now, whether you like it or not. Why don't you both kiss and make up?"

#

"How long do you suppose Proteus—if that's indeed whom I'm to blame—has been masquerading as my brother?"

Zorin glanced back in surprise from the liquor cabinet, where he was raiding Dex's stash of top-shelf Mogadon whiskey. For a while, Dex had been muttering orders into his wrist unit about manual passcodes and fallback protocols and disabled biometrics and whatever the punk else he thought might keep his evil twin from impersonating him back on Mogadon or trying to take over the fleet.

But, mostly, the kid had been quiet since Nero skedaddled.

Too quiet.

Just standing at the viewport with his back turned so Zorin couldn't see his face.

But he didn't need to see the hidden grief in his face or hear the buried pain in his voice to know what the guy was feeling. Or the question he was really asking.

*How long has it been since Proteus murdered my brother?*

Zorin splashed a generous slug of reactor-fermented whiskey in a tumbler and schlepped it over. He figured the kid could use it.

"Cato might still be alive, Dex. Far's I know, Proteus can pretty much imitate any life form he wants, but he's no telepath like Ben. If he's gonna pass, he needs to learn about the… construct he copies. Either through observation or torture. To hoodwink you and your whole fleet the way he did, I reckon he'd need to keep Cato alive a good long while."

Dex shuddered and lifted a hand to shut him up.

Zorin pressed the tumbler into his palm and waited until the guy's fingers closed around it.

Their shadowy images floated in the polyglass against the star-streaked blur of space. His own ugly mug, spiked with unruly hair, looming a good cubit over Dex's burnished and brutal beauty. Grief furrowed Dex's brow and hardened his jaw.

But his eyes were locked on Zorin like lasers.

And just the wavering image of Dex Draven looking at him like that—alone, raw, grieving—punched every button he had. Buttons he'd busted out of the brig and flown parsecs away to protect.

*He was a kid when you knew him way back when. Barely legal. Your protégé. Your best friend's son.*

*You had every reason in the world to walk.*

Zorin cleared his throat and shuffled around to put his shoulder to the window and his back to the bulkhead. Which pretty much gave him a VIP ticket for the space wreck happening in Dex's head. He curled his hands into fists so he wouldn't break down and touch the guy.

"Drink up," Zorin said gruffly. "And don't you give up on Cato. If Proteus thinks he still needs him, chances are he's still got him."

"That's bloody unlikely and you know it." Dex tipped the glass and tossed back a stiff swallow. The whiskey's peaty bite zinged through the air. "Although it certainly explains how the Swarm slipped past my perimeter to ambush Kaia on the *Angel*. And it explains how someone knew enough about my own movements back on Mogadon, even when those movements were classified, to rig my shuttle with explosives. Cato enjoys privileged access to the Mogadon defense mainframe—access I've just given orders to revoke. If my so-called brother surfaces anywhere in the Empire, he'll be promptly detained. As for my *actual* brother…"

Dex pushed out an unsteady breath. "How in blazes can I mourn him… yet still feel so bloody thankful he didn't betray me?"

Zorin didn't know whether it was the hoarse timbre of choked-back grief in his voice or the hot glitter of pent-up tears in his eyes.

All he knew was, he was a goner.

"Stars, kid," he rumbled. "You're killing me."

Without asking, he grabbed the glass from Dex's loose grip and tossed back a hefty swallow to fortify himself. The radioactive kick shot straight to his head.

*Your girl wants him. You want him. Neither one of you wants to amble away this time, do ya, big guy?*

"I'm not a kid." Dex reclaimed the glass and took another swig. "I always wanted to tell you that. You never saw me as an adult and it always drove me straight to bedlam."

"Oh, I saw you all right," Zorin muttered. "You're hard to miss. Tell you true, I never saw anyone else." He just about lunged for the whiskey. "Gimme that, will ya? I shoulda just brought the bottle."

Dex handed it over without comment. And the guy still looked so goddamn lost, even after Zorin's big reveal, that he bolted the rest of the glass just to brace himself.

"Come on, kid. Don't look like that. It'll be okay." He got rid of the glass somehow and gave himself permission to touch. Just this once. Just enough to grip Dex's muscled shoulders and give him a bracing squeeze. "It's gonna be okay."

"Like hell it will." Dex gave him a lopsided grin, but his heart clearly wasn't in it. "You're a dreadful liar."

But he wasn't shrugging free, and the breadth of his shoulders under those shiny epaulets was a temptation Zorin wasn't any good at all resisting.

"Sure it will." Like they were acting on their own, his big battle-scarred hands slid up the hot suntanned skin of Dex's neck to burrow in his tawny hair. "After all this is over, we'll look for him. Your brother."

Gods of Olympus, was he even making sense? All he knew was Dex was nailing him with a vivid blue stare that glittered with grief from barely a cubit away. And his own mating scent, the familiar whiff of steel and predator, was rising dark and potent from his hide and making a mock of whatever good-old-boy charade he thought he was pulling.

"Don't," he heard himself say. "Don't cry. You're making me crazy. We'll find him."

And just to top off the whole damn mess, he leaned in like Dex was ten years old and kissed him roughly on the forehead.

A startled noise rose from Dex's chest. His hands clamped on Zorin's waist. Zorin's grip tightened in his hair. And he was way too old a soldier not to know when he'd lost the battle.

"Oh, hell with it," he muttered.

And just kissed the guy the way he'd always wanted.

Their lips collided, rough and awkward, Dex's mouth like hot silk under his desperate clinch. The guy's lips softened with what had to be surprise. Zorin exerted every molecule of willpower he had—*take it slow, don't spook him*—and gentled his touch, coaxing, teasing, damn near pleading rather than just taking the way he was burning to do. The way every instinct in his body told him Dex needed.

Another muffled noise rose from Dex's throat. Finally, with a sigh that felt like surrender, his lips parted.

A primitive surge of elation roared through Zorin like a blast wave. In a flash, the careful contact between them ignited.

Dex tasted like whiskey and heat and despair and Zorin couldn't take it—he couldn't—so he deepened the kiss and really laid one on him. And if Dex didn't like it, he shouldn't be gripping Zorin's waist hard enough to sear through his starmetal and he damn well shouldn't be kissing him back.

Zorin cradled his head to hold him and met the hot electric slide of his tongue with a lifetime of bottled-up hunger. His whole body was tingling like he'd been struck by lightning. His hands clenched harder—pulling Dex's hair, pulling him closer. The guy's grip tightened in unmistakable demand and dragged their hips together. Their bodies collided and fused like atoms in a Mogadon reactor, throwing off heat and power. Dex moaned into his mouth and Zorin growled in response. Fireworks were going off in his head like a victory parade. Under his armor, his swelling cock was tight with heat.

Even through his armor, Dex had to feel him—feel how much he wanted him—all up close and personal like that. Had to know Zorin was rigged to blow.

But he still didn't pull away.

And Zorin really, really wanted to know how far he could take this rocket ride between them.

Mars, he didn't want to stop.

But this was no way to treat a guy who'd just suffered a crippling loss. He needed not to be an asshole about this.

"Juno, queen of the gods," Zorin breathed, stopping the kiss through superhuman effort and surfacing for air.

Dex panted against him for a bit, chiseled face fractured and open, cobalt eyes burning with hunger and need. Then, inevitably, Dex released him and stepped back stiffly, hard hands straightening his jacket and smoothing the hair Zorin's rough touch had disturbed.

"What in the name of all the gods was *that*?" Dex demanded hoarsely.

"*That*," Zorin said, doing a little panting himself, "was a good eight years overdue. Cripes, you know how long I spent telling myself you didn't kiss me back the last time? That I made it all up and that's why you shot me. This time right here? Don't even pretend it didn't get us both off. And if I thought your head was in the right place, I damn well wouldn't have stopped."

Dex wasted no time putting a room's worth of distance and the width of his desk between them. When he spun to confront him, the ruthless mask of the First Indomitable was soldered back in place.

"If you expect me to thank you for not getting me liquored up and seducing me in my own ready room while I grieved for my murdered brother," Dex snapped, "you'll be waiting quite some time. You can rest assured, grief or no grief, I would never have let matters spiral so far beyond the pale."

Still thoroughly sexed up and now ticked off to boot, Zorin allowed himself an eloquent snort. "Kid, if I wasn't such a good guy, I'd have had you bent over that desk and clamped around my cock in a hot tick. And I guarantee you woulda liked it."

"Not bloody likely!" Dex fired back.

Which only made him burn to walk over there and prove it. Especially with Dex blushing fiery blazes at the visual.

Shoot, he needed to get out of there before he did something crazy. Like make the guy come until he saw flaming comets. And to hell with his hang-ups and to hell with the consequences.

Next thing he knew, Dex would be nuking him.

Zorin pushed a hand roughly through his hair and motored for the exit. Right before he hit it, he swung back.

Just to get one last thing off his chest.

"In case you're wondering, that's another reason I lit outta here all those years ago. I had it for you so hard I couldn't see anyone else, and you never even knew I was alive. Then, at the end, you hated me for your dad. But you damn well know I'm alive now, don'tcha?"

Dex tried to say something, but Zorin wasn't having it.

"You know I'm mating Kaia soon as this shindig's over." He forged ahead and said the rest. "She's mating me, but she's in love with you, knucklehead. Far's I can tell, you're in love with her. And I already told you how I feel about both of you. You decide you wanna do something about all that, you come on over to the *Relentless* and find me."

# CHAPTER SEVEN

## The Confession

Four hundred down. Just one more farking hundred to get rid of.

Nero sat curled in the window seat of his temporary digs on Dex's flagship—the room's nanosteel lines and razor-sharp angles still cold and inhospitable as all seven Mogadon hells despite the colorful smattering of Valyrian comforts he'd strewn about. Chin propped on knees, he brooded as a purposeful queue of transport shuttles streamed past, stuffed to the vents with rejected Tombola suitors. The psychic fallout of the rejects' sullen rage burned through the polyglass against his mental barriers.

A rage stoked with thwarted lust to the point of combustion.

He should feel profound satisfaction. Somehow he and Dex between them had finagled the feat of whisking another hundred of Kaia's dangerously disgruntled suitors safely out of the running and off Dex's ship. By midnight tomorrow, they'd be down to fifty.

Few enough for Dex's armed muscle to manhandle if it all went to shit.

By rights, that ought to please him. But clobbered by exhaustion and hammered by grief, all Nero felt now was numbness.

The comm link embedded in the wall was still flashing its silent signal. He hadn't listened to the feed. Didn't need to.

All he needed to know was the sender's ID to grasp the bottom line.

Valyria's prize stallion was being summoned home to service another fertile mare.

*And with Dex hellbent on denying who he is and what he wants, and Kaia gone dark and radio silent with that pirate, there's no earthly reason in the nine unknown realms for me to stay.*

A soft *plink* tugged at his attention.

The electronic blip of the doorbell.

He gave serious thought to ignoring it. It was well past midnight, and he'd done his bit for galactic peace today and then some. Thanks to a willing assist from one of those redheaded acrobats who looked like Kaia from a distance, none of her suitors even knew the maharani was MIA—

Another insistent *plink* peeled out.

Nero muttered a vile curse, uncoiled to his tired feet, and strode to the portal with real annoyance simmering in his gut. He punched the entry panel, fingers dancing with purple sparks.

The door slid open to reveal Dex swaying on his doorstep. With all the gleaming buttons of his jacket undone, an open bottle of Mogadon whiskey dangling from his fist—and a smoking heat in his gaslight gaze that Nero had seen on plenty of guys who pitched up on his doorstep after midnight.

A heat that shocked all seven hells out of him coming from Dex Draven.

"Comets!" Nero blurted out.

"Mind if I come in?" Without waiting for permission, Dex pushed in. Because ruling half the known galaxy did that to a guy.

Nero's options were to allow it or let Dex run right into him.

Either of which would violate the strict no-contact rule he'd instituted once he realized Dex was never going to give him what he needed. Nero had loved him since they were kids. But now that he'd seen firsthand from the inside what a lifetime of exposure to Max Draven's virulent prejudices had done to his son's head, it was time for Nero to accept the truth.

Dex just wasn't capable of that kind of love.

Not when it involved another man.

Right now, after half a bottle of Mogadon whiskey, it looked like he knew Dex's limits better than Dex knew himself.

Alarm bells ringing in his brain and shrieking through every synapse, Nero folded his arms protectively across his chest.

"Look, Dex, it's really late—"

*"Ben,"* Dex gritted through clenched teeth, in a voice like shattered stone. "With Cato dead and Kaia gone, you're the only living soul left on this ship I can trust. If you send me away tonight, I swear I won't be responsible for the consequences."

Hearing coolheaded Dex Draven about a blink away from losing it stretched Nero's own nerves to the splitting point.

"All right," he said warily. "You can stay for a tick. But only because of Cato."

*And only for a tick. I mean it, Dex.*

But if Dex heard the caveat, he wasn't acknowledging it.

Which was classic Dex.

Dex made a beeline for the window seat and crawled into it, one hand sliding over the Valyrian ice-tiger pelt Nero had flung over it. His golden head turned to scan the room, checking out the lush furs and opulent furnishings Nero had ordered over from his envoy ship.

"Nice." Dex's neon eyes wandered over the vivid dyes of the hand-woven rug to Nero's bare feet, then rose slowly to take in the rest of him. "This place suits you. I like that you're… comfortable on my ship."

And despite all his resolve and all his good sense and that farking summons still flashing on his comm link, Nero felt the same rush of heat in his skin, the same hitch of breath in his chest and the same coil of need in his cock that he always felt with Dex.

He cleared his throat and propped a hip against the wall. Keeping a good six cubits of empty air between them.

"I take it you've given them a heads-up on Quorum?" That topic seemed safe enough.

Dex's head dipped in an absent nod. "I've beamed a transmission to the Imperator's secure channel. Warned him to secure his airspace and hunker down. Marcus will ping me when he responds."

"Any more news from the *Relentless*?" A subject that seemed like another safe bet.

"Had another transmission from, uh, Zorin." Dex cleared his own throat and took a swig from the bottle. "Kaia's been sleeping all day. Claims he'll tell her about Cato—Proteus—when she's conscious. Once she realizes I didn't lie to her face and use novicide against the Syndax, I trust forgiveness will be forthcoming." His voice hardened. "If it isn't, I'm bloody well flying over there myself to collect her."

Nero turned that over in his head. Trying to gauge exactly how much Dex had been drinking. He wasn't sure he had the fortitude to handle Dex drunk, with all those formidable Mogadon barriers lying in shambles at his booted feet.

Although if he was drunk enough, maybe he'd pass out. Then Nero could summon Marcus to cart him off.

"Wondering what I'm doing here at this godforsaken time after the day we've both had, aren't you?" Dex met his gaze with a wry smile, and Nero recalled with a jolt that they'd started sharing thoughts. "To answer your question—yes, I've been drinking. Yes, I'm a bit drunk. In fact, I'm finally drunk enough to ask why you took off like that ten years ago."

Nero found himself suddenly glad he was leaning against the wall. Because he needed it to prop himself up.

"You want to discuss that *now*?" He eyed the flashing comm link and pushed out a sigh. "Gods and demons, Dex. What does it matter anymore?"

Dex leaned forward with a growl. "It matters to me."

Nero flung up a hand in exasperation. "Did you and Zorin even—?"

"I'm not here to discuss me and Zorin," Dex purred, low and lethal. "I'm here to discuss me and *you*, gorgeous. That's what he calls you, isn't it? I can tell you like it."

Dex was definitely drunk. Drunk enough to be dangerous. But probably not drunk enough to be dissuaded from this disastrous discussion. And suddenly the whole wretched business was royally flipping Nero off.

*Why the farking hell is Dex doing this? Now, at the end of everything?*

"You want to know why I left? You really want to know?"

Dex's eyes narrowed to glacial slits. "I'm not in the habit of repeating myself."

"And *I'm* not one of your jack-booted sidekicks, Commander!" Nero fired back. "Know what a Valyrian lifebond is?"

Dex blinked and leaned back in his seat. And he looked so jaw-droppingly gorgeous—all burnished hair and gleaming buttons and black jacket against the striped cream-and-jet pelt—that Nero felt his mouth go dry.

"Lifebond," Dex repeated. "That's what you and Kaia have."

"It's an unbreakable bond—psychic, sexual, genetic, instinctive—completely involuntary. A Valyrian gets exactly one in a lifetime. When you bond with the wrong lifemate—when you can't *be* with the lifemate you've bonded—you're both doomed to a permanent hell."

Dex took a slow swig. "That's why Kaia hasn't been happy. You either. Because you left her too."

"I met her after I left you. And this isn't about her." Nero dragged a breath past his suddenly hammering heart. Was he really going to spill the secret he'd been hugging to his heart for half his lifetime? The secret he hadn't even told Kaia?

Gods of Solaris, Dex wanted to know, didn't he?

"After me, before the biowar. I've got it. Go on." Dex looped an arm around one booted leg and nailed him with a nuclear look hot enough to melt steel. "And while you're at it, gorgeous—why are you standing all the way over there?"

The lightning flash of Dex's possessive stare sent a jolt of electricity through every nerve.

"Don't play games with me, Dex." Nero strode forward, braced his hands against the lush fur, and leaned right into Dex's space. The heady nip of Mogadon whiskey hit him hard, spiked with the dark spice of Dex's mating scent.

Nero felt either drunk or crazy. Which wasn't a safe way to feel when you had a Precursor's power.

"If I hadn't left when I did," he shot out, fast and fierce, "I would have bonded with *you*. Gods, I could feel it happening. Feel myself falling for you harder and deeper every day that summer. Falling for you even though I knew you'd never reciprocate. Never let me in. But, like a Prime Class fool, I thought I could somehow… change things. That I could change *you*.

"Right up until that last flipping night in the shower, when I let you see exactly how much I wanted you. I thought I could make you feel something you obviously don't feel and never could—"

Dex clenched Nero's tunic and dragged him close. He ended Nero's furious protest with a searing kiss.

A kiss that sucked every scrap of oxygen from the ship.

When they'd kissed before, Dex had been hesitant. Nero could have pushed away if he wanted. But there was nothing hesitant in Dex's kiss now. Nothing but hunger and dominance and absolute possession.

And pushing away wasn't even an option.

All the breath rushed out of his lungs. Nero's world slid away under his feet and the walls spun around him. Somehow he was sprawled between Dex's thighs, hands clutching the powerful muscles of Dex's quads.

Dex was kissing him like he wanted to crawl down Nero's throat and devour him from the inside.

And Nero was giving him everything he wanted, moaning under the insistent thrust of Dex's tongue, feeling the sharp bite of Mogadon whiskey sting his senses, smelling Dex's mating scent seep through his skin. A desperate, debauched, debilitating desire pounded through his limbs and weakened his legs.

"Wait!" he gasped between kisses that were hot enough to swell his cock against his breeches.

Somehow he had to stop this. Dex was drunk, and his own heart far too fragile.

"No more waiting." Dex spread his thighs and pulled Nero between them, hard hands cradling his head to hold him. "I swear to Jupiter there's never been anyone like you. Your eyes are glowing."

"That happens." Nero sucked in a desperate breath. "I'm Valyrian—"

"Do you know my mating scent's all over you?" Dex drank in his gasping breaths with deep searching kisses that made Nero's head spin. "Anyone who gets anywhere near you is going to know *I've* been all over you. And there goes my fearsome Indomitable reputation. I swear to gods you're driving me daft."

"Dex—I bonded—with Kaia," Nero panted in a last-ditch effort to save his own sanity. "This thing—with you—I don't know what this is."

Dex's hands were gentle in his hair. Pulling him closer.

"Yes, you do," he whispered. "You know."

And he did know. He knew.

There was just no future in admitting it.

"By the seven devils," Nero said from the heart. "What do you *want* from me?"

"Everything," Dex whispered against his mouth. "Ben. Don't leave me alone tonight."

Nero's heart was breaking. Breaking for Dex and for himself. Because Dex was going to regret this in the morning.

And that was really going to hurt.

In utter despair, he tore free from those drugging kisses that would haunt his dreams and bowed his head against Dex's broad chest.

"Demons, Dex! You're drunk and you're grieving and you're horny. I can't read you right now. And you have more landmines in your Mogadon psyche than a war zone. I need you to spell out what you do and don't want."

Dex's hands slid down his back, gripped his hips, eased him closer. Until they were heartbeat to heartbeat, hip to hip, practically cock to cock.

And it was all Nero could manage not to grind into all that hard heat.

"I want to see you," Dex whispered. "I want to see *all* of you. I want to know if you look the way I remember when I wake hard and aching for you in the night."

Nero closed his eyes and shuddered. Because he knew in his soul he was going to give Dex every last thing he wanted.

He'd give him tonight. Give him everything he had to give. Then, after tomorrow, he'd give Dex what he wanted most.

He'd hightail it for Valyria and never come back.

"All right, Dex," he breathed, feeling his body harden and heat with anticipation. "All right. I can't deny you a mother-loving thing when you're like this. Not tonight. Just… give me a tick, okay?"

"Take your time," Dex rumbled, releasing him to lounge back in the window seat.

And the deep masculine growl of anticipation in his voice made it damn near impossible for Nero to breathe.

Swallowing hard, he uncurled to his feet and peeled off his tunic. Despite the jumble of caution clamoring in his head, hearing the breath catch in Dex's throat was one of the most sublime sounds he'd ever heard. He hooked his hands in his breeches and looked up beneath his lashes.

And the sight of Dex Draven sprawled gracefully across the tiger's pelt with his jacket open, all suntanned sinew and corded throat, tawny hair falling over electric eyes and that straining bulge of arousal pressing against his trousers, stole Nero's breath all over again. Suddenly the intoxicating knowledge shot through him that tonight, if he played his cards right, he might finally live out a few of his own buried fantasies about his boyhood best friend.

At least this once.

Before the end.

For no earthly reason, he felt shy—he, Ben Nero who was never shy, except when it suited one of his little games with some surly brute in a rented room. Now scorching heat climbed into his face. He found he couldn't look at Dex as he worked open the laces of his breeches. He was violently aroused—there would be no hiding it. He'd probably be a total turnoff for a guy like Dex who was used to having the only cock in his bed be his own—

"Easy," Dex whispered, following his jumbled thoughts. "I'm not going anywhere. I'm through running away from this."

Nero's heart twisted with hope and fear.

Because he couldn't. He couldn't afford to let himself believe Dex was finally ready to love him.

He couldn't.

He slid out of his breeches. Fiercely resisting the desperate instinct to hide the jutting erection that sprang into view, already begging for the hard hot friction of his hand—

"Gods of Olympus." Dex shoved the bottle aside and unfolded to his feet. "*Gorgeous* doesn't begin to describe you. You're mesmerizing. You're an angel. Come here."

Flushing with pleasure, Nero ducked his head and closed the distance between them. He didn't dare touch him, and he definitely kept space between the guy and his cock. He was already so painfully erect—shaft jutting hard and eager, skin stretched taut and purple, balls drawn tight and tingling—he was about a heartbeat away from losing it.

Dex's calloused hands skimmed his ribs and traced the flat plane of his abs. Nero squeezed his eyes shut, breathing hard through his mouth.

"Easy," Dex whispered again. "I'm going to give you what you need."

His lips grazed the hollow of Nero's throat, already damp with sweat. Just as his battle-hardened hands slicked down Nero's back to grip the tense muscle of his ass. His cock leaped at the contact.

Nero groaned and moved in close, hands sliding under the open waist of Dex's jacket, solid muscle rippling just beneath his shirt. He was starving for the feel of Dex's skin under his hands, the taste of Dex's sweat on his lips, the sound of Dex's shout in his ears when he pushed aside all his hang-ups and exploded in Nero's—

*But maybe that's not what he wants. All that Mogadon garbage about male submission…*

"Comets, Dex," he moaned. "I don't want to cross a line—"

"Go ahead and cross one. Cross a hundred. If I can't go there, I'll tell you," Dex rasped against his throat, fingers winding tight in Nero's hair to hold him. One hand dragged his hips hard against the electric bulge under Dex's trousers in a wordless demand that made Nero ache to rock against him.

*Except maybe that's too much. He doesn't even know where the lines are himself.*

But Dex had told him to go ahead, hadn't he?

Nero wasted no time pushing off Dex's jacket and peeling him out of his shirt. Which finally gave Nero the visual he was craving. All that suntanned skin stretched tight over slabs of muscle, hard ruddy nipples over sleek pectoral strength, bulging shoulders and biceps that made him want to sink his teeth in.

The pale square of the silicon bandage over his ribs to remind him life was fragile and fleeting.

As fleeting as this moment with the two of them.

Dex's skin was hot silk under his fingers. Just getting his hands on all that off-limits real estate sent fire streaking through him.

Especially when Dex caught his hand and pressed it hard against his sizzling heat. Fireworks exploded in Nero's head. Because Mogadon males came supersized, and he could already tell the guy was big enough and hard enough to fill whatever part of him Dex wanted.

"Is this what you want?" Dex growled, grinding into his touch.

Nero moaned in response and worked him through the fabric. Dex's hand tightened in his hair and a groan clawed up his throat. Nero's own cock was jerking with jolts of need in desperate want of tending.

But he was afraid to scare Dex off by asking.

"Come and get me," Dex gasped. "Oh gods. Like that—gods! Don't hold back."

"Slow down." He still couldn't seem to breathe. "It's your first time… doing this. I'm trying… to be… careful."

"I don't want you careful. I want you desperate." Dex's voice turned dark and brutal. "I want you on your knees with your mouth wrapped around my cock until I tell you to stop."

His hand clenched in Nero's hair to push him to his knees. And it was all Nero could manage not to come on the spot. His tongue dragged down the salty length of Dex's chest and licked the taut plane of his abs. Dex shuddered and gripped him tighter in urgent command.

If Dex decided he wanted to dominate him, if he wasn't holding back—if he claimed the pilot's seat on this rocket ride between them, he'd have Nero begging for mercy.

And he'd bet Dex would like making him beg.

Naked on his knees before the star of every guy-on-guy wet dream he'd ever had—even with the guy in question still wearing pants—hand wrapped around his own shaft and mouth watering at the prospect of Dex's come shooting down his throat, Nero trembled with a shiver of raw need.

"You giving the orders now, space cadet?" he heard himself say huskily, barely recognizing his own voice.

"That's how it works in my bed. You'll have to get used to it." Dex's voice too was three octaves lower than usual. The sound tightened Nero's hand on his shaft and wrung a whimper of longing from his lips. "And you'd better not come until I tell you. Now stop talking and suck my cock."

#

Dex held his breath while Nero worked his trousers open. But only because panting with need wasn't a good look on a First Indomitable.

And he desperately wanted to look good for Nero. He needed to atone for ten years of hurt.

His cock sprang free from captivity, rigid and dripping with need, and Nero swallowed what sounded like a moan. Dex wished like hell he could see the guy's face and not just the fall of his sleek black hair.

Then Nero's lips grazed the head of his cock.

And Dex just stopped thinking.

The hot silk of that sinful mouth closed over his tip, tongue flicking his slit, lapping at the precum he couldn't contain. Dex clenched his jaw against a ferocious surge of need. No way he wanted this over before they'd even begun, before he even had the chance to know—oh bloody *hell*—

Nero's hand closed around his shaft, jacking him slowly in a tempo that matched the rhythmic suction of his mouth. Dex gripped his head to hold him, smoothed back his long hair so he could savor the erotic thrill of seeing his own cock, shiny with saliva and his own need, thrusting in and out of Nero's gorgeous mouth.

"Oh gods, Ben, like that—gods! I want you—want you so much—"

"Take a breath, space cadet," Nero breathed against his cock, squeezing the base to slow him down. "I've waited for this night way too long. So much I want to show you."

"No more teasing," Dex growled, about to lose his mind. "Hands behind your back."

Nero went still, kneeling gracefully at his feet, starlight glittering on the sweat that slicked his smooth skin. Dex wanted to lap it off the supple lines of muscle that bridged his shoulders and broadened his chest.

Then just keep working his way down.

Nero's elegant cock jutted before him, longer than Dex's but not as thick. Maybe all Valyrians were built that way, though he was the only Valyrian male Dex had ever wanted. Less carnal brutality than a Mogadon cock, Nero's was all supple grace. And just the thought of getting his hands on him, working over all that hard length while Nero thrust desperately into his grip—making Nero plead and beg for him until they were both savage and mindless with need—made his entire body tingle like he'd been zapped with his own taser.

Nero gazed up at Dex with smoldering eyes that glowed with heliotrope fire. His tongue swiped across the creamy wetness that coated his lower lip. The visual jolted through him and made his balls clench.

"Hands behind your back," Dex repeated roughly.

A visible shiver swept through Nero. He bowed his head and clasped his hands behind his back.

"You're good at this, aren't you?" Dex rumbled, hands curling around his head to anchor him. "You're bloody perfect. Now stay just like that for me."

And he did what he'd been dreaming about for ten blooming years and sheathed himself deep in Ben Nero's perfect mouth. Slick heat encased him all the way down his length. A surge of electric pleasure coiled in his balls and rolled his eyes back.

Nero's tongue wrapped around his length. His mouth closed around his shaft and started working him over. Dex groaned and gripped tighter, holding him in place, bucking into his mouth in a haze of urgency until his cock nudged the back of Nero's throat.

Nero gagged a bit but kept working him, diligent and earnest like the fate of the galaxy hung in the balance. His throat rippled around Dex's cock—accommodating him, swallowing him, taking everything Dex had to give him without a whimper, submitting to this brutal domination.

Head tipped back, teeth bared with pleasure, barely holding back by his fingernails the raging climax that wanted to boil from his balls and shoot down the guy's throat, Dex gasped out, "You're so bloody perfect—oh gods Ben—tell me—tell me you love me."

That eager mouth froze around him. Linked the way they were—physically and psychically—Dex felt the recoil slam through him like an asteroid collision.

With a hiss, Nero twisted free and scrambled to his feet.

Leaving Dex suspended halfway between shock and climax.

Nero dragged a hand across his wet mouth. "Go to hell, Dex. And while you're at it, you can finish off your own damn climax and get the hell out!"

"Wait one bloody tick." Despite having all seven hells shocked out of him, Dex grabbed Nero's wrist as he spun away and dragged him up hard against his furiously aroused body. Their cocks collided— Dex's slick with saliva, Nero's slick with want.

They both groaned at the contact.

"Blast it." Staring straight into those incandescent eyes, Dex wrapped both arms around Nero to hold him and struggled to clear his head. "Talk to me. What the devil just happened?"

"You just happened—same as always," Nero snarled and tried to twist free.

But he'd never been any match for Dex in a fight.

And, turned on like they both were, the slick slide of cock on cock made this one fight Dex had every intention of winning.

"Let go of me, Dex," Nero panted, psi fire spilling from his eyes. He could hurl Dex through the nearest wall and half a parsec into space if he wanted, but Dex didn't think he would. "You have to have everything—always—but you're not having *that*."

"*That* meaning… your love?" Suspended between desperate arousal and complete mystification, Dex chuffed out a breathless laugh. "By all the gods, what else do you think this is?"

"Damn you, I said no!" Nero writhed against him in a frenzy, but his eyes were glazed with lust. "I've given you everything else. I'm *not* giving you that."

Pinning his struggling body in place with one arm, Dex worked a hand between them and wrapped his fist around both of them—his cock and Nero's. At the first spark of contact, Nero shuddered and went rigid. Dex followed his gaze down. The sight of their two cocks, swollen with need and roped with creamy fluid, arced through him. Under his own calloused grip, the smooth silk of Nero's skin sheathed his potent hardness. Rhythmic surges of pleasure rolled through him as his fist jacked them both.

Gods on the mountain, he was losing his mind.

Especially when Nero groaned and thrust into him, gripping Dex's hips for purchase. Dex leaned in to claim his kiss-swollen lips and tasted the musk of his own come on Nero's desperate tongue.

Jupiter, he could do this all night.

"You know bloody well what this is," Dex panted between kisses, jacking them both harder and faster. "I just need to hear you say it."

"Go to hell," Nero groaned. "Good gods, Dex—just shut up. You're going to make me come—going to make me come so hard—"

"Not yet. And I'm giving the orders."

He felt a shiver work through Nero and tingled with a savage thrill. Having Nero submit to him like this in bed was going to work out exceedingly well.

For both of them.

Dex pushed him back a few steps until they both toppled onto the bed, sinking deep into sleek dappled pelt, Nero's urgent hands pulling Dex down on top. Dex crawled over him—pushed between his legs—wrestled through a mental jumble of confusion and resistance. At his feet yawned an abyss of desperate craving.

He hovered on the brink.

He'd never done this with a guy. But he'd been to more than enough saturnalias to understand the mechanics.

Every Mogadon guest room came fully equipped with a discreet stash of lube and prophylactics in a bedside drawer. All he needed to do now was lube Nero up, slide the guy's legs over his shoulders, work his way one breath at a time into all that tight heat, and thrust into him until they both saw stars.

But this was Nero.

His best friend.

Dex couldn't—couldn't dishonor him like that—no matter how badly he wanted—how badly he *needed*—

"Oh, damn your Mogadon hang-ups." Nero sighed. "There's more than one way to do this. Come here, space cadet."

He gripped Dex's ass and pulled them together, cock to cock. Lightning need sizzled through him and took care of the rest. Dex thrust against his shaft, slick with precum and saliva. Nero's ridged head sparked a delicious friction down his length that drew his balls tight against his body. Nero was moaning into his mouth and rutting against him with desperate, indecent haste—fast and urgent—just the way Dex wanted him.

A tingling tightness shot down his shaft.

Barely holding it together by the skin of his teeth, Dex pinned Nero's arms over his head and growled into his mouth.

"Stop being so infernally stubborn and tell me, damn you. I need to hear it."

"Meteors." Nero opened his violet eyes from a handspan away and nailed Dex with a look he drowned in. "You honestly need to hear me say it?"

*"Tell me."*

The bittersweet knowledge of surrender rippled over Nero's face. "I love you, all right? I've always… loved the hell out of you."

A shout of triumph clawed from Dex's throat. His entire body convulsed. Raw pleasure seared through him like a lightning bolt and spurted from his cock in hot gouts that soaked Nero's abs and chest and slicked the skin between them and thoroughly claimed the guy as his.

He came what felt like buckets. He never wanted this to end.

"Now," he groaned. "Oh love—come for me now."

Crying out his name, Nero shuddered and arched into him. A flood of liquid heat engulfed Dex's cock and belly in rhythmic spurts. He buried his face in Nero's neck and held on to him for all he was worth.

Because there was no way in the nine unknown realms he was ever letting Ben Nero go now.

And let all seven devils take the consequences.

# CHAPTER EIGHT
## The Crucible

It hadn't taken long to get her naked.

Just twelve clicks of shut-eye to refuel her engine, a stiff hit of Kryllian firewater to blow through the fumes, and a solo plunge in a steaming bath to ease her jangled nerves.

Kaia could only thank her lucky planets Dex and Zorin hadn't blasted each other to subatomic particles while she slept the day away.

Immersed to her chin in water that reeked of minerals, she stretched her aching body in what appeared to be Zorin's private bath and gazed around with lively interest. The echoing chamber with its domed ceiling, mosaic floor, arched porticoes all dripping with damp, crumbling with age, and wreathed with steam was a purely Mogadon setup.

A setup fit for a First Indomitable.

Because the *Relentless* was obviously a stolen Mogadon ship. Battered and rusting and a bit worse for wear, but all rigged out with heated atria, cold plunge pools, and a sunken basin big enough for an orgy where she wallowed in her current hot soak. One full wall was a battle-scarred sheet of floor-to-ceiling polyglass.

Beyond the sleek raking lines of the *Inevitable,* streaking fiercely through space at their side, floated the cloudy rose swirl of a nebula she knew.

A guidepost she recognized.

It meant they were getting closer to Quorum Central Starbase. Closer to Kryll, whose merchant princes owed their staggering wealth to the planet's prime location at the galaxy's commercial crossroads. Closer to the Quorum, the judicial body she was hoping like hell would sanction her scandalously unconventional mating—the same Quorum who'd once forbidden her match with Nero.

Closer to her father the Patriarch, who represented Kryll on the Quorum.

Closer to her fate.

Despite the *caldarium*'s soporific heat, a chill of trepidation shot through her and knotted her much-abused muscles. Kaia rolled her shoulders, tucked a fallen curl into the pile at her crown, confirmed her waterproof bandages were weathering the deluge, and made yet another deliberate effort to loosen up.

But the unrelenting pulse of arousal that tightened her nipples and throbbed between her legs definitely didn't help.

Neither did the fact she hadn't actually seen Zorin since he decanted her exhausted, fertile, frisky, still fully clad body from his cyberport to his bed and went charging straight off to the *Inevitable* to confront Dex.

And the vid feed she'd found blinking when she woke—the recording where Zorin unloaded those mind-blowing revelations about Cato and Dex and Proteus, not to mention the currently unknown whereabouts of the Zephyrs and their biological payload—raised way more questions in her feverish brain than he'd answered.

She appreciated the fact the guy had a pirate ship to run and all. But she sure hoped he'd find a tick or two in his busy schedule to show up in person and clue her in.

Maybe Zorin was a tad less eager to seal the deal between them than she'd thought.

Or maybe he was just more eager to finish off Dex and win his war than he was to climb into her bed.

After all, how well did she really know him? She was flying at hyperspeed through uncharted space. Running on instinct and prophecy. Taking risks and making choices for all four of them.

Choices with galactic impact.

*Steady on, samurai. You already screwed up big time by trusting Cato and not trusting Dex—and it just about got you killed. Either you trust Dex to keep the peace and Zorin to keep his promise and Nero to keep both of them away from each other's throats—or what the flip are you doing here?*

Itching with nerves, she uncurled to her feet and sloshed across the pool to press her palms against the polyglass. The bone-deep cold of space seeped through her fingers and the steamy heat of paradise lapped at her hips.

But it didn't do smack to warm her.

*You rolled the dice, angel. Now you need to pull up your big-girl panties and play the numbers—*

"Venus rising from the sea."

The deep rumble of Zorin's voice rolling from the shadowy atrium sent her spinning with a gasp. Not to mention diving to get her important bits under water. Though if he'd been lurking there long, he'd probably already gotten a good eyeful.

Not that she minded.

This whole fertility thing made her more than happy to find herself suddenly sharing a Mogadon *thermae* with a Syndax pirate.

At least this particular Syndax pirate.

"Gods, Zorin, you scared the spit out of me!" Trying for nonchalance, she raised her arms to tighten the knot of hair at her crown. "What did you say?"

"Old Mogadon myth from the dark days. Way before we lit out for the stars." His voice deepened to a drawl that slid like silk against her overstimulated senses. "Take it as a compliment."

With the *thermae* barely lit by the turquoise glimmer of underwater lights, she could hardly make him out through the shadows and the steam. But she could have been blind and deaf and still known he was there.

His unavoidable presence filled the chamber's echoing confines in a way that had nothing to do with his physical size.

And the knowledge that she'd placed herself so completely in his battle-hardened hands—the knowledge that he wanted her and she wanted him and she'd already jettisoned her decade-long vow of celibacy with a headlong eagerness that was flat-out humiliating—not to mention the knowledge that she'd trusted her life to a space pirate with a notorious reputation for taking what he wanted and keeping it?

Let's just say this rampant speculation wasn't doing much to manage all those frisky hormones her fertile body was kicking out.

Feeling way too hot, she smoothed damp tendrils from her flushed face and tried like hell to clear her head.

"Um, I got your message. About Proteus. Pretty staggering stuff— but it definitely explains those spacebots that stalked me. What's the latest on him and those Zephyrs? I've got a score of my own to settle with that shapeshifter."

"Still MIA. So no need to go running off into battle just yet, samurai."

She liked that he sounded positively indulgent of her bloodthirsty leanings—like he planned to give her the shapeshifter's head for a holiday gift.

*That's the advantage of choosing a pirate for a consort.*

"My bio sensors at the base are sniffing for novicide," he went on, "but they're not getting any hits. Still, my boys on Quorum know the drill. All nonessentials have been evac'ed, defensive patrols are on battle alert, and my docking crew's holed up in a safe space. All thanks to you, sweetheart."

His voice warmed, and a flush of pleasure spread through her. Still, her overdeveloped conscience wouldn't let her accept unqualified praise for her impulsive acts.

She'd punked it all up big time. And she wasn't sure Dex would ever forgive her.

"I'm half Valyrian." Her shoulders lifted in an awkward shrug. "No way was I going to stand around braiding my hair while Dex launched the next biowar. Except it wasn't Dex, was it?"

"Seems not."

Leather creaked in the shadows as he leaned against the wall. For once he didn't appear to be wearing his ubiquitous blast armor.

Which made her really curious to get a better look at him. Staying low in the water, she drifted across the basin in his direction.

"Zorin?" she whispered.

"I'm listening."

"Thanks for keeping your promise. Thanks for not letting me down. Thanks for talking to Dex rather than blasting him out of the sky." Her heart twisted and burned with guilt. "Gods of my father, I should have trusted him. Even if trust has never really been my strong suit. Dex has to be royally flipped. Right?"

Under the dribble and drip of water, she heard his slow exhale.

"Dex is an interesting fella. All this ruckus gave him one heck of a lot to think about. You want my two bits? I'd say he's more focused right now on getting you back in his bed than pointing fingers. He's a first-things-first kinda guy."

The breath snagged in her throat—an audible catch she prayed he wouldn't notice. Because just the thought of being back in Dex's bed—

a wrathful Dex growling demands in her repentant ear while she begged for his hands and his mouth and his cock all over her—was enough to shoot her oversexed body straight into the stratosphere.

"He trusted me and I ran away," she whispered, quite a bit less than steady. "And he doesn't trust easily." *Actually, he doesn't trust at all.* "He has to be flipping furious."

"He's used to being the guy who calls the shots." Damn and blast, she couldn't read anything in his tone. "This whole notion that you're safer over here with me? That's a pretty tough pill for a First Indomitable to swallow. Believe me, I oughta know."

*Right. Because Zorin used to be First Indomitable himself. Until his exile.*

Which only reminded her this wasn't a guy who played games.

She'd reached the edge of the basin. And between the swirling steam and the cloaking shadows, she still couldn't see him, beyond the hiss of leather on steel and the gleam of starlight on skin and the overwhelming sense of mass and menace held carefully in check.

She folded her arms on the rim and propped her chin on her forearms.

"*Am* I safe with you, Zorin the pirate?" she breathed.

Finally—*finally*—he pushed off the wall and prowled into the light. And just the sight of him without his ubiquitous armor sucked every molecule of oxygen from her lungs.

Gods, the sight of him.

Massive frame sheathed in fighting leathers and space boots and a shirt that showcased the tribal tattoo around his bulging biceps. Knife strapped to one thick forearm, blaster buckled in casual menace around leather-clad hips, all spiky hair and battle scars…

He made *dangerous* and *disreputable* look downright delectable.

"Safe isn't what flips your switch, sweetheart," he growled, aquamarine eyes glittering like neutron stars. "Or you'd never have looked twice at a guy like me. You're not your play-it-safe twin sister. You're looking for strength and violence coupled with a conscience and ironclad control. That's why you fell for Dex and it's why you fell for Nero.

"But they'll have to wait their turn." His eyes darkened to navy, and a shiver of danger shot through her. "You're on my ship now. And, like any Syndax, what I claim as mine—I know how to keep."

Her entire body hummed with anticipation. Hummed hard enough to make the water ripple. Barely six cubits away, his monumental form loomed over her, smelling like starmetal and violence, big hands loose at his sides, face hard and predatory.

She knelt at his booted feet and burned for him.

"Jupiter," he rasped. "Your eyes are glowing. You're so goddamn gorgeous, you're practically incandescent."

She dragged in a breath past her suddenly stumbling heart. Time to trust him—*really* trust him—with the truth.

"If I'm glowing," she whispered, "it's because… I'm fertile. Remember what I told you about Valyrian biology?"

"Yeah. You said you couldn't conceive unless you wanted the hell out of me. You telling me that's why your eyes just went ultraviolet?"

Gaze holding his, she dipped her head in a nod. "Hormonally speaking, you flipped my switch. When I saw you the last time—with all that, um, foreplay?"

He vibrated with a visible ripple of predatory hunger. His pupils widened and his nostrils flared to breathe her in. She gazed up at him with parted lips, barely daring to move.

When he spoke, his voice was so deep it made her shiver. "Last time we were alone, you held me off. Still wanna wait until after the ritual?"

*After the ritual? I can't even wait until after dinner, big guy. In fact, if you don't put your hands on my body right now, I might literally self-destruct.*

And even though she practically hurled the thought at his head, he only pushed out a breath that sounded like humor.

"You and Nero. All this mental chitchat's a nifty trick for a war dog like me. But I'm an old-fashioned kinda guy." His voice thickened. "I wanna hear you say it."

Damn if that didn't make her hotter.

Carefully she cleared her throat. "You already know I've been with Dex. So if I conceive…"

He waited.

"There's even an outside chance—just a long shot really—that, um, the kid could be Ben's. With forty-three offspring and counting, gods know he's virile. We did fool around, and… he *really* wants to be the father."

He waited.

"Plus there's a lot I don't know about Valyrian fertility. My mom died young—and besides, I'm half Kryll. Maybe those rules don't apply to me."

He waited.

Gods, she was babbling like a bubblehead. She licked the iron zing of mineral water from her lips and locked onto his expectant eyes.

"Listen, Zorin. What I'm saying is—if you want your own shot at siring my son, like the prophecy says… um… now would be good."

"Let's get one thing straight." With a suddenness that made her gasp, he crouched to cup her chin in his big palm. "I have every intention of siring your son. Shoot, I'd love a shipload of kids if you're up for it. But that's just a fringe benefit." His eyes dropped to her parted lips. "Kid or no kid, I want you for *you*, sweetheart. Just like you want me for me."

His thumb rubbed the breathless curve of her lower lip. "That's the only way this works. Got it?"

"I do want you, Zorin," she gasped, pulse pounding in her throat. "So bad I can barely breathe. And I'm telling you… we don't have to wait."

The rough rasp of his thumb against her mouth was like setting a spark to rocket fuel. Holding his darkening gaze with hers, she encased his thumb in her lips, grazed the pad with her teeth, wrapped her tongue around his length. He tasted like salt and steel. The primitive whiff of wolf rising from his skin sent goose bumps shooting down her spine.

"Out," he said hoarsely. "Out of there before I drag you out."

And the thing about him looking so dangerous with his tattoos and his weapons and his leather was that he looked more than capable of violence.

Knowing she was playing with fire, she sank her teeth lightly into his thumb. "Or you could come in."

"Plenty of time for that later. Right now I'm gonna make you come wrapped around my cock so many times you lose count. And I'm not gonna have you slipping outta my arms like a damn mermaid while I chase you around that tub like a bar of soap. *Out.*"

The carbon-steel command in his unyielding voice made her shudder with need. Lowering her lashes, she released him and swam toward the submerged steps.

Now that she'd driven him to the breaking point, the thought of rising naked from the water left her insanely flustered. But this wasn't some rogue samurai or fugitive thief she could toy with. He was one of the galaxy's dominant powers. She'd teased him and taunted him and enticed him from the moment they'd met. Tonight he'd make her fulfill all those promises she'd been whispering in his ear.

Every last one.

He lurked like a leather-clad colossus six cubits away, silent as a stealth ship as he stalked her through the steam.

"Don't be afraid." His deep rumble echoed from the wet walls. "You're mine now. By day you'll rule the Syndax horde at my side—and by night I'll bring all your bad-girl fantasies to life. And you got plenty of those, don'tcha?"

Her body burned with more than thermal heat.

"One or two," she whispered. "How'd you know?"

"Cuz I know you. Knew you the moment I met you. You think I don't know you were just floating in my bath dreaming about Dex and how hard he's gonna fuck you when you're back in his bed?" His words roughened. "I'd be pissed as all get-out if I wasn't having a few choice fantasies about Dex myself. Ever since I did what you wanted today and kissed the living daylights outta him."

"You did?" Breathlessly she waited for more. "Oh, come on—you can't just leave it there! Did you—did he—?"

"Let's just say we both liked it enough that neither one of us wanted to stop. That turns your crank, doesn't it?" His lids dropped over his wolfish gaze. "There's plenty more where that came from. Now stop dawdling and come here."

And there it was, that hint of humor and tolerance under all that steel that said *Zorin* to her. It finally brought her to her feet.

Foam clung to her curves. Not enough to conceal. Just enough to tantalize. Slowly she climbed the steps, putting a sway in her hips.

"Oh, Juno," he rasped, eyes claiming every handspan of exposed skin. Her breasts swayed and her nipples peaked and her clit tingled beneath his gaze. "You're bare as an egg."

"Is that a problem?" Her voice was so throaty it barely sounded like hers.

He made an inarticulate noise.

"It works better with a cybersuit." She tried with mixed success to contain a grin. "Am I your first cyber samurai, big guy?"

"First and last and only." Before her silicon-bandaged feet could hit the floor, his hands closed around her waist and dragged her from the water, hard against his dangerous frame. "And that's a goddamn promise."

Her soft squeak of surprise as her feet left the floor was muffled by his mouth. Her breath rushed out as their lips collided.

He kissed her like he'd been waiting a lifetime to do it and now was his one and only chance and he damn well meant to make it matter.

The demanding heat of his mouth opened her up and consumed her. Their breath mingled in a shared moan as the slick fire of their tongues came together. The dark taste of predator made her head spin—tinged with the caramel smoke of whiskey.

Naked and dripping and panting with need, she twined her arms around his neck and wound her legs around his waist and whimpered into his mouth as she kissed him back.

Her fertile body was burning to feel his cock inside her. Which meant he was wearing way too much. Desperate, she clawed at the tight shirt stretched across his mighty shoulders.

"Zorin—*please*—"

A deep groan rumbled from his chest.

"Slow down a little, sweetheart," he breathed between hot hungry kisses. "A girl like you's a lotta excitement for an old guy like me."

"You're not old. You're perfect for me—for all of us." Her feverish hands dragged his shirt up his back until her palms hit the plane of naked skin stretched over muscle.

The frisson of contact made them both moan.

"And I don't want to wait," she finished with a gasp.

"Well, I intend to make this last. And I guarantee I'll make it worth the wait."

Muscle rippled under her hands as he hoisted her higher. He nuzzled his way down her throat between her breasts while she shivered and clutched his shoulders.

Did he even know how much his monumental strength turned her on? Desperate for more of him, she squirmed in his grip.

"You need to trust me on this one," he breathed against her skin. "This is still pretty new to you, ain't it? I'm a big guy and you're tiny. The only way this works is I get you good and ready."

His lips closed around one swollen nipple. A jolt of electricity streaked through her.

"That's supposed to slow me down? Good gods, Zorin…"

And then she pretty much lost the ability to say anything. He was licking and sucking and tasting and she was mesmerized by the sight of her own tight golden nipples, shiny with his saliva, thrusting forward and begging for his mouth. Her hands threaded through the rough spikes of his hair, sand sprinkled with silver, in a demand that echoed her gasping pleas for *oh gods Zorin please…*

Now he was carrying her through the *thermae*, steamy walls and ancient arches seeming to shift around her, muscle flexing in her heated grip. When they finally hit the bedroom, she barely registered the cool air that encased her wet skin.

He sank to the edge of the bed and eased her down to straddle his hips.

The spectacular bulge of his cock nudged her clit.

And she thought she'd lose her mind.

His rough hands pulled the clip from her hair so it tumbled down around them in a cloud of scented jasmine. Groaning, he buried his face in her neck, breathing her in, the hard sting of his lips leaving his mark of ownership on her skin.

She seized her moment to skim him out of his shirt and—

"Wow," she panted. "Just wow."

He was all bulging muscle and sleek skin and black ink, the tattoo that banded the bulwark of his biceps as wide as her hand. The spiky tips of another tattoo wrapped around his ribs from whatever was inked across his back. The pale starburst of an old blaster scar spread across his massive shoulder and a knife scar scored the hard plane of his abs.

*"Wow,"* she whispered again.

"You're good for a man's ego," he chuckled as she unbuckled his belt with indecent haste and got his blaster out of their bed. "Stars, the way you look at me."

He started to unstrap the knife, but she whispered, "Leave it. I like it."

"Like I said," he murmured, "safe isn't what revs your engine. Is it?"

"Guess not," she admitted with a grin.

While she worked on his zipper, easing the metal tab over that bulge that left her breathless, his hands slid up her thighs and spread her wide. She stilled, staring down at her own pussy, slick and swollen and glistening with need, clit engorged and begging for his hand.

*Little more exposure and a lot less control than you're used to, angel.*

Feeling heat flash through her, she tried to close her thighs, but he held her legs open with a low growl and looked his fill. The potent kick of Mogadon pheromones poured from his skin. Helpless to prevent it, she rocked her hips into him. Gods, she could come just from—

"Zorin—please—I need—"

"I know what you need. You need to come tonight so hard and so often you'll never want to spend another night without me. You need to want me so much you'll beg Dex to come over here and spend his nights in my bed so you can have us both inside you."

"Oh gods, yes," she whispered.

"Yeah, it gets to me too." He pushed out a breath. "But that's gonna take some doing."

"Ben too," she gasped.

"You're an insatiable little thing, ain'tcha?" He chuckled. "Not that I'm complaining. Now tell me if you like this. We'll start off nice and easy."

His thumb circled her clit. She rocked into his touch with a cry.

"That sounds like a yes." His voice rumbled deep in his chest as he just kept doing it—touching her without touching her. Even as he worked a finger into the tight pulsing heat of her channel. "How about this?"

"Yes. *That.* Oh gods Zorin—like that—"

Mindless and gasping with need, she rose to her knees and rutted against his hand, face buried in the powerful column of his neck. His free hand wrapped in her hair and pulled her head up.

"Let me see you, sweetheart. I wanna see your face when I make you come."

"More—harder—I need—"

"Maybe you need this?" He worked a second finger inside her and she rode him with desperate abandon, breasts bouncing and head tipped back. "Gods, you're gonna feel out of this world when I'm buried deep inside you. Now you tell me if I'm hurting you. I mean it."

"You'll only hurt me—if you stop—oh gods—"

His free hand slid down her back, dipped into the slick heat between her legs, and smoothed her own wetness up the crease of her ass. When his finger found her tight pucker—uncharted terrain except for that one incendiary dream—she clutched his shoulders and cried out.

"Oh no, I can't—please—please don't—"

"Sure you can," he breathed against her breasts, tonguing the tight furl of her nipples to sweeten the deal. "If you want Dex and me in the same bed, you're gonna need to take both of us. Because neither one of us is any good at going second. That *is* what you want, ain't it?"

*"Yes."* The scorching visual made her whimper. She'd never dreamed that part of her could be so sensitive. The sound caught in her throat as he breached the tight ring of muscle with a slight burn that made her moan again.

"Relax for me, sweetheart," he coaxed her. "Imagine how good you're gonna make Dex feel the first time he comes in your tight little hole."

Gods, he was going to kill her if he didn't let her come.

She was riding his hand—possessed and stretched and filled in both places—the wet sounds of her own arousal clearly audible under her desperate cries as she bucked against his fingers. Her rear channel stretched to accommodate him down to the third knuckle, squeezing just the way she would when she milked his cock. His thumb found her swollen clit and she disintegrated. With nowhere to hide from his burning eyes, she arched her back and pressed her tingling nipples in his face and begged him to take her.

"Good girl," he breathed, suckling her nipples. "I think you're ready for me now, aren't you?"

"So ready—I'm so ready—"

"This first time, I want you on top." His hoarse command made her shudder with need. "Now come here and take my cock."

Then she was scrambling forward, straddling him on the bed, dragging his leather pants down far enough for what she needed more than oxygen. His fully engorged cock sprang free, glistening and slick with his own need, to slap against his belly and make her whimper.

He was bigger than Nero. Even bigger than Dex. She needed both hands to hold him, hot and heavy and pulsing in her grip. But the slide of her fingers over his slick length made him clench the blankets in both fists and thrust into her palms.

And the sight of his powerful tattooed body, flat on his back and writhing with pleasure, jaw clenched to keep from spilling in her hands, was almost enough to send her over the edge.

Eyes heavy, lips parted, she swiped a finger across his dripping tip and slid her wet finger into her mouth. The salty musk of his taste spread over her tongue and made her hum.

"Gods, Kaia. Put me inside you," he growled. "Now—do it now."

Trembling with craving, she straddled him and fitted his thick shaft against the aching need at her core. She knew a moment of desperate uncertainty—she'd never done it like this, he was only her second time, he was so much bigger than anything she'd imagined.

Just the head of his cock made her stretch to take him.

But she was slick and wet and ready for him… so ready… that she worked herself down his cock a finger at a time. Breath hitching with every thrust.

"You're perfect, sweetheart, so gods-damned perfect," he praised her. "So tight and hot and needy."

"Please—Zorin—I can't—can't wait any longer."

"Need you so much—you're gonna make me come so hard."

His hips rolled against her, burying him inside her to the hilt. A deep groan tore through him. His hands gripped her derrière and urged her on.

"I'm so close," she whimpered. "Oh gods."

He found her hand and pressed it to her aching clit. Sitting astride him, she rocked into her own hand and rode him. He pistoned into her harder, faster—the rapid slap of flesh on flesh accented by his breathless curses and her own urgent cries. Truly, truly, she was flying apart, spinning like a top under his centrifugal force.

"Kaia. Look at me." Blazing silver with need, his eyes locked on her, compelled her, held her in a grip she'd never break free from. "Give me a son."

She was spinning… burning… flying… pleading… hearing him shout as she cried his name… shuddering into the kick and spurt of his cock inside her.

It went on and on forever. Like he'd never stop coming.

The pleasure obliterated her and blew her apart. Knowing at that moment she'd give him anything and everything he wanted.

Always.

One child. Ten. A thousand.

*Yes. He's part of this. I can never walk away from him now. It's Dex and Nero and Zorin.*

*It's all of us.*

Somehow then she was crying. Soft gasping sobs that made zero sense. Because she'd never been a fan of useless, self-indulgent tears. But all this excess emotion crashing through her needed to come out somewhere. And he was cradling her against his sweat-slick chest, arms wrapped tight around her trembling body, hand cupping her head to hold her close.

"Don't cry. You'll break my heart. I'll conquer worlds and lay them at your feet."

"That's such a Syndax thing to say," she sniffled. "I don't need worlds laid at my feet. I don't even know why I'm crying."

"Sure you do," he whispered. "And for the record, I'm damn near crying myself."

Her thighs were slick with his come and her own craving. She ached deep inside from taking him. But she burned with an unquenchable need that only conception would satisfy.

She snuggled up against him with a shuddery sigh.

"Ssshhh," he soothed her. "Good girl. Just rest a few ticks. I know what you need."

"What's that?" she hiccupped.

One rough, possessive hand smoothed down her spine while he whispered in her ear to make her shiver.

"We're just getting started, sweetheart. And you need to conceive. Soon's you catch your breath, I'm gonna make you come for me all over again."

# CHAPTER NINE
## The Masquerade

Nero needed to move. Despite the fact that every molecule of his being was screaming at him not to budge.

He'd been dreaming half his life about what it would feel like to wake up with Dex Draven in his bed. And he was flat-out flummoxed the guy hadn't just ghosted him and tiptoed off during the night.

In fact, he'd done the exact opposite.

Nero lay sprawled on his stomach in the ruddy dawn of Valyria's red sun, thanks to the artificial climate control in his quarters, one arm flung overhead in the tangled mess they'd made of his bed. With Dex's solid frame sprawled snoring right on top of him. Chest pressed to his back, face buried in his hair, one muscled thigh shoved possessively between Nero's.

But what really got him was Dex's arm thrown over his, his calloused palm pinning Nero's to the mattress. Their fingers laced tight while they slept.

All of which meant he wasn't going anywhere until Dex felt like letting him.

And when Dex woke up and pushed him away, he'd leave a smoking crater where Nero's heart used to be.

*Gods of Solaris, what an infernal farking mess. First I let Kaia trample my heart to a pulp under her sexy little cyber boots. Then I let Dex pour rocket fuel over what little I've got left. All he needs to do now is toss a match.*

*And I'll go up in flames.*

A heartfelt groan rolled from his chest.

Which turned out to be a major mistake.

Dex pulled in a slow breath and whispered into the back of his neck, "You're still here."

As if he needed any further evidence that the feel of Dex's mouth on his body still made him rock hard in a heartbeat.

"You're in my bed," Nero pointed out irritably, trying to ignore the swelling ache of his cock pinned hard against the mattress. "On *your* flipping battleship. Where the punk was I supposed to go?"

"Nowhere. You're right where I want you." Dex sounded thoroughly satisfied with himself and this entire outcome.

It was all Nero could manage not to groan again.

Instead he battened down his mental barricades against the inevitable rebuff. If nothing came in—if nothing went out—then nothing could hurt him.

At least that was the theory.

Regrettably, his body hadn't read the briefing memo. Subtly he shifted to ease the incendiary heat in his mindlessly idiotic, relentlessly insistent cock before he lost every vestige of personal dignity and started rutting into the mattress.

Which turned out to be another monumental mistake. Because the movement only lodged his ass against the rigid blade of Dex's cock. They both moaned at the contact.

"For punk's sake, Dex! Have a little mercy," Nero muttered, hands knotting into fists in the tangled sheets.

*Any second now, you're going to go all Mogadon on me and freak the hell out—*

"Still not a morning guy, are you?" Dex breathed in his ear. Which only made him shiver all over. "What's the matter, gorgeous? Did I keep you up too late?"

A memory raced through him. A memory of how searingly good it felt to thrust against the slick friction of Dex's cock. A memory of Dex's explosive climax spurting all over him. Not to mention the surge of intense satisfaction it gave him to make the hopelessly unattainable object of all his secret fantasies finally lose his mind and cry out with pleasure in Nero's bed.

Feeling his breath go rough, he muttered an exasperated curse.

"Come on, Dex. You have a ship to run—and a Tombola to finish. Today's the masquerade. We need Zorin to ease up on the caveman complex, and Kaia to get her shapely ass back on board this ship before her suitors start a riot. Now let me *up*."

Desperate to end his torment, he pushed hard against Dex's solid weight.

That burst of defiance turned out to be his final mistake.

Dex growled and rocked into him, his taut heat wedging into the crack of Nero's ass like he was gods-dammed made for it. His fist clenched hard in Nero's hair to hold him still.

Nero barely contained a whimper of longing.

"The blasted ship and the blasted Tombola can wait. I'm not done with you yet. Stay still." Dex's teeth closed gently around Nero's earlobe in not-so-subtle warning. A sting of mingled pain and pleasure made Nero suck in his breath. "You and I need to talk. About what happened last night."

Here it came.

The big rebuff.

Practically panting with need, acutely aware this entire encounter was about a breath away from careening off the rails, Nero made a desperate attempt to fend it off.

"You're full of surprises, aren't you, Dex? First you manage to wrestle all those mighty Mogadon hang-ups into momentary submission just long enough for an actual guy-on-guy hookup. Then, after years of avoidance, you actually want to talk about it?"

"Damnation, Ben!" Now he actually sounded offended. "This wasn't some bloody random hookup and you bloody well know it. And you're bloody well right I want to talk about it! Hells, I've been trying to talk to you for two days about—"

The warble of his wrist unit peeled out. With a curse, Dex released Nero's hair and muttered fiercely into the comm link, *"Not now."*

"There's nothing to talk about." Nero sighed against the clutch of heartbreak splitting his chest. Too damn late now to fend anything off. He'd just have to suck it up and lick his wounds on the long flight back to Valyria. "It was a one-time thing. I get it! Now get the hell *off—*"

"Does this feel like a one-time thing to you?" Dex's hard hand slid over his ribs and closed unerringly around the throbbing ache of Nero's cock.

Which turned out to have a mind of its own. Same as always wherever Dex Draven was involved. Helpless to prevent it, he groaned and rocked into Dex's fist.

"Damn it, Dex," he whispered. "You're too flipping good at this."

"And you're too perfect." Breath rough and quick in his ear, Dex thrust against his ass. "You're so blooming perfect for me, Ben."

And feeling the guy's cock—already slick and pulsing with need—lodged hard against his hole sucked every particle of good sense out of Nero's head as effectively as if he'd just thrown open a portal and jettisoned his brain into the vacuum of space.

He'd always known Dex would never go for this. Never break down and give Nero what he needed at his most primitive, fundamental level. Because what he needed was nothing short of complete submission to Dex's total possession. The possession that sprang from Dex emptying his cock and shooting his seed so deep inside Nero they'd never be free of each other. If there had ever been the slightest scintilla of a chance the military ruler of the Mogadon Empire might actually be on board for that plan…

But there wasn't. Of course there wasn't.

Yet stubborn hope made him a mindless idiot for his boyhood best friend.

Same as always.

"Dex," he panted, thrusting into that knowing fist. "I can make this—easy for you. Do you want me to—?"

The cheerful carol of that farking wrist unit nearly made Nero tear his hair out.

"For flip's sake, Dex! Don't you dare answer that."

"Commander?" The tinny voice of some youthful functionary over-rode his desperate demand. "Sir, you ordered a sit rep as soon as we—"

"Belay that order, prefect. My hands are… rather full at the moment." Dex's breathless chuckle sounded in Nero's ear. "Not quite so blasted eager to go bolting out of my bed now, are we?"

"Go to hell, Dex." His seeking hand found the corded length of Dex's thigh, slid up to grip the luscious globe of his ass, and pulled him in tighter.

"Sure that's what you want?" His slick tip lodged right up against Nero's tingling pucker.

And despite the complete lack of any of the customary preliminaries to get him opened up and ready, Nero had to smother in his pillow a long low groan.

"Ah, sir—I'm not quite hearing you?" that infernal voice persisted. "We've found those missing Zephyrs."

"Damn. We'll have to make this quick," Dex whispered in his ear. "Are you ready for me?"

His pride seethed with rebellion at the notion of being Dex's morning quickie. But a far more prominent part of him surrendered completely to the plan.

Abandoning every atom of good sense and self-respect and Precursorial dignity, he arched his back and ground into Dex's hard heat.

"There's lube in the drawer," he panted. "Know what to do with it?"

A frisson of discord eddied through the fog of arousal that clouded both their brains. Just a ripple of recoil.

But he felt that recoil like a slap in the face.

*"Ben."* Dex's tone was raw with denial. "I can't—*do* that to you. I can't—disrespect and—dishonor and—*disgrace* you like that. I can't. Not ever."

*Disrespect.*

*Dishonor.*

*Disgrace.*

That was how a quintessential Mogadon male like Dex felt about the union that was the greatest act of intimacy and love Nero knew how to express.

Gasping with pain and shock, Nero released his desperate clutch and struggled furiously to wrench himself free.

But Dex was having none of it.

"Easy," he whispered into Nero's neck, licking the sweat from his skin. "I can still give you what you need. And you're still mine. Aren't you?"

"Go to hell!" he snarled, twisting savagely in his grip.

"You're *mine*," Dex gritted, grimly undeterred. His determined hand tightened around Nero's aching cock. "Let's prove it. To both our satisfaction."

A few hard, fast strokes brought him right to the edge, his entire body tingling, his balls clamped tight. He was so slick with his own precum they could both hear the wet slide of Dex's quickening hand riding his shaft. Even over his own desperate panting.

"Gods—oh gods—please! I don't—want you like this—"

"Yes, you do," Dex groaned against his ear, breath harsh as he bucked into the crack of his ass, slick with the man's own eagerness. Every thrust sent lightning bolts of need straight down Nero's cock and made him cry out. "You want me the same way I want you—any way, any place, any time I can get you. You still love me?"

"I never loved you!" Nero gasped in one last desperate act of self-defense. "I just—lied through my teeth—to get in your pants."

"Don't be absurd! I was already bloody naked and out of my mind with rutting you when—"

Savage with craving and despair, Nero caught Dex's burnished hair in a frantic fist and pulled him in for an openmouthed kiss that blazed with a bonfire of pent-up longing and throbbed with a lifetime of need.

"You do love me," Dex panted into his mouth, undeceived. "You do. Promise me you'll never stop. I need you so much, Ben. Need you so farking much."

"Oh comets—oh gods—oh *Dex*—"

He didn't know if it was giving away how he felt or shouting Dex's name when his climax boiled through him or the rhythmic jets of seed shooting from his balls and spurting all over Dex's hand.

He didn't know anything.

All he knew was the deep, animalistic, intensely pleasurable groan that shuddered through the powerful body behind him and the hot spurt of Dex's release.

Panting with exertion and slick with sweat, Dex collapsed across his back, his hand going slack around Nero's shaft. Between harsh ragged breaths, he pressed repentant kisses to Nero's trembling shoulder.

"Gods of Olympus, Ben," he gasped out. "When are you going to stop fighting me? You damn well have to know—this isn't a casual fling. Not for either one of us."

Nero knotted his fists and slammed his barriers back down. Because the word *love* didn't appear in the Draven dictionary. Dex's head right now was one monumental mess.

Barriers or no barriers, Nero would have to be blind not to sense the howling storm of grief for his brother that Dex was fighting his way through. And comatose not to know Dex was hurting because of Kaia. The same way Nero himself was hurting. His lifemate's defection was a gaping hole in both their hearts.

Right now, his bed was Dex's port in the storm.

But it wasn't going to last.

"You know," Dex pressed him. "Don't you?"

Nero answered without words from deep in the no-man's land in his head. Deep enough in that Dex would never hear.

*I know the thought of fucking me revolts you. And I know you had to get space-faced drunk before you could bring yourself to my bed.*

"About those Zephyrs, boss?" A new voice crackled from Dex's comm link. Deeper, older, and grimly persistent.

Dex pushed out a breath and rolled to his back. Leaving Nero lying in a pool of rapidly cooling semen. Grimacing, Nero grabbed a fistful of linen and started cleaning up.

Though he couldn't help but notice the thoroughly proprietary look in Dex's cobalt eyes as they raked over him. Looking way too satisfied at leaving the Valyrian Precursor in such a soiled and sated state— thoroughly claimed and ravaged and reeking with Dex's mating scent.

A look of complete possession that left Nero tingling. Already halfway ready to drag his tongue down Dex's body until they both got hard and went at it again.

*Gods know that wouldn't take long.*

And despite all his unbreachable barriers, something in his face or his head gave Dex a predatory grin.

"Go ahead, Marcus," Dex murmured, his eyes never leaving Nero's.

"We found those fighters—all three of 'em —adrift."

Dex's smile vanished and his gaze turned hard. "Do we have Cato?"

"That's a negative. Cato's still MIA. But every man jack on those three flight crews is dead."

"Damn." Dex sucked in a breath and pushed up to sit. "Are you certain? Have you dispatched a medic?"

"We don't need a medic in there. Just a guy with a mop. Poor bastards are smeared all over the cockpit." Together, they waited through an uncomfortable pause. "Boss, it's classic Swarm."

"Right." Crisp with command, Dex sprang to his feet and reached for his pants. "What about the novicide?"

"Tanks are empty. All of 'em. Your, uh, brother released his payload somewhere—we're just not sure where. We're trying to download some kinda flight path from their databanks."

"Here's what I want." Moving with brisk efficiency, Dex scooped up clothes and boots and beelined for Nero's bathroom. "I want every bit and byte in those databanks gone over with a microscope, am I clear? And I want that Tombola hall secured and guards placed on every one of the final hundred from now until they're off my ship. Send a shuttle over to the *Relentless* ASAP to collect the maharani and that infernal Syndax. The ritual resumes at twelve hundred sharp. Make it happen."

Without waiting for assent—because he took absolute obedience for granted—Dex switched off the comm link and tossed over his shoulder, "Mind if I use your shower?"

"Make yourself at home," Nero muttered.

But the hiss of water swallowed his sardonic tone.

By the time a fully showered and impeccably uniformed Dex emerged, Nero had pulled on tunic and breeches, thrown a fur over the incriminating ruin of his bed, and busied himself in the galley brewing a stiff pot of *chaco*.

Having spent ten futile ticks trying like blazes not to imagine Dex Draven naked in his shower.

"I can't stay. I've got suitors queued up in my ready room. And I want to inspect those Zephyrs and their databanks personally before Zorin turns up." Dex snared the steaming cup Nero poured him and gulped a hasty swallow of the potent brew. "Ben, you and I need to talk. I promised Kaia—"

"No time," Nero murmured blandly. "You said it yourself. See you later at the masquerade."

"I suppose that'll have to suffice." Dex sighed. "Don't be late—and make yourself beautiful. Gods know that won't be difficult."

Before he could avoid it, Dex leaned in to give him a hard careless kiss.

And even that—being taken and used as an object of careless enjoyment by his boyhood best friend—revved his engine to a fever pitch. Same as always.

He swallowed a wistful sigh.

Dex paused with one hand still gripping Nero's waist and breathed him in with a frown.

"You'd best have a proper shower yourself before you leave this room," he muttered. "Every head on this ship is supplied with a cleansing agent that's engineered to mask the scent. It isn't perfect, but it helps."

"The *scent*?" Nero stared.

"You've got my mating scent all over you. No Mogadon with a nose could miss it. Sorry." Attention clearly elsewhere, already cataloging the day's duties and demands, Dex spared him a brief smile. "The cleansing agent will help."

The shock of rejection slammed through him like a body blow.

Nero was privately astounded how much it hurt.

And fiercely determined to hide it.

"Oh, right. Because no one's supposed to know."

"I… regret the necessity." Clearly sensing his mounting wrath, Dex gave him an apologetic grimace. "I'm afraid I've never been any good at this."

"You mean *relationships*?" Nero's tone dripped acid. "I hadn't noticed."

"Come on." Dex reached for him, but Nero slid deftly aside. "You know how precarious my position is—mine and Kaia's. Just two nights past, I barely survived an attempted mutiny. Not to mention multiple assassination attempts. Yet I'm solely responsible for Kaia's safety—and yours—while you're aboard this ship. As I'm acutely aware, my fleet and I are all that currently stand between the two of you and another smack of Swarm assassins."

"Get a clue!" Nero snarled. "I don't need your farking *protection* any more than you need mine. And you're the alpha in this floating fortress. Don't tell me half this ship doesn't already know you spent last night rutting in my bed. The rest will know by noon."

Dex looked inclined to argue. At least about the not-needing-his-protection part. Instead, he sliced a glance at the time and sighed. "Just use the cleansing agent. That's a start. We'll sort the rest out later. You, me—and Kaia."

And the chasm of naked yearning that split Dex's soul and surfaced in his face made envy burn in Nero's throat like alkali. They'd barely been apart a day, but Dex was on fire with longing for Kaia. The same way Nero knew—by the echo of an ache in his own chest—that Kaia was yearning for Dex.

Somewhere in the middle of this interstellar mess, his lifemate and his best friend had fallen in love.

For some damn reason, his eyes were stinging.

He hoped like hell Zorin could handle it when Kaia hurled herself into Dex's arms and the two of them went at it. Comets, he hoped he could handle it himself.

Maybe Zorin would take Nero as a consolation prize.

Except, after the night he'd just had and the number Dex had just done on his heart, Nero was through being anyone's consolation prize.

Right now he needed some consolation himself. Needed it more than oxygen.

Before Dex could sniff out the emotional carnage he'd left in his wake, Nero cleared his throat, turned away, and buried his face in the bitter chocolate steam of his *chaco*.

"Well?" The pressure of Dex's eyes burned into his back. "The masquerade. Will you be there?"

"I'm still your neutral second. I'll be there," Nero said gruffly. "But we dock at Quorum in three days. Then this Tombola's history."

*At which point I've got a one-way ticket home on a Valyrian cruiser to sire my forty-fourth offspring for the breeding program. Where you'll never carve my heart to ribbons again.*

*Either one of you.*

Behind him Dex's voice rang steely with determination. "We'll have to find some way to make this infernal affair work—you, me, and Kaia. Because I have absolutely zero intention of losing either of you."

*It's not up to you, Dex. Not this time.*

But that was one thought Nero managed to barricade.

And Dex marched off to discharge his Indomitable duties without hearing a thing.

#

Though he kept the impulse to himself, Zorin wished heartily he could spend the whole day in bed. Because all the gods knew neither one of them had gotten much in the way of sleep last night.

Not that he was complaining.

Sprawled comfortably in the pilot's seat on the *Relentless*'s aging shuttle, with Kaia's compact body tucked between his spread thighs and her capable hands on the yoke, he couldn't hold back a grin of satisfaction.

Last night she'd blown every fuse in his body. Including a whole circuit board he didn't even know he had. And based on how many times he'd made her shudder and sob and fall apart around his tongue and hands and cock, he figured it was fair to say he'd returned the favor.

135

His girl would be electric in the sack under any circumstances—one reason out of a million why Dex and Nero couldn't keep their hands off her. But this whole fertility kick?

It made her insatiable.

She couldn't seem to get enough of him. And, given all the mileage on his ugly carcass, he was flattered as all get-out.

*Yep. Definitely not complaining.*

"This shuttle handles like a cargo scull in an asteroid belt," Kaia muttered as they jolted into a pivot toward the *Inevitable*'s sleek superstructure, floating against the vast glittering night of space. "We should have taken the shuttle Dex sent over. One of these days, you're going to have to learn to trust him."

"It's not him I don't trust, sweetheart. We *think* Proteus was behind those hits on your life and Dex's—maybe even mine—but that doesn't mean he's the only threat on the gameboard. Don't forget the Mogadon and the Syndax are still at war."

"Fair point," she sighed.

And just because he could and because she'd let him—and because he couldn't keep his big paws off her hot body for more than a few ticks at a time—he slid his hands around her sleek bare tummy and nuzzled the side of her neck.

And the way she shivered and gasped and wiggled her tight little ass against his rapidly hardening shaft made every cell and molecule in his makeup sit up and say howdy.

Sure, they'd just done the dirty so many times he'd lost count. Right before they boarded, he'd come buried deep inside her so hard he saw stars.

Now, mileage or no mileage, he found he was plenty ready for another go-round.

Too bad they had company.

Six of his best boys packed the jump seats in back, leather creaking, chains rattling, muttering and farting and sweating and generally needing serious time with soap and a scrub in the *thermae*. He didn't plan on letting that lot get any more of a gander at his girl than they were already getting, thanks to those sexy Syndax threads she was rocking.

Mars, they were only human, fueled by testosterone and edgy with all the pheromones he was kicking out in this confined space. Even if they did worship her with canine devotion after the way she'd saved their collective butts on Quorum.

He leaned in to punch a button on the rusting console. The rattle of the geriatric ventilation unit kicked in, pushing out a gust of stale-smelling oxygen from life support.

Which should take the edge off.

He hoped.

"I'm perfectly well aware you're still at war," Kaia murmured, tone pointed. Rubbing her sweet backside into his boner just to jerk his chain, the little space vixen. "You and Dex need to do something about that. As in *today*. Particularly since your temporary ceasefire ends in three days when the Tombola's over. We're running out of time."

"Be a good girl," he whispered in her ear, hands sliding over her metal-studded belt and black leather miniskirt to grip her bare thighs. "You're gonna sweet-talk Dex into peace talks for me soon as the two of you get horizontal."

"Mmmm." Her thighs parted under his touch—a bold invitation he could barely resist, even with his boys salivating at the prospect. "What makes you so sure he'll listen?"

"Pretty sure you'll have his undivided attention." His voice turned raspy. "Maybe I'll even help if you ask me nicely."

He still wasn't sure at all Dex would go for it—his girl's naughty fantasy of getting all four of them in the sack, matched and mated with her fanatical father's blessing?

But damn if he wasn't primed to give it his best shot.

"We'll talk to Dex at the masquerade," she murmured.

It took a lot of muscle to coax the balky shuttle onto a glide path for the flashing maw of the *Inevitable*'s landing bay, so he leaned in to help, but she shrugged him away and capably finished the job herself. A thoroughly Syndax instinct he fully approved.

*Yeah, you done good, big guy. You couldn't have found a better consort and a better queen for the horde if you gods-damned planned it. She's made for you.*

Which sure came in handy, given the fact he was toes over nose in love with her.

Heck, he'd fallen for her on Day One, when she defied her godlike dad to protect a scared kid. He'd fallen for her harder after the way she leaped at his unconventional Tombola bid—because he got her ferocious need for freedom from civilization's petty rules. So perfect in every single way for the Syndax and for him.

And he'd fallen for keeps when he watched her face—transformed, transcendent, exultant, enraptured—the first time he made her climax.

His heart felt too big for his chest. Like it was beating outside his skin. He felt like he stood a hundred cubits high. He was crazy in love for the first time in his whole flipping life.

Unless he counted falling for his former protégé eight years ago. Which he didn't.

Because that would mean while he'd been racketing around the galaxy raising hell since his exile, punching every one of Dex Draven's buttons, he'd been jonesing for the guy the whole time.

He cleared his throat and pushed a hand through the rough spikes of his hair. Which dislodged the carnival mask he'd shoved up over his brow.

"About this shindig today," he murmured in her ear, just to feel her shiver. "I was gonna bone up on the protocol last night. But you kept me kinda busy, sweetheart."

"Sorry," she whispered, low and throaty.

"I'm not."

And it was all he could manage not to unbuckle the sleek leather halter stretched over her succulent tits and work her nipples until she moaned and begged for more.

*Not now, dickhead. Screw your head on straight. You're flying right into the kill zone. We're down to the last hundred—and those suitors of hers are desperate. You gotta keep your girl safe.*

He cleared his throat and his head. "Why don't you give me the down-low."

Her fingers danced over the aging console, transmitting their call sign to Dex's flight control like she'd been flying Syndax shuttles since she was five.

"The masquerade's the capstone contest. How we narrow the field to the fortunate fifty. Just you, me, Dex, Nero, and the final candidates for my bed. So far, it's been all about might and money. Now it's all about seduction and sex."

"Sounds like a Mogadon orgy." He scanned the flashing blue lights that filled their viewport and framed the harsh glare of Dex's landing bay.

Which used to be *his* landing bay. But that was a lifetime ago.

How many of his old enemies were waiting for him inside?

"Why do you think my father wanted Dex running the show?" Her tone cranked tight. "According to Kryll tradition, the masquerade has the highest per capita fatality rate of any Tombola event—except for the blood games, which go down tomorrow. Those are to the death. You'll have to fight again. Gods, Zorin…"

Under his hands, she shuddered with a tangible tremor of trepidation.

"I survived the pit before," he reminded her gruffly. Because he loved that she was actually worried over his sorry ass. "Tomorrow I'm gonna do it again. Right now we gotta focus on the masquerade."

Clearly she wasn't buying it, but his girl followed his lead in front of his crew. Her hands clenched around the yoke. "Basically, by tonight? Every candidate still standing will be horny, drunk, and desperate. This is the day a Tombola bride is statistically most likely to end up kidnapped, raped—or killed."

A fist of angst gripped his gut, while adrenaline donkey-kicked him in the chest. That primitive drive to protect what was his—the oldest instinct in the Mogadon genome. Now that ferocious spike of protectiveness just about brought him out of his chair.

"That won't happen to you. And that's a farking promise."

His boys in back rumbled with agreement and aggression.

"That's why I need you to work with Dex today, big guy." Kaia kept her eyes nailed on the landing drone, guiding their nose into the bay between sinister rows of sleek golden Zephyrs. Just like the ones that might've already dumped novicide—or something worse—on his folks at Quorum.

"You, me, Dex, and Nero," she repeated adamantly. "It's all four of us. That's the only way we get this done."

He made a conscious effort to unclench his fists. "How come we're all wearing masks for this hootenanny?"

She pushed out a scornful snort.

"The masks are supposed to make it easier for my suitors to woo me. Since hypothetically I won't know who they are, I'm supposed to choose the final fifty based on charm and chemistry—unimpeded by mercenary factors like money.

"But I'm a telepath." She edged her voice in cynicism. "Yeah, they're all aching to get inside my cybersuit. Especially with the

Mogadon candidates kicking out enough pheromones to make a mastodon horny. But none of them want me for *me*. They want the Kryll Corona. They want the power and prestige of having the Patriarch's daughter in their beds."

A hard shiver worked through her. "And for the Kryllian candidates, they want me in chains."

The steel of absolute certainty settled in his spine.

"Not gonna happen, sweetheart. Cuz you're not taking a Kryll consort. You're taking *me*."

Once he might've been able to sashay away from all this.

Not anymore.

The stakes for him had shot through the roof. And his resolve had rocketed through the stratosphere.

The end of the war. The end of his exile. Security for the Syndax. Peace for the galaxy. Raising a passel of kids with Kaia. Waking up every morning next to the girl he loved.

Not to mention waking up next to that brooding Valyrian with his silky hair and his sulky mouth and his cataclysmic psychic powers. Elegant and electric, mesmerizing and magical, Ben Nero was a bonus he hadn't expected—a birthday surprise Zorin knew in his bones an old pirate like him didn't deserve.

But waking up next to Dex… getting his hands and his mouth all over that powerful sun-bronzed body he'd been fantasizing about forever… hearing the way the galaxy's greatest general would sound gasping with pleasure if and when Zorin finally eased his straining cock inside him…

Shoot, he needed to think about something else. He needed to get his head straight.

"That's what we both want," Kaia breathed, following his fantasy without effort, her glowing eyes tinting the shadows lavender. "But my father has to agree. That's why we need to conceive. He'll see it as the Ninety-Nine Gods blessing our union. That's our insurance policy."

Her electric tension leaped between them. "We *need* to conceive, Zorin. If we don't, we need to get Kylie out. Out of Kryll's most impenetrable harem… the one no living soul's ever broken into. Somehow. Otherwise he'll make her… make my sweet little sister…"

"Syndax shuttle." The comm link crackled with a grim Mogadon voice. "Proceed directly to Bay Six and await further orders."

He pushed out a breath and grabbed the comm. Kept his cadence nice and easy.

"This is Zorin. Maybe you've heard of me. I got the maharani—and I'm pretty sure you've heard of *her*. We'll mosey on down to Bay Six like you want. But we don't take orders. We give 'em."

"Commander Zorin." The Mogadon traffic cop sounded slightly chastened, but firmly resolved. "Afraid you'll have to take these orders. The First Indomitable wants a full security detail on the maharani before she sets foot out of that shuttle.

"And he definitely wants to talk to you."

#

"Just how flipped at me do you think he's going to be?"

Kaia's question, forced through a throat tight as a clenched fist, fractured the brittle silence that hovered between her and Zorin like a secret. She didn't care for the windowless closet Dex's armed goons had decanted them into. One of the seedy little rent-a-rooms above the Blind Tiger, achingly similar to the dive where she'd hooked up with Nero.

She didn't care for the no-nonsense way they'd been separated from Zorin's boys—left standing in the hall since there was no room inside for six scowling Syndax.

And she definitely didn't care for the wait Dex was putting them through.

All of which told her he was flipped.

Which meant she was punked.

Zorin sprawled on the narrow bed with his back against the wall and his big boots on the blanket. Because there was nowhere else to sit. Watching her pace their crowded digs like a chained tiger herself.

"Thought you wanted to trust the guy," he said under the muffled grind and pulse of asteroid punk. One scarred brow hitched at her agitation. "How about we give him the benefit of the doubt?"

"I do trust him. All I'm saying is why the wait?"

Beneath the dim sputter of the lone light, she paused before the dingy mirror and tugged nervously at her short skirt. In the rusty womb of the *Relentless*, wearing some Syndax girl's discarded party threads had seemed like a bold plan. Because all those scheming suitors might as well start accepting that Kaia was out of play.

That she belonged to Zorin.

Now—when it was way too late—the provocative choice of black leather boots and micromini, a black leather halter that barely buckled over her breasts, a studded metal belt riding low on her hips, and miles of bare golden midriff seemed disastrous.

She felt way too exposed. Even with her saber strapped over her shoulder and a Syndax knife stashed in her boot.

"We'll be lucky to survive this bloodbath." She propped her saber against the wall and gathered her burgundy curls in an anxious twist. Just to be combat-ready. "Even if we're all four on the same page. If it turns out we're not…"

"Leave it loose," he rumbled, lids lowered to half-mast. "That just-bedded-by-a-Syndax fashion statement delivers exactly the right message. Besides, sweetheart, it suits you."

"Blast." She dropped her hands with a sigh and kept right on pacing. "This is all my fault, isn't it? Why didn't I just *ask* him—"

The *shuss* of the door shooting open brought her spinning around, heart wedged hard in her trachea.

"My apologies for keeping you waiting," Dex began briskly. "I'm afraid there's been a bit of a security hitch in the Tombola hall. These accommodations may be a trifle austere, but at least they're discreet. And therefore secure."

As the door whooshed shut behind his solitary form—shutting out the curious faces of Dex's praetorians and Zorin's pirates—Kaia caught a single searing glimpse of gold buttons and shining epaulets and burnished hair before her body toggled to autopilot and launched into a run. The familiar spice of Dex's scent shot euphoria spinning through her. His hard arms closed around her and dragged her roughly against his powerful frame.

"Dex, I'm so sorry—" she got out on a gasp.

Before her words were swallowed by his blazing kiss.

She whimpered into his mouth and gave him everything, arms wrapping around his neck, lips parting beneath his need, tongues sliding together with the bitter bite of *chaco.* His hands closed under her thighs to lift her and she wrapped her legs around him. The world swaying around her, he backed her to the table and sat her on top.

An altitude that suited her just fine. Because it fitted the slick heat under the gusset of her panties right against his bulging cock.

"I'm sorry—I'm sorry—I'm sorry," she said between frantic kisses, fingers threading through his hair. Her eyes drank in the chiseled planes and angles of his face, brutal and burning with passion. She couldn't seem to get close enough.

And every time her mouth said *I'm sorry*, her heart said *I love you*.

"You're forgiven," he muttered, gripping her thighs to haul her hard against him. "This time. But don't you *ever* do anything like that to me again. I mean it, Kaia. Next time, I want you to try trusting me."

She wondered if that was his way of saying *Darling, I love you to the moon and back.*

Sometimes telepathy sure came in handy—but as a half-Kryll hybrid, she couldn't always control it. Which meant she really needed to hear him say the words.

She just hoped someday he'd oblige.

"I won't," she panted. "I mean I will. I promise. But only if *you'll* promise not to shoot up my ship next time."

"I was trying to protect you. Aiming for your cyberport because I could hardly aim for *you*." Between hot, greedy kisses, his mouth curved against hers in a rueful smile. "Suppose it's my turn to apologize, isn't it? For my… lamentable penchant for violence."

"Maybe it's a job requirement for First Indomitables." She nipped his lower lip just hard enough to sting. "But I'll let you make it up to me. Where's Ben?"

"Dealing with your unruly suitors and our precipitous change of venue."

Calloused hands spanning her bare waist, Dex eased off long enough to get a good look at her Syndax garb. His gaze narrowed on the halter barely buckled over her breasts. His eyes kindled with gaslight flames. "What the devil are you wearing?"

"A Tombola gift from her future consort." Zorin had slipped up right behind her—quick and quiet as a hunting wolf. "I figure we're done keeping secrets. Kaia's made her choice. Howdy, Dex."

Dex's head jerked up to meet his gaze. The air between them crackled with an arc of electricity.

Trapped between their solid heat, Dex standing between her thighs and gripping her waist, Zorin looming close enough behind to feel his breath in her hair, Kaia thought her skin would ignite.

Especially when Zorin's big hands closed over his and pushed her into Dex's arms. "It's okay, kid. I know you missed her. I don't mind."

Dex pulled in a harsh breath and bent his head to claim another desperate kiss. Hunger tore through her and need pounded between her legs. Against her bare skin, Zorin's fingers threaded through Dex's. A degree of intimacy with his supreme rival Dex seemed willing—at least under these particular circumstances—to tolerate.

So aroused she could barely breathe, she rocked her hips into Dex's straining fly.

"Kaia." He pushed out a hoarse groan and licked into her open mouth. "You're still… fertile. Aren't you?"

"You bet your imperial boots she is," Zorin murmured. "Till she conceives, she's hotter than the core of a Mogadon reactor. She needs all three of us right now. On her side—and in her bed."

Chest heaving, Dex lifted his head to look at him. Too hot to wait, Kaia leaned in to kiss his sun-bronzed throat and licked the salty sweat from his skin.

Zorin eased closer, starmetal armor pressing into her back. His voice rasped rough with passion. "I already told you I'm all in. How about you?"

Dex's hand closed around her head to press her harder into his neck. Her frantic lips parted to suck a bruise onto his skin. He hissed under her mouth, hand clenching in her hair until her scalp tingled.

Which, in her current condition, only made her hotter.

"Let's lay all our tokens on the table," Dex grated in a voice like gravel, heart thundering under her hands. "She's not the only one who needs something from me. Is she, Zorin?"

Zorin's hands clenched on her waist. "You want me to come right out and say it? I'll do ya one better. How's this?"

Kaia lifted her head in time to see Zorin lean in to claim him with a brutal kiss. A purely masculine, purely dominant, purely I-know-what-I-want-and-I'm-taking-it kiss. She didn't think she'd ever seen a hotter kiss.

A kiss to which Dex seemed far less stridently opposed than she expected.

Matter of fact, he hardly seemed opposed at all.

Glimpsing their twining tongues, hearing their throaty groans, feeling their urgent need telegraphed through their hands on her body, just about shot her core supercritical.

Dex surfaced gasping from that incendiary kiss. Zorin's teeth scraped slowly over Dex's lower lip—sucking it into his mouth in a power play that made her shiver—before Zorin released him.

By the time he did, they were both panting.

Dex licked his lips, candescent eyes glazed with passion. "Why don't you tell me precisely how you fancy this wildly unconventional arrangement is supposed to work. I mean after the Tombola. Even assuming I replace Cato in the roster and assuming her father agrees—an outcome that is far from certain, Apocrypha precedent notwithstanding. You know the rules on Mogadon."

"I'm Syndax. We do polyamory in the horde whenever. So I don't have any rules." Zorin shrugged against her back, blunt fingers finding the hem of her halter. "And your buddy the Imperator's the Mogadon head honcho, so you can make your own."

"You make it all sound easy." Dex snorted. "And, public appearances to the contrary, the Imperator and I don't always agree. He happens to want this war with you and your Syndax. It forms a handy pretext for raising taxes. And you know he's never been one to flinch from a good bloodbath."

But he wasn't pulling away.

And his eyes were locked on Zorin's hands like tractor beams, watching him toy with the buckle between her breasts.

She swelled and tingled under Dex's combustible gaze, nipples pressed hard against the leather. When Zorin eased the prong open, she breathed out a soft whimper of craving.

"You're not a kid anymore, Dex. You said so yourself." Deftly Zorin released the buckle, and Kaia shivered as her breasts sprang free beneath Dex's transfixed gaze. "I'm not the one who's afraid of this. And neither is she."

And while Dex gripped her waist and looked his fill, Zorin leaned in to circle her wrists and pin them together behind her. The move arched her back and thrust her breasts forward.

The brazen exposure made her moan.

"Question is," Zorin drawled, "are you and me gonna give our girl what she needs?"

"Damn if I'm going to say no to that," Dex muttered, filling his hard hands with her breasts. His thumbs found the tight nubs of her nipples. Heat streaked through her, zinging straight to the wet ache between her legs.

"Is this what you want, darling?" His eyes smoldered as they took in her flushed skin and heavy lids and breathless mouth. But his voice was tender. "Both of us together? With you? Right now?"

She was panting so hard she could barely speak.

"Yes—please—I need—both of you inside me."

Triumph flashed in Dex's eyes like a supernova. Zorin growled and leaned in to kiss him again. Their mating scents rose deep and dark—spice and steel, passion and predator. Zorin pinned her hands while Dex played with her nipples, tweaking and rolling and pinching. Twin jolts of pleasure zipped down her thighs and lifted her hips in a wanton plea for more.

"You see how much she wants you?" Zorin said, guttural with passion. "How hard she's gonna get off, having me hold her down while you're bucking inside her? Then, once you shoot your load deep inside her and get her all slick and soaked and ready for me, I'm gonna take my sweet time and ride her long and hard, just the way she likes it. While you watch till you're ready for round two."

*Maybe with me this time if I'm lucky, kid.*

She couldn't tell if Dex picked up the thought. A low groan of naked need rolled from his throat and he shuddered between her thighs.

"Sounds like… a bit of a mess," he whispered against Zorin's lips.

"She'll love it. Won't you, sweetheart?"

Head lolling against Zorin's chest while Dex worked her over, Kaia gasped out something affirmative. She barely registered the skip and thud of music when the song changed below.

But a not-so-distant bellow of rage prickled her skin with a frisson of violence.

Grasping for the fraying edges of her survival sense, she struggled to sit. "Angels and asteroids! Those suitors… they're all still waiting down there, aren't they?"

"Let them wait," Dex growled, hot hands sliding up her naked thighs. "I'm burning to know what exactly you're wearing under this indecently short skirt. And at the moment, I'm in no mood to wait myself."

She swallowed a breathless, slightly hysterical giggle. "Well, but—we—we can't do this *now*. Can't just keep them all—stewing in their own juices—"

"Like Chiron's coldest hell we can't." Dex gripped her thighs and held her spread. "Darling, you're begging for this. Tell us we're right."

She loved the fact he'd said *we* instead of *I*.

And her exposed and helpless placement under their four hands—arms pinned behind her, breasts bared and thrust forward, legs spread and held wide, skirt riding high on her thighs—sent a dizzying dose of danger and desire shooting like a drug through every synapse.

They were two of the galaxy's dominant powers. They knew exactly what they wanted. And clearly what they wanted right now was to pin her down and take turns rutting between her thighs while she begged them both not to stop.

Zorin whispered in her ear, "I don't think we're gonna give you any choice, sweetheart. Not with your eyes glowing like lamps and all those sexy sounds you're making."

His focus shifted to Dex, voice rough as sandpaper. "She needs your cock inside her. Right the hell now. Let's see what you got—"

The hiss of the opening door barely made a ripple in the steam of arousal rising from their skin.

It took Nero's strangled gasp and the psychic impact of her lifemate's shock to send her shooting upright.

"Ben!" she cried, her intense surge of pleasure at seeing him spiked with carnal awareness of just *what* he was seeing—breasts exposed and flushed with passion, nipples taut and jutting for attention, thighs spread wide and wanton, Dex and Zorin with their hands all over her.

"Gods and demons." Nero's purple eyes swept over her, nostrils flaring to take in their mingled scents as a juggernaut of Mogadon pheromones slammed into him. *"Kaia."*

Behind the glittering jet mask, above the raven sweep of his carnival cloak, dark and deadly as a fallen angel, his sculpted features hardened with lust.

The impact of her lifemate's arousal swept over her and sucked her under. Her hips undulated in a tidal wave of need.

"Howdy, gorgeous," Zorin rasped. "Don't be shy. She's been missing the bewhosis outta you."

Nero's smoking gaze slid from Kaia to Dex and his face went wary. "No."

"Ben." Dex extended a hand, his voice a deep rumble of desire that made her tingle. "I've been waiting for you. And so has she. Come over here and show me how you—"

"I said *no!*" Nero flung out a hand that told Dex to keep his distance more clearly than an electric forcefield. Purple sparks flared at his fingertips, and a gust of wind lashed his cloak in warning. "Good gods, Dex! Has it completely escaped your mind we've got dozens of drunk and desperate men at each other's throats down there? One of your gods-damned Mogadon just knifed one of the Kryll over one of your gods-damned acrobats. I had to throw him through the wall to bring him down, and the psi fire's still burning. Right in front of a live camera on interstellar news."

"Bloody hell." Dex pushed a hand through his hair and straightened his jacket with unsteady hands. "Bloody *hell*. I, ah, beg your pardon. I—lost my head. I'll be down directly."

"Fine." Without so much as meeting his gaze, Nero pivoted to leave.

"Hold on a tick." Buckling her halter, Kaia slid free of Zorin and hopped down from the counter. "Ben—wait."

While Dex muttered orders into his wrist unit, she raced across the room and wrapped herself around Nero's stiffly resistant form. The seductive incense of musk and sandalwood twined around her, laced with the potent bite of Dex's mating scent.

Which was one hell of a turn-on. Just in case she needed another stimulus.

Her mind reached for his by instinct—

—and ran *smack* into a wall she couldn't breach.

After that first powerful surge of shock and lust, he'd slammed down all his barriers.

Now she read nothing in his head but caution.

While she staggered and clung to him for reassurance, his hands closed gently around her shoulders and imposed an unbridgeable distance between them.

"Ben, what's wrong?" Eyes wide with pleading, she curled one hand around the smooth plane of his cheek. "You can tell me. You know you can tell me anything. Just like always."

"Kaia. Please." His voice was stripped raw, eyes behind his mask hollow and empty as the void of space. "I can't do this. Not anymore."

"Do what?" An instinctive, unreasoning fear raised every hair on her neck. "Talk to me. What is it you can't do?"

"You. Him. *This.*" Wildly he swept out a hand to encompass the seedy dive reeking of pheromones and sex.

Jerky with agitation, he stepped back from her touch.

Limp with dread, her hand fell away.

He sucked in a breath and steadied his voice. "Look, angel. We'll talk later. Right now I need to go down and make this cosmic circus safe for you. If that's even possible."

And before she could say or do anything to hold him, he was gone. Leaving her with nothing but the alarming memory of his body gripped rigid in her arms and his mind locked tight against her.

Heart hammering hard with panic, she spun to face Dex. "Blast it! His barriers are jacked from here to the thermosphere. What in the seven devils—Dex—what have you done to him?"

A wash of ruddy color crept up Dex's neck.

"At this point, just about everything," he muttered.

She studied him with fascination. "Gods of my father, are you actually *blushing*? Meteors, did you and Ben *finally*—?"

"Kaia." That was Zorin, firm and steady as a stone at her shoulder, strapping her saber into place. "Give the guy a little breathing room. We could all use it. Nero's right. We gotta screw our heads on straight and finish this jamboree."

She knew he was right. Her head dipped in a nod that acknowledged it. But knowing he was right didn't make it any easier to quiet the clamor of questions jostling for answers in her head.

As he beelined for the door, Dex shot him an inscrutable look. "Thanks."

"Anytime, kid." Zorin reached past him to punch the exit panel. The door shot open and the electric pulse of asteroid punk plinked in. "Let's finish this thing. All flipping four of us."

# CHAPTER TEN
## The Apology

That hole he'd blown through the wall was still smoking.

Even three clicks later.

Nero took a certain professional pride in that fact. He hoped like hell it sent an appropriately cautionary message to the eighty-two Tombola candidates who were still ambulatory—after three knifings, an accidental blaster discharge, and two bare-knuckle brawls—and thus still actively competing for the vacancy in Kaia's bed.

From his vantage at the bar of the Blind Tiger—their Plan B venue since Dex's guard found that bomb rigged with toxins in the Tombola hall—Nero gestured to the tattooed tomboy behind the counter for another shot of Kryllian firewater. She scrambled to comply with an alacrity he found gratifying.

And no, he didn't mind one bit the apprehensive looks he kept getting from the candidates since he'd hurled that piss-drunk Mogadon through the wall.

*By all the gods, I hope they are afraid of me—and by extension, afraid of Valyria. I hope they're farking terrified.*

*All except Kaia.*

His gaze sliced across the gin joint's spinning lasers and jungle holograms to the crowded dance floor, steaming with body heat, where a dozen copper-haired acrobats boogied with a dozen sexed-up candidates in a cloud of artificial fog. Despite the visual clutter, he zeroed in instantly on his lifemate, dutifully shimmying with one of her suitors.

His battered heart twisted tight.

That glittering gold mask she'd slid into place, framing her lavender eyes, didn't do space dirt to disguise her.

Not with those Syndax leathers she was rocking on her sleek

tawny body and the Syndax leader looming ten cubits away. Looking like he'd disintegrate any guy who looked crosswise at his girl.

Any guy except Dex.

Just the thought made Nero's shaft stiffen. He'd been fighting a raging hard-on ever since he walked in on the three of them going at it. And the sight of Kaia with their hands all over her—all but naked, gasping with pleasure, her golden skin and burgundy hair and lilac eyes glowing with fertility and passion—had just about killed him.

He'd give ten years of his life to be the guy who slid his aching length into her liquid heat. The guy who sired her son and fulfilled the prophecy. The guy who shared her bed while Dex made love to them both.

But Dex would never give him what he needed. That fiasco in his bed this morning—and the humiliating directive in his galley right after—had only cemented his conviction in place. All Dex could offer Nero was a few desperate tumbles spiked with secrecy and shame and, ultimately, heartbreak. He'd made his distaste for anything more abundantly clear.

While Kaia'd done everything but transmit an interstellar broadcast to signal she didn't want that either.

Not from Nero.

The guy who'd left her. The guy who'd betrayed her. The guy who'd destroyed her.

And, consequently, the guy she'd never trust.

Even if he burned to drag her into his arms and prove her wrong—

"It's no good, you know, gorgeous."

Suddenly Zorin was towering over him. Deftly intercepting the shot glass the barkeep slid down the counter toward Nero, the Syndax tipped its contents down his own gullet.

"I'm sorry?" Bemused, Nero eyed the empty glass.

He wasn't used to looking up at anyone, but he had to tip his head back to meet Zorin's ironic gaze.

Steel eyes framed in the cold shell of a titanium mask made his pulse skip and his chest clench. Mask or no mask, no one in the joint was going to mistake the giant space pirate with his blaster and space boots for anything but a galactic menace.

With a wry grimace at the music's decibel-defying pitch, Zorin leaned to murmur in his ear.

And suddenly Nero felt way too warm behind his own mask.

"The cleansing agent," Zorin drawled, breath soft on Nero's neck. "You still smell like Dex from half a room away, and you better believe these Mogadon know it. Lucky guy."

"Me?" Nero snorted, too bitter to hide it. "Lucky? I'm fathoms deep in love with a guy who needs to pound half a bottle of whiskey before he can bring himself to touch me. A guy who thinks loving me back would be a disgrace."

"Actually, gorgeous, I'm thinking the lucky one's Dex." Zorin's big hand landed lightly against his cheek. "And he damn well knows it. We all do. An old war dog like me'd never have a chance with a guy like you."

And just the fact that the space pirate wasn't afraid to touch him in the middle of a roomful of Mogadon, while Dex barely even looked at him when anyone else could see, poured oil on Nero's scorched and smoking heart.

"You sure about that?" Nero whispered.

Blunt fingers gentle on Nero's skin, the pirate adjusted the mask his touch had dislodged, smoothed a wistful palm over Nero's hair to finish the job, then dropped his hand with a sigh.

"Oh, I get that you'd put up with me for Kaia's sake. Tell you true, I been meaning to talk to you about that."

"Oh?" Nero eyed him warily.

*Great. Just flipping great. One more smoking hot Mogadon who's about to explain why he can't share my bed.*

Zorin propped an armored hip against the bar and scanned the scene with narrowed eyes. He took in Kaia's gyrating form—rocking hard enough to keep her surrounding suitors at bay. Then Dex's watchful vigilance, chatting up the Kryll candidates while his gaze never veered from Kaia.

"This thing with the four of us?" Zorin murmured. "It's gonna be complicated as all get-out. Just about the only chance in the universe we got to make it work is if we're all honest as hell."

"That sounds comfortable," Nero muttered under his breath. "I can hardly wait."

"Look, gorgeous. You barely know me. I'm twice your age—"

"Hardly that." Nero snorted a reluctant laugh.

"I'm too old for Dex," Zorin said patiently. "Not that it's slowing me down much going after him these days. For him and me, I figure it's now or never. But you're younger than he is, ain'tcha?"

"Little bit, yeah," Nero admitted. "But Kaia's even younger, and she doesn't seem to mind. Which is putting it mildly."

"We're talking about *you*. I'm too old for you—and the scourge of the galaxy to boot. Or so they tell me." One side of Zorin's mouth lifted in a rueful grin. "I just want you to know you don't have to worry about me expecting anything or making any, you know, assumptions. You can be with Kaia without having to be with me. I can give the two of you as much space as you need."

And the whole time he was talking, exuding sincerity from every neuron, giving Nero every chance in the world to walk, Zorin was looming over him in that same possessive, protective, I'll-die-for-you way he was always looming over Kaia. With his intense eyes nailed on Nero like he didn't want to miss a breath.

Completely unencumbered by any of Dex's space junk, Mogadon, keep-your-distance public baggage.

Dex who was breaking Nero's heart.

"You'd let me do that?" Nero checked, just to be sure. "Share your consort's bed without sharing yours? You wouldn't want—what Dex is getting?"

"If that's what makes you happy, sure." Zorin's massive shoulders lifted in a self-deprecating shrug. Which totally charmed the hell out of Nero. "Oh, I'm not saying I don't have a few X-rated fantasies, same as the next guy. But I get that that's all they are—pipe dreams. I know a guy like me doesn't get to fly off into the sunset with a guy like you."

"You sure about that?" Nero repeated, low and husky.

Because his entire body was tingling.

Zorin's nostrils flared and his eyes lightened to silver. Nero held his gaze to reinforce his message.

Slowly, like he didn't want to screw it up, Zorin ventured, "You telling me there's a snowball's chance in a sun storm you'd actually…"

"I'm not saying I'd make it easy, big guy." Nero looped a hand in Zorin's utility belt and tugged, plenty light enough to resist. "You'd have to roll the dice and take your chances."

Behind the metal mask, Zorin's face turned hard and hungry. Instead of resisting, he stepped in close. Close enough for Nero to get a potent whiff of mating scent.

The scent of an apex predator.

"Dance with me," Zorin growled.

Caught between laughter and protest, Nero glanced at the crowded dance floor. The candidates were all over the acrobats. The orgy couches in the shadows were starting to see some action—all heaving bodies and entwined limbs and the salty musk of semen.

And now Kaia was dancing with Dex. In that quadrant of the dance floor, those two only had eyes for each other.

Nero didn't see any other guy-on-guy pairings, not without a girl involved. Because this wasn't a Mogadon orgy—not quite—and it *was* a Mogadon battleship. But it wasn't like his proclivities were any big secret. Like he'd already said, half the ship knew he was sleeping with Dex.

And the other half suspected.

But if his omnivorous tastes gave anyone offense, he was well beyond giving a shit.

"What the hell." Nero threw caution to the solar wind and grabbed Zorin's hand. "Let's do this."

And because clearly there was a Solarian god somewhere who liked sexually omnivorous Valyrian telepaths, the music downshifted from asteroid punk to a grinding ballad just as they hit the floor.

He slid Zorin a sidelong look. "You still up for this?"

*Because Dex definitely wouldn't be.*

"Yeah, well I'm not Dex." Picking up his thought—a sign of affinity Nero definitely noticed—Zorin eased Nero into his arms. "Whaddaya say, gorgeous? Let's show him what he's missing."

For the scourge of the galaxy, he had a gentle touch. Which surprised all seven hells out of Nero. And it was the easiest thing in the world to slide his arms around Zorin's hard waist, rippling with power under the starmetal mesh of his armor, and touch him back.

A high-octane shot of intoxication bubbled through his blood. Heady as a hit of pure oxygen in deep space.

A rare eddy of…

*Happiness.*

Nero tried like mad to keep his head. Tried to keep an eye on the double-takes their guy-on-guy action was attracting. Like that swarthy Mogadon brute—one of Dex's praetorians, the one he'd been eyeing, the one who'd give his last paycheck for a click alone with Nero, but only if none of his war buddies found out. His hot eyes were devouring their entwined bodies like he didn't care anymore who knew, if only it meant getting some of what that farking Syndax was getting.

But he looked away when he saw Nero watching.

For the most part—here, now, deep in the Tombola endgame—the candidates still on their feet were way more interested in brawling with each other and showing off for Kaia than they were in anything Nero might be doing.

Zorin angled their joined bodies in a way that gave them both a clear view of Kaia, still wrapped in Dex's arms. But Nero kept his eyes on the prize—this battle-scarred pirate with his square jaw and his once-broken nose and the mouth that was starting to make him shiver.

Seeing the direction of his attention, the guy looked surprised.

"Now don't take this wrong. I'm gratified as heck. But I didn't think you'd trust a scoundrel like me to keep an eye on your girl."

"She's my lifemate. I don't need to be watching to know if she's okay." Nero tapped a gloved finger to his temple. "I just hope Dex knows what he's doing. Because he doesn't look anything like her Tombola master now. He looks like what he is—the guy first in line for her bed."

"Right up there with me," Zorin said easily, without an atom of envy. "And you. Yeah, he knows what he's doing. He's king of the hill around here, and most of the final few are Mogadon. He's telling them all to back the hell off. That they don't stand a chance. And you can bet your boots those bozos haven't forgotten that any joe who reneges before midnight won't have to pay the whatchamajiggy—the munificence—the price of admission to the Patriarch's party."

Nero nodded. They'd scrounged up that arcane withdrawal clause from the annals of the Kryll Apocrypha as a safety valve—a twelve-click window when any remaining candidate could pull out, no questions asked, and get his money back.

A safety valve they prayed would blunt the edge of the bloody body count exacted over the next two days of the contest.

Zorin was a dream to dance with. A badly needed balm to Nero's bruised ego. The man knew how to hold a guy close without groping him. The powerful pheromones he was kicking out were enough to make anyone with a nose euphoric. And the feel of that big body surrounding him—all that spectacular strength and menace held in check by an older guy's patience and Zorin's basic decency—made Nero really wonder what it would take to drive the Syndax leader over the edge in bed.

How it would feel to be the focus of all that tender violence.

All of a sudden, Nero was burning to find out.

Hypnotized by the music's heavy pulse, he eased close and breathed deep, filling his head with the musky scent of predator. He was about one breath away from running his tongue down the guy's throat just to find out how he tasted.

Zorin growled under his breath and angled their hips together. Nero sucked in his breath and pushed out a low groan. That mesh armor the Syndax was sporting barely contained his colossal cock.

And Nero wasn't the only one getting hard.

"Easy, gorgeous," the pirate breathed. "You can have my full attention any time you want it. And that's one promise I intend to keep. But right now, you and me? We gotta keep our heads together. Kaia's fertile and repentant as hell. Now Dex—he's over-the-edge possessive and a little bit vengeful after the way she lit outta here yesterday. We gotta have their backs. Because those two aren't gonna make it through this thing."

Nero made a focused effort to get his brain out of his breeches and followed Zorin's gaze. In deference to her suitors' sensibilities, Dex was just managing to keep his hands off Kaia's shapely ass as they swayed through the dance. But their mouths were barely a handspan apart, eyes locked on each other like nuclear warheads on a target.

When those two finally came together, the blast wave would incinerate everyone in a thousand-parsec radius.

Shivering with arousal, Nero wrenched his gaze away and watched Zorin watch the crowd watch Kaia slip through their collective grip.

"And you don't have a problem with that?" Nero blurted out, suddenly burning to know. "With your former protégé and your future consort falling crazy in love? Not to mention me being part of it? You're in love with her yourself—I can feel it. Doesn't it bother you? Having to share?"

"Nah. She's got enough love in that no-holds-barred rebel heart of hers for all three of us." Zorin gave him his wry one-sided grin. "Including you. You make them happy, gorgeous, that kinda makes me happy too."

"Huh."

That attitude made Zorin a pretty remarkable Mogadon. And probably the perfect consort for Kaia with her fierce independence. Perfect the way Nero himself could never be.

His wounded heart contracted in a spasm of anguish.

"How about you?" Behind the industrial shell of his mask, Zorin's eyes were kinder than a pirate's had any right to be. "Does it bother you?"

He could have lied. Could have leaned on the guy's head a little and made him believe it.

But he couldn't lie to himself.

"Only because I'm not part of it." Nero's acrid admission made his throat sting. "I torpedoed my last chance with Kaia years ago. When I rolled over and submitted to the Senate. When I chose duty over love and left her. When I let her believe I died. Now you've had her, Dex's had her—comets, you'd both have had her together if I hadn't blundered in."

He pulled in a shaking breath and steeled himself. "But *I haven't*. Did you know that? Yeah, we've fooled around plenty, but she's never let me inside her." His voice fractured under the strain. "I'm her lifemate. I'm the one who told her she's fertile—because she didn't even know! And she hasn't let me near her ever since."

Face thoughtful behind his mask, Zorin rubbed Nero's back with an absent hand. "Ever tried telling her you're sorry? For what you did way back when?"

"Not exactly." Nero grimaced. "Blast! I, uh, told her our first night on Mogadon I didn't regret it. That I'd do it all over again."

Zorin's brow furrowed in a sympathetic wince. "And you wonder why she's flipped? She's a proud woman, you know, and stubborn as the dickens. You wanna get her back? You're gonna have to apologize—and you're gonna have to mean it."

"Sincerity won't be a problem. I know I screwed up, believe me. I've known it for years. But Kaia doesn't own the monopoly on being proud and stubborn." He searched that steady gaze, desperate fear and painful hope tangling his thoughts in a twist. "You honestly think if I apologized it would make a nanoparticle of difference? Because I don't think I can handle any more rejection."

*From either one of them. Which is exactly why I'm leaving.*

"She just figured out she's in love with Dex. She's still figuring out if she can fall for me. But loving you?" The pirate's calloused hand squeezed his nape. "That's like breathing for her, gorgeous. It's so central to her whole existence she doesn't even think about it. You want my advice? Give it a whirl and see what happens."

Gods and demons, he wanted that. Wanted it so bad he could hardly bear to hope. But he owed it to her, didn't he? That monumentally sincere, better-make-it-matter, long-overdue apology? And she deserved to hear it.

Even if it didn't change her mind.

"Good boy," Zorin breathed. Clearly having zero problem—Syndax or no—reading a Valyrian's thoughts, or at least *this* Valyrian's thoughts when Nero didn't bother hiding them. "I just made you happy, didn't I? I think I can maybe do a whole lot more of that. If you let me."

"Maybe so," Nero murmured, feeling dazed. Even though he still couldn't bring himself to believe Kaia could ever forgive him.

But he could… just… barely… bring himself to hope.

Of course, even if by some astronomical chance his lifemate did forgive him for ruining both their lives, that still left him grappling with his other great unsolvable.

Dex.

Dex with his fierce competitiveness and his daredevil courage and his damnable stiff-necked integrity. Dex with his loneliness and his loyalty and his loveless past. Dex with his buried passions and his buried hang-ups. Dex who demanded every ion of his love—but was terrified to love him back.

"Aw, shoot." A lightning charge of vigilance leaped from Zorin to Nero. Cold tentacles of alarm slithered down his spine.

"What is it?"

But Nero knew what it was—what it had to be—even before he spun to search the crowd.

A search he already knew down to his DNA would be futile.

"They just skedaddled, didn't they?" Zorin gave him a squeeze and set him free—much to his regret. "Like I said, those two were never gonna make it through this thing. We gotta get 'em back here before all the wannabes notice the maharani's missing and suss out why. And for that, we gotta find 'em."

"Actually, that part won't be a problem," Nero murmured, already tingling with the electric charge of his lifemate's arousal. Those two certainly hadn't gone far. Not nearly far enough, in fact, for secrecy. "Welcome to one of the many advantages of having a telepath for an ally. You can leave finding them to me."

Zorin rolled his big shoulders and looked attentive. "You just tell me where. I'll tippy-toe outta here and get 'em."

Nero raised a sardonic brow. "Actually, you'd better not. At the moment, I don't think they'd appreciate the interruption."

#

"Do we know yet who set the bomb in the Tombola hall?"

That was the question she'd been burning to ask Dex all day. Besides, Kaia needed a break from the obligatory ordeal of dancing with an endless assembly line of smarmy, handsy, increasingly creepy candidates under Dex's incendiary eyes.

And it wasn't the physical exercise that was making her gasp for breath. It was the vengeful, possessive, you're-mine-and-you-know-it promise of imminent reckoning in the First Indomitable's molten stare.

A reckoning that was way overdue for her headlong flight from the *Inevitable* and its electrifying commander.

Dex pivoted away from a pair of discouraged-looking Kryll to give Kaia his undivided focus. "To be precise, it's not an explosive, but a dispersal device. One theory points to Cato—Proteus—having placed the device in the Tombola hall and loaded the sprayer with paralytic toxin. In that case, he'd have rigged the timer before he escaped."

"And anyone within range when it went off would have suffered slow paralysis and suffocated when their lungs stopped working." Kaia's skin crawled and her stomach squirmed. "I didn't even know the Swarm used toxin weapons. Wouldn't toxins… poison their food supply?"

"I suspect it was an opportunistic choice. Paralytic toxin was part of my father's arsenal. Cato—Proteus—would have had full access." Dex's gaze wandered over her nearly naked torso, slick with heat and exertion, then narrowed on her worried face. "A competing theory is that Proteus left an accomplice on board who placed the device. Perhaps even another shapeshifter."

Centipedes of alarm skittered across her bare skin. "So you're telling me he, she, or *it* could be watching us right now?"

"Unfortunately, there's no way to know. Listen to me, darling." He moved right into her space to cup her chin in his palm. A power move for the benefit of her stalking suitors. "Proteus isn't a god. He's a mere mortal, albeit one with abilities whose parameters we haven't yet fully grasped. I've kept you safe so far. And I fully intend to keep doing it."

The fierce intensity in his tone sent heat streaking down her spine like a meteor shower. Straight to the hot pulse of need between her thighs she was trying like blazes to ignore.

Fighting to keep her head in the game, she worked to resist Dex's magnetic pull—if only for discretion's sake—and looked around for Zorin. With the protective bulwark of the Syndax leader's big body looming over her, and Dex exerting all his formidable powers of persuasion to induce her unwanted suitors to withdraw—to say nothing of Ben hurling unruly combatants through walls with a thought—she ought to feel secure.

Proteus or no Proteus.

In truth, she felt anything but.

While she sweated freely in the gin joint's humid heat, every instinct in her body was clamoring that the shapeshifter and his Swarm legions weren't finished with her. With any of them.

*Not even close.*

Her distracted gaze locked on Zorin looming over her lifemate near the bar. Looking like he found the sinister beauty of brooding Ben Nero in glittering jet and a raven's mask every bit as deliciously distracting as she did...

"Do you believe me?" The hard edge of urgency in Dex's voice snapped her focus back to him with an immediacy that left her dizzy. "Do you still believe I'll keep you safe?"

Her samurai instincts whispered a warning.

*I don't believe anyone can keep me safe. We've got the Swarm gunning for us, the Patriarch breathing down our necks, a ship full of desperate suitors plotting how to get past you into my pants, and a fugitive shapeshifter packing enough novicide to exterminate the human population of a good-sized planet.*

And the stakes—for Kaia, her sister, the galaxy, and the men she loved—couldn't be higher.

"I believe you, Dex." Even though she knew she shouldn't—not here and definitely not now before an army of frustrated suitors—she slipped her hand into his and laced her fingers through his calloused grip. "I believe in the four of us. We just need to hold it together a little longer. We're done once we reach Quorum Central Starbase if—" she swallowed hard "—*when* we persuade my father."

Because the imminence of her first physical encounter with her father since she'd fled his custody all those years ago was enough to make anyone queasy.

"I swear I'll protect you from him. I swear it on my life." Voice vibrating with intensity, Dex pulled her in close, hands sliding around her naked waist to claim her. "Damnation, I can't keep my hands off you. Dance with me."

Bemused, it dawned on her she was witnessing a phenomenon no one else in the universe, with the possible exception of Ben Nero, had ever been permitted to witness.

The First Indomitable of the Mogadon Empire, the dominant power of half the known galaxy, in desperate need of reassurance. And he needed it in a way that maintained his invincible façade in front of eighty-odd men who burned to challenge him.

But if she gave him what he needed—showed this roomful of his rivals she was his and they were space dust—she'd set off a freaking firestorm.

"All these suitors," she breathed. "Too many of them still haven't pulled their bids. Do you really think we should?"

"Gods of Olympus, Kaia." He pinned her with a savage stare. "Whatever damnable argument you're mustering to fend me off—I don't want to hear it. I want you closer than my own breath. Dance with me."

Heart beating way too fast, she managed a coy look. "As my Tombola master?"

"As your future bloody consort. I want every man on this ship to know you're mine."

That clinched it. The galaxy's dominant power definitely needed reassurance. And that unexpected flash of hidden vulnerability made her ache to give him exactly what he needed.

Even if giving him what he needed led to violence.

The grinding beat of the music slowed, and the frenetic rhythm eased. Feeling like she was floating in zero gravity, she drifted into his orbit, arms winding around his neck, lungs filling with the drugging spice of his mating scent.

She didn't even need telepathy to know what he was feeling. She read his desperation to protect her and his driving need to possess her in the tension of his hands, insistent at her hips, pulling her into his cock.

Arousal thrummed between them. The heat of his combustible stare seared through her to incinerate all her secrets.

"It's all right," she murmured, fingers grazing the back of his neck. "I'm safe. I'm not running. And I'm so… so sorry for yesterday. I never should have doubted you after you promised not to use novicide. You told me you abhorred it, and I should have believed you. Talked to you instead of running. I guess I'm still figuring out… this whole trust thing."

The ghost of a smile came and went in his hard face. "That makes two of us. I'm not exactly accustomed to, ah, this whole trust thing myself. Hence the regrettable incident with my blaster and your cyberport—for which I'm hopeful you'll forgive me."

Her heart gave a painful ping. Because she seriously doubted the words *forgive me* typically got much airplay in the Draven lexicon.

"I guess we both need a little absolution. You for your overactive trigger finger, and me for that stunt I pulled." Blast, she'd really blown it, hadn't she? "It's just—biowarfare's a hot button for any Valyrian. And I thought you were going to kill Zorin."

"I've no intention of killing Zorin," Dex muttered. "At least not immediately."

A fragile flame of hope flickered in her heart. "Thank gods. Because having the two of you at each other's throats has been killing me. Dex, he wants to negotiate. He wants peace between the two of you—"

"That'll be up to him." His eyes flashed with neon lightning. "I'm willing to tolerate your Syndax lover—for now—if and only if he can manage to refrain from his litany of military provocations and cease his annoying incursions on Mogadon planets in the colonies. Which is an exceedingly tall order for a rogue like Zorin.

"Still…" A muscle flexed in his jaw. "I do believe I grasp how you… feel about him."

"Yes." A mischievous smile tugged at her lips. "I am rather… taken with him. What I really want to know is—how do *you* feel about him?"

*Because I'm pretty sure he's in love with you, Dex. He loves you so much he sacrificed his own future and went into exile to protect you. And watching the way you kissed your boyhood idol in that rent-a-room this morning, like the fate of every lifeform in this sector depended on it... let's just say it makes me suspect you're not even close to being over whatever you felt for him all those years ago.*

Dex's gaze slid past her to zero in on the quadrant of floor where Nero was dancing with Zorin—one of those minor sensations Nero created so effortlessly. Lust and tenderness and envy chased across his chiseled features.

Envy of Zorin. Envy of Nero. Envy of their ability to be together in a roomful of Mogadon without inciting an insurrection.

Dex sighed beneath her hands, a wistful fondness softening that hard edge of anger toward his former mentor he'd honed like a blade.

"Ben wants him. That much is patently clear. And these days I'm rather inclined to give Ben whatever his heart desires." His tone deepened. "In fact, I'm inclined to spoil him. The same way I'm inclined to spoil you."

Dark gold lashes dropped over his gaze as he eased her closer. Her breasts grazed his jacket, epaulets flashing platinum in the laser lights. Desire and anticipation arced between them, amplified by their psychic connection. Around her wrists, the Valyrian torques pulsed with secret warmth.

"I'd like to see that," she whispered, sounding as breathless as she felt. "You giving Ben whatever he desires."

*Especially whatever he desires in bed.*

"When I finally have the two of you at my mercy, I assure you, you're going to do a lot more than watch."

A predatory image flashed from his mind to hers. An image of her and Ben kneeling naked at his feet. Dex's rough command bringing their mouths together, tongues tangling in a molten kiss.

Kaia's breath stuttered and her knees went weak. Dex's hard hands slid down her bare back to steady her—igniting a sensual thrill that was *almost* enough to distract her from how neatly he'd sidestepped her question about Zorin.

And, because their souls were entwined right now just like their bodies, he plucked the thought right out of her fevered head.

"I've told you I'm prepared to tolerate him," he rasped, voice thick with the residue of their shared fantasy. Which told her exactly nothing. "If only because I need the bastard alive and standing shoulder to shoulder with Ben and me when we face your father."

If there was anything that could pop the sexual bubble of a Dex-Kaia-Nero erotic fantasy, it was the needle-sharp reality of her father.

"Maybe we should talk about how that scene's going to go down, space cadet. You know, when we pitch up on Quorum with the final ten? Because it isn't just my father we'll have to persuade. A maharani's mating needs to be ratified by the Quorum of Four. Which is exactly why I couldn't mate Ben nine years ago. First the Valyrian Senate opposed it. Then the entire galactic Quorum voted it down."

Prickling under the prod of the jealous eyes that probed them—the eyes of all those thwarted suitors—she tried to impose a prudent distance.

But Dex was having none of it.

He raked their malevolent viewing audience with an arctic stare that held them all at bay and exchanged a cool nod with Marcus. The reliable right-hand man who held Dex's praetorian guard, strategically seeded through the crowd, armed and alert for action.

"I've the situation well in hand." Dex's words rang crisp with assurance, but that wasn't what the tight battle-ready coil of his body was projecting. "I know historically the Quorum of Four hasn't been your ally, but we'll have them in our pocket this time. The Mogadon vote is the Imperator. By Mogadon tradition, he rules the civilian Empire by hereditary right, while the Council of Indomitables controls the military. And I command the Indomitables by right of combat. When properly handled, he and I are allies. I'm confident he'll take my side."

"I know he took your side against Zorin, even though Zorin was First Indomitable himself when he, um, killed your father." Her head tilted. "Which makes me think our Syndax might not exactly be the Imperator's favorite guy."

His face tightened in reluctant acknowledgment. "Zorin's a freedman's son. The descendant of slaves. While Imperator Claudius is admittedly a bit of an elitist. Unfortunately, Zorin's piratical exploits in the outer colonies since his exile have done nothing to redeem him."

Her tummy knotted with trepidation. "The Imperator's above you in the food chain, right?" The words felt foreign on her tongue. Because she didn't like the thought of an apex predator like the Imperator lurking anywhere above Dex in the food chain. "And *he*'s the guy who's waiting for us on Quorum? How do you know he'll go for this crazy scheme?"

"Let's say he's suitably intrigued by the prospect of an alliance with the mighty Patriarch. Having the Kryll maharani mate his First Indomitable is a prize he won't want to relinquish. No more than I do, albeit for entirely different reasons." He leaned in to sear her forehead with a kiss—another of those possessive gestures he was making like a public service announcement to stake his claim. "Claudius is an ally. And the Syndax rep is Zorin's man, who'll vote the way he's told. Full stop. That's half the Quorum right there."

"It's the other half who worry me," she pointed out. "And the very real prospect of a deadlock. Because we need three votes for a majority, and my father *is* the Kryll vote. Plus I don't think Ben's said a word to anyone on Valyria about all this. He was pretty standoffish and skittish when we were all, um, upstairs. Does he even know you want him as a consort?"

"We haven't had time to discuss it—but he certainly knows I want him." A wolfish gleam sparked in his eyes. He leaned in to whisper in her ear. "We'll tell him the rest tonight. Just the three of us on an orgy couch. Gods on the mountain, I can't wait to see the two of you together."

The hot brush of his mouth against her ear made her shiver with carnal fever. Not to mention the psychic impact of what *he* was feeling.

His sexual hunger to seal the deal sliced like a shark through the vast ocean of tenderness he felt for both of them, but didn't know how to name. To Dex at his deepest level, his Valyrian lovers were angels, so exquisite with their glowing eyes and exotic pedigrees and impossible abilities they'd break any man's heart. He was desperately proud of them, fiercely protective…

And starkly terrified in his secret soul that they'd both leave him.

That they'd leave him alone.

A poignant sense of his lifelong loneliness reared up and crushed her heart like a tin can. He'd always been alone. Always—until now. Her throat swelled and her eyes burned. In that moment, she knew she'd never leave him.

Any more than she'd ever leave Zorin.

Which meant they really needed to figure out a foolproof plan to placate her father. Not to mention a way to mollify her savage suitors.

She shivered in his arms.

Which of course he noticed.

His arms tightened to pull her close. And their bodies fit together the way they always had. Thigh to thigh. Hip to hip. Heart to heart.

They were so nearly the same height she could stare straight into his nuclear eyes.

"Darling." A rueful smile softened his hard-planed face. "You're still worried sick, aren't you? What can I possibly do to reassure you? Name it and it's done."

Deep in her belly, a flutter of unease took wing.

"For one thing, it would help if I conceive. If I turn up that way before the Patriarch, with one of you the father? A Kryll maharani with three consorts—and those three a Mogadon, a Valyrian, and a Syndax? He's the god of neutrality… or so he earnestly believes. I think he'd buy it. With the Mogadon and the Syndax to back him, we'd have a majority on the Quorum. It won't even matter if Valyria votes no."

Her voice spiraled high and tight with urgency. "But I *have* to conceive. I have to, Dex! And not only to persuade my father that our mating's divinely ordained. Because wanting you—wanting all of you like this…? Well, it's not like I'm not enjoying it." Heat rushed over her skin at the certain knowledge of exactly how much she was enjoying it. "But not being in bed with you right now? It's literally killing me."

Beneath her desperate hands, a subterranean quiver ran through his powerful body. The leashed violence so carefully contained behind his impeccable uniform.

Laced with a potent undertone of payback.

Between the heightening danger of the Tombola finale and their imminent endgame with her father, Dex Draven was already wound tight as a trip wire. When she ran away, she'd torqued him to the breaking point. She'd rejected him. She'd hurt him. Now she was all but begging him.

Begging him to take her.

Which pretty much meant she was triggering every genetic Mogadon instinct in his DNA.

Dex sucked in a sharp breath. A single slicing gesture launched his guard into action. Dark and discreet, a line of armed men pivoted to shield them from her scowling suitors.

Opening a narrow path from the dance floor to a guarded door.

"Wanting me in your bed is one need I can definitely accommodate," Dex growled in her ear. His arm slid around her waist, spinning her toward the exit and drawing her hard against him. "And I assure you I'm eminently capable of making you conceive. Right bloody *now*."

# CHAPTER ELEVEN
## The Reckoning

Kaia's heart was somersaulting with more than exertion when Dex pulled her breathless body through the door to a private balcony. Below her spread the hangar bay's vast expanse. A superpower arsenal blazing with ultraviolet light.

Packed with row after row after row of Dex's deadly fleet. All those blinding Zephyrs, glittering gold with fierce raking lines and knife-sharp angles, racked and ready to rumble.

*Stars and planets, look at them. Battle-ready and armed to the eyeteeth.*

*Every last one.*

Awestruck, she slipped forward to grip the rail. Her eyes swept the scene, echoing with the clatter and tramp of flight crews and maintenance drones, edges blurred by distance. The sharp chemical tang of oxidizer stung her nostrils.

Dex could launch an interstellar war with a word. In fact, he'd already launched one back on Mogadon. Only the current exigencies of the Tombola stayed his hand.

That, and his promise to her, and whatever he felt for Zorin.

She hoped like hell that would be enough.

A cold artificial wind gusted over them, lifted the silken mass of her sweat-damp curls, and sent it streaming behind her.

A sudden shiver ghosted through her.

Dex closed the balcony door between them and the Blind Tiger to muffle the music's grinding beat. His hands wrapped around her waist and his breath filled her ear.

"How does it feel?" he murmured. "Having all that lethal firepower leashed and ready to launch at your command?"

"My command?" Surprised, she glanced back at him. "It's your fleet."

"And I'm yours," he said matter-of-factly, lids dropping over his burning gaze. "With the power of the Mogadon Empire and the Valyrian Precursor and the Syndax horde at your booted feet, you're about to become the galaxy's premier power. The ultimate arbiter of right and wrong. Because might equals right in this universe."

A flicker of humor chased across his chiseled face. "So, maharani, I trust you'll use all that formidable power wisely."

Aghast, she swung back to the scene, brain scrambling to weigh his words.

"I've… never thought of it like that." And she wasn't sure she liked it. What would she know about wielding all that power? "For punk's sake, I've been a fugitive for years! I'm a circus acrobat with a samurai sword. The only place I've ever felt powerful is in the cyberverse with a utility belt full of exploits. And strapped in the pilot's seat on the *Angel*."

"Your father's an infernal *god*." His voice thickened and his hands slid down her leather-clad hips. "What do you think that makes you?"

"Not a goddess," she scoffed. "Asteroids, Dex, you know I've been helpless as an infant since this whole thing started—"

"Helpless? You're far and away the most formidable woman I know. I certainly wouldn't want you as an enemy." His breath quickened. "Perhaps that's why I find you so bloody compelling."

His hands found her bare thighs. Her pulse skipped and sped. Her mental churn fell away under the relentless pulse of arousal.

That sweet burning ache he roused in her without effort. The ache she was so desperately helpless to resist.

*"Dex."*

"Darling." His breath in her ear went ragged. "Time to satisfy my insatiable curiosity and discover exactly what… if anything… the galaxy's premier power is wearing under this indecently short skirt."

His hands slid beneath her hem and found her silky panties. Before she could even begin to protest, he'd skimmed them down her thighs. A gasp tore from her throat.

Her eyes shot to the scene five flights below. At this altitude, cloaked in shadows, she prayed their presence wasn't obvious to the crews and techs who bustled among the Zephyrs far below.

Most of the attention, thank gods, seemed to be focused on fueling the Hurricane, Dex's mobile weapon of mass destruction.

Still, she and Dex were hardly invisible if anyone cared to look.

His mouth grazed her inner thigh. And her combustible core went supernova.

"Dex!" she yelped. "H-hold on a tick—"

"Be a good girl and step out of these for me." His firm touch curled around her booted ankles and eased her out of her panties before she could say *brazen exposure.*

Breath short and quick, she gripped the rail and closed her eyes. Behind her, she heard his slow inhale and wondered if he was breathing in the musk of arousal from her panties.

Her temperature spiked ten degrees at the thought.

He voiced a low rumble of appreciation. "Saturn. You smell like heaven—and you smell like Zorin. He's been inside you, hasn't he? And considerably more than once."

"Yes." The admission spilled out in a whisper. Because she couldn't even think of lying. Not to Dex.

Not with the way she loved him.

"Of course he has." One heartbeat at a time, his hands eased up her knees to spread her legs wide. "How long has it been since he's had you?"

"N-not long." Her whole body trembled with the strain of restraint. "Right before we, um, boarded the shuttle to come over here."

He breathed out a low curse, hands sliding up her inner thighs, bending her forward over the rail, thrusting her bottom toward him.

Her tongue flicked out to moisten her parted lips. "Does that... bother you? Knowing he was just inside me?"

"*Bother* me? That's one way to put it." Voice rough, hands certain, he peeled up her skirt. The kiss of cool air against her derrière made her twitch, hands moving instinctively to shield herself from roving eyes.

"Don't move a muscle," he growled in warning, hands kneading her naked ass. "Gods, what a vision. Has he had you this way?"

"From behind?" Her mind leaped to last night. To the feel of Zorin's firm fingers spreading her open despite her *pro forma* protests, stretching her pucker, telling her she'd have to learn to take both of them...

The visual leaped between them—her mind to his—and another hoarse groan shuddered through him.

"Thoughtful of the guy," he whispered, uncoiling to loom over her from behind. "Getting you all ready for me. I'll wager you made him come buckets inside you, didn't he?"

Heat burned in her face as her whisper slipped out. "Yes."

"Good girl." He nuzzled her neck and sank his teeth in a gentle bite. "I'll say this much for the man. He knows how to make love to you and make you like it, doesn't he? Not to mention knowing how to dress you."

His hands ghosted over her ribs to find her breasts, barely contained in her leather halter. Already swollen and tingling for his touch.

She arched into his palms.

Which was all the invitation he needed to slip her buckle and expose her, nipples peaking tight against the cool air.

She whimpered a protest that really wasn't one, too aroused even to look down at the flight deck to see if anyone was looking up to watch her. Gripping the rail and panting, legs spread wide, skirt up around her waist, ass cocked high in invitation as her fully clad lover tugged and tweaked her nipples.

Her breasts seemed fuller than usual, nipples flushed and chafed and tender. Every glancing touch sparked a pang of response between her legs that had her moaning and writhing against him. Dex weighed her breasts in his hands and groaned with approval as he worked her. She rocked back into the rigid blade of his cock, straining the cloth of his crotch.

She didn't even care anymore if anyone was watching. After all, she was wearing a mask, wasn't she?

As long as Dex did something soon about the burning need between her legs, she'd let the whole ship watch if they wanted.

"Oh, Dex, *please*—I need—"

"I know precisely what you need. Stand still for me. Just like this." Pressing a final searing kiss to her shoulder, he released her tingling breasts and dropped to his knees behind her. His next openmouthed kiss burned the tender curve of her bottom.

It was all she could manage not to beg.

Especially when he crawled deftly between her legs, spread her wide, and pressed his mouth to her drenched and aching pussy.

She flung her head back and bit her lip hard against a sharp cry of pleasure.

His tongue lapped the juices spilling down her thighs—hers and Zorin's, she knew it—but it didn't seem to bother Dex a bit. In fact, he was loving it. As her taste hit his lips, his deep moan vibrated against her flesh. She was tender there too, a bit sore from being so thoroughly stretched and ridden by Zorin. But not too sore to revel in it when Dex's tongue dipped inside to probe her, taste her, claim her again and again.

And now she did cry out and beg and shudder and gasp with the electric shock of his tongue thrusting inside her, again and again, slick with her arousal and his saliva and Zorin's... oh *gods*...

"Don't you dare come without me. That's an order," he rasped against her flesh, strong hands holding her up while she bent over the rail with her ass in the air and her legs turned to marmalade beneath her. "He's all I smell and taste inside you... Zorin... his spunk and your pleasure. The next time he has you, I want him to smell and taste *me*."

He surged up before her, lifted her, staggered a few steps to get her back against the wall. Her hands fumbled desperately at his belt and zipper. His cock spilled into her eager grip—hot tight skin stretched over all that throbbing length—a lightning flash of contact that made them both moan. Their mouths met in a breathless kiss that tasted of Zorin's musk and her salt and Dex's domination.

"Tonight—it's all of us together," she panted between kisses. "It has to be. Watching you and Zorin—dance around each other—both of you—wanting each other—"

He filled her slick depths with a smooth thrust that sheathed him deep inside her and silenced her demands. A cry ripped from her throat that pulsed with mingled pain and pleasure.

"Sorry, darling," he breathed against her lips. "I'm a beast, aren't I? You feel so phenomenal, I swear you make me lose my infernal mind. Want me to stop?"

"No! Don't you dare stop. I need you." Her fingers skimmed his intent and worried face. "Just—be a little more—gentle."

And if she'd harbored any doubts about the First Indomitable of the Mogadon Empire's ability to be gentle, they dissolved under the tender frenzy of his kisses. Slowly he rocked into her, grazing her clit with every careful thrust, hands gripping her ass to hold her steady, eyes burning into her like ultramarine flames. Gauging every breath, every shiver, every flicker of her response. Setting his rhythm to match hers.

But she could sense how much the effort cost him. Sense it in his ragged breath, his trembling hands, his erratic thrusts as the climax rushed toward them.

"Oh gods oh Dex dear *gods*—"

"Darling," he gritted through clenched teeth. "Tell me you're ready. I'm so—so close."

"So ready." Her entire body thrummed with the deep building throb of orgasm. Vaporizing every atom of doubt and caution to release the immutable truth in her heart. "Oh Dex. I need to—need to tell you—"

"Tell me what?"

"I love you."

Something fractured in his face. She thought it was the reinforced titanium shield he'd been gripping all his life to keep everyone in the universe a million parsecs away from his heart.

"Bloody hell, Kaia. I thought you'd never bloody say it." His brow furrowed with wrenching need. "Promise—promise you'll never leave me. Never again. Promise me."

"I promise—I promise—*Dex*—"

Her world fell apart and her flesh pulsed around him and a shrill cry spiraled from her throat. Beneath her desperate clutch on his hips, his measured rhythm turned jerky and frantic. Once more he thrust in deep, and wave after wave of his hot release spurted deep inside her.

She held him through the high-voltage jolts of climax that surged through them while they trembled in each other's arms. While their frantic hearts slowed and their shaky breaths steadied and the world around them seeped slowly back.

She held him while he cradled her face and groaned, "Give me a son, darling. Give us a son to rule. Your son and mine."

"We're certainly trying," she said on a breathless laugh. "No one can say we're not."

He pressed his mouth to her ear, drew in a shuddering inhale, and whispered softer than breath, "There's nothing I won't give you now. Even… if it works for Ben, and I hope it might… even Zorin in our bed. You can tell your pirate… I agree. I want all of you here with me tonight."

A laser-sharp thrill of triumph shot through her and shredded her post-coital lassitude. Suddenly she was quivering with a sense of possibility that left her poised on tiptoe with expectation. A bare inkling of what they could achieve together. All four of them.

Starting with a lasting peace.

Now she was breathless with more than exertion and sex.

She was breathless with hope.

"I think that's something Zorin will want to hear from *you*, space cadet." She wiggled free of his arms and buckled her halter. "Let's go finish this Tombola and find him… um… as soon as we find my panties."

#

Nero ducked with a curse to dodge a cobalt pulse of blaster fire. He flung out a hand in defense. A purple current of psi fire exploded from his fingers and coursed across the brawling chaos of the dance floor, sending acrobats cartwheeling and candidates scrambling in all directions.

The fist of violet fire slammed into his attacker and sent the drunken fool flying backward over the bar. Liquor bottles shattered under his explosive impact.

Then a gang of those disreputable convicts Dex was using to backstop his praetorians swarmed the bastard and disarmed him. Roughed him up plenty in the process.

No more Tombola for that guy. In fact, he'd likely wake up in Dex's brig. Or his infirmary.

If he woke up at all.

Even if the guy'd been gunning for someone else in the melee, when someone fired a blaster at his ass, Nero didn't pull any punches.

And he had to admit those convicts Dex had dragooned from his brig at Kaia's suggestion were about five hundred times more effective in a bar fight than his painfully overtrained, rabidly treasonous, stiff-assed praetorians—

The rapid *thump-thump* of fists hammering flesh brought Nero spinning toward the orgy couches. Where another brawl was breaking out over one of the redheaded acrobats.

*Seems I've made a career pivot to an illustrious gig as a bar bouncer.*

Comets, this whole ship was a cosmic powder keg. When Kaia disappeared with Dex on that balcony, she'd pretty much tossed a match.

Which was why he'd broken up three bar fights in the last twenty ticks. Broken them up without real effort, because her disappointed suitors were all flipping terrified of his psychic muscle.

Now he stalked toward the heaving mass of men on the orgy couch, sparks smoldering at his fingers. Taking surly satisfaction from the way candidates fell over their own feet fleeing him.

His rivals, all of them. None of them worthy even to touch her hand.

Much less sire her son.

Scowling, Nero clenched a fist and spread his fingers. A core of magenta death pulsed in his palm. A megaton warhead of destruction that would bring down this entire battleship if he willed. The Senate of Psychics hadn't made him Precursor—Valyria's deadliest weapon— for a lark.

*Yeah. And it's a bar fight, Precursor. Maybe a little overkill?*

Appalled, he closed his fist to extinguish the deadly flame. And watched a couple of Zorin's leather-clad pirates wade into the latest brouhaha to break it up with brutal efficiency.

Grimly Nero rolled his drum-tight shoulders and willed himself to unwind.

Of course he got the reason he was wired to blow. And it went way beyond the musky cocktail of violence and pheromones that laced the air like a hallucinogen.

He was done in by the psychic shock of sexual climax that still hummed through every synapse of his lifemate's currently sated body. And horny as all nine realms after being hammered with surge after surge of domination and triumph spiked with sex—the psychic signature that spelled one whopper of an orgasm for Dex.

After last night, Nero was in a position to know.

Damn it to Hegemon, he wanted to be out there on that balcony with them. Not lurking in the hall making sure no randy candidate blundered out to where Dex was doing his level best to sire Kaia's prophecy son.

Nero needed them. Needed to be with them. Needed them like oxygen.

Except, with the way things currently stood between them, Kaia wouldn't care what he claimed he needed. Wouldn't let him anywhere near her. Not while she was fertile.

Which meant he needed to stay the hell away.

Nero eased into an alcove with a decent view of the Blind Tiger. Across the way, Dex's dragooned felons actually had that guy he'd blasted halfway to the Beta Sector on his feet and ambulatory. Bellowing over the din about lodging a protest with the Patriarch.

A threat that would give Kaia the cold chills.

Nero started forward with a muttered oath. Blast, he should've just killed the guy—

*Take it easy, tiger.* The amused rumble of Zorin's inner voice settled into his roiling thoughts like a hand rubbing the nape of his neck. *I got this.*

Bemused, Nero watched the Syndax pirate amble up to the blustering Kryll and sling an arm around his shoulders. Soon Zorin was schmoozing the guy in a back booth. Something about a Syndax escort to protect the guy's next trade caravan through the no-man's-land Omega Sector at cost. The battered, half-concussed Kryll was actually looking interested.

And that easy current of psychic connection between Nero and Zorin that let him listen in on every word?

Color him intrigued.

Zorin wasn't Dex. Nero barely knew the man. But damn if he didn't know already the pirates' head honcho would be electric in the sack. There was a reason Kaia'd been prowling around all morning looking like a cream-fed cat.

*He'd almost be worth sticking around for. At least sticking around long enough to figure out if there could maybe be the spark of something more between us than sex. Except even if Kaia does forgive me for nine years of neglect, there's no way I'm sticking around to be Dex's dirty little secret—*

A hand touched his shoulder.

Nero spun with a snarl, psi fire cresting in a tsunami of raw power. Ready to send candidates flying in all directions like the blast wave from a mega bomb.

"Eureka! Found you." Like lavender moons, Kaia's incandescent eyes glowed up at him—secret joy lighting her from inside like a lamp.

Nero reeled in the billowing wind of psychic violence a heartbeat before it howled out to wreak mayhem. His psi channels burned with backlash and the acrid scent of charred flesh seared his sinuses.

"Ouch! I felt that." Through watering eyes, he saw her grimace in sympathy. "Sorry, Ben. Are you all right?"

"Just peachy," he choked out.

Gods and demons, he hadn't dealt with a backlash like that since his youth at the Psi Academy. Where, incidentally, Kaia'd already had his thoughts twisted in tangles. Even way back then.

"I know," she said contritely, following his thoughts the way she always had, unless he blocked her out. "You've always been dutiful. And I've always been a distraction, haven't I?"

He sighed in tacit agreement.

She was so flipping beautiful she made his chest hurt. Always had, even as a girl. Even before he fell ferociously in love with her. And now more than ever—glowing with health and fertility, tremulous with hope that somehow this whole galactic mess would work itself out and she could have Dex and Zorin and her happily-ever-after.

"I thought you'd know it was me." Faced with his silence, her brow crinkled with concern. "Either way, I shouldn't have surprised you like that, should I?"

"Probably not," he said hoarsely. "Keeping a roomful of randy suitors under wraps while you and Dex fuck like marsh rabbits just cubits away hasn't exactly been a walk in the woods. I'm wound pretty tight here, Kaia."

Her tawny face flushed rosy with repentance. A riptide of guilt eddied through her. Which meant it eddied through him.

Damn and damn again, he needed to keep his barriers jacked way the hell higher if he wanted to survive this Tombola.

*Only for a little longer. Then it's bye-bye baby and you're back to Valyria.*

*But first you owe your lifemate an apology.*

*And it better be one hammering good one.*

"I'm so sorry, Ben." Eyes swimming with tears, she touched his sleeve. Keeping it low-key for the sake of their volatile viewing audience. And even that limited contact was enough to make his shaft stiffen. "I've been saying that a lot lately, haven't I?"

A sudden, savage yearning for her twisted his heart and squeezed until he gasped. His yearning to hold her… yeah, claim her, sire her son, there was always that… but beyond that, a basic yearning just to touch her. To *be* with her. He couldn't stand here another nanosecond and not be with her. Not be hers.

The devastating certainty of knowing Kaia and Dex were together without him—loving each other without loving him too—was just about killing him.

Yet he knew when he left, he'd die all over again.

Which meant he was pretty much punked.

"Well, at least you're not scrambling to let me off the hook." Her lilac eyes searched his face for clues. Because he wasn't letting a molecule of insight leak through his barriers. "Somehow I've screwed this whole thing up big time, haven't I?"

"There's a lot of that going around," he said wryly, his soul raw. "Listen, angel. You and I—we need to talk—"

"There the two of you are. Hiding from me in this alcove." The low rumble of Dex's voice behind him, husky with satisfaction and crisp with command, was enough to finish the job and give Nero the full-blown boner he'd been fighting all day.

He sucked in a breath and steeled himself for the visual punch of seeing Dex up close and sexually sated. Somehow he kept his head together while Dex and Kaia reunited. Dex's arm sliding around her waist to claim her, Kaia's supple body melting into his hard length, Dex murmuring intimacies in her ear.

Nero had never felt anything but contempt for jealous theatrics in his hit parade of casual flings. And he flat-out refused to fall prey to some tawdry display of jealousy himself. Or any other equally useless emotion.

Including blind rutting lust.

Even with enough pheromones pumping through the air to make the entire ship frisky. And with Dex's electric eyes wandering over Nero's glittering Tombola rig like he was already fantasizing about peeling him out of it.

*Preferably with his teeth...*

Feeling his blood heat to the boiling point, Nero cleared his throat and battened down his hatches.

"While the two of you were off playing hooky on that balcony," he said, more harshly than planned, "one candidate was knifed to death. And four more wound up in the infirmary."

"While six have withdrawn their bids entirely," Dex pointed out. Clearly in command of his obligations as Tombola master, no matter what he'd just been doing on that balcony. "Marcus is refunding their money and getting them the hell off my ship. With this kind of attrition rate, we'll have no difficulty culling the herd to the final fifty—maybe even fewer, if we're exceedingly lucky—by midnight."

"Just in time for the blood games," Kaia said tightly. A visible shudder rippled through her. "After which my father steps in. We'll see him at Quorum. With my sister waiting in the wings in case he doesn't care for the outcome."

Crowd or no crowd, caution or no caution, rebuff or no rebuff, Nero couldn't help himself. No more than he'd ever been able to help himself where Kaia was concerned.

Holding her anxious gaze with a stare she couldn't break, he stepped into her space, slid an arm around her waist, and eased her up against him.

And she softened and yielded and melted into his arms the way she always had once he got past her prickly armor, a sweet sigh of surrender spilling from her lips, eager arms winding around his waist. The sharp tang of ozone and the lush sweetness of jasmine rose from her hair. Under his hungry hands, she was all sleek muscle and silky skin. His senses sizzled with the frisson of psychic connection.

Same as always.

"We're going to protect you, angel," he rasped, throat aching with the impact of her fear. "And we're going to save your sister. You and me and Dex and Zorin."

"I know," she breathed, face turning into his neck. Still, she shivered under the Patriarch's cold shadow in the overheated room like a fever victim.

His grip tightened around her. Brushed up against Dex's hard hand still holding her. Acting on instinct, he opened his other arm to Dex and pulled him in close. Dex's arms closed around both of them, enfolding them in his steady strength.

For a heartbeat then it was the three of them together, locked tight body and soul against the whole flipping universe, Nero's psychic power and Dex's unyielding strength and Kaia's unquenchable fire. All of them holding each other up.

The way they were meant to be.

His battered heart flickered with a fragile flame of joy.

"Love you so much," he whispered to both of them, one hand rising to press Kaia's face into his neck, head turning to find the heat of Dex's mouth.

The distant *choom* of blaster fire whined through the club. Another flipping fight. An unwelcome intrusion tearing through the gossamer fabric of intimacy.

Shredding it like tissue.

Dex cursed and pushed him away with a hard hand against his chest. That rough heedless shove transmitted everything his best friend felt. The cold shock of anger—

And the blistering heat of shame.

"Damn it to the devil!" Eyes blazing sapphire, Dex dragged a hand across his mouth and tugged his uniform straight, every motion crisp and cracking with fury. "You know full bloody well we can't do that here."

Gasping, Nero reeled back in shock. The impact of that rejection slammed through him like a gut punch. Pain, savage and deadly as a wounded bear, clawed his heart to shreds.

Kaia stumbled in her platform boots and Nero steadied her with a shaking hand. Her startled face turned from him to Dex.

Dex raked a sharp gaze over their viewing audience—attention currently divided between the latest brawl and two bare-breasted acrobats putting on a sexy show on an orgy couch. When he turned back to confront Kaia's reproachful face and whatever was written on Nero's, his eyes flickered with awareness and chagrin.

"Damnation, Ben," Dex muttered. "I didn't mean—"

"I know what you farking *meant*," he snarled, putting plenty of distance between them. "You don't need to write me a gods-damned memo. I know your precious Mogadon reputation could never survive word getting out that you like a little cock on the side. I get it!"

Dex's face flamed with embarrassed heat. "Blast! Will you please stay put for once in your life and listen—"

"Just forget it." Nero dragged his gloves out of his belt and rammed them on his hands. Because all it would take at this point was one more atom of aggravation and he'd blow this entire ship to kingdom come.

"Oh, Dex," Kaia breathed, tone eloquent with sorrow as she stood stranded awkwardly between them. "Ben, don't run away. He... he didn't mean it."

"I said *forget it!*" Nero pivoted away—fists clenched, mood murderous—and plunged blindly into the dangerous crowd.

Because if he had to look for another microsecond at Dex's sickeningly ashamed expression—ashamed due to what he felt for Nero—he was going to self-destruct.

And take this entire farking sector with him.

#

"Twenty-nine candidates left on the ledger," Marcus reported grimly to Dex. "And pretty damn determined to stay there, boss. We'll need another winnowing in the pit tomorrow. This time to the death, according to that punking book. We'll be shipping the next set home in body bags."

Distracted and on edge, still cursing himself for that moment of catastrophic overreaction with Nero, Dex barely heard a word over the monotonous grind of asteroid punk. Gods on the mountain, he'd *felt* the impact of his own harsh words. Felt his own scorching shame hammer into his best friend like a groin kick—

"Hey boss, you listening?" Marcus again. "Afraid there's some kinda trouble on Quorum."

"Damn it, man." His eyes never veered from the bar where Nero was chatting up one of his praetorians. A surly brute, mean-tempered, a real bully and an outright butcher in battle. Too crude even to bother wearing a mask to the party.

For some bloody reason, Nero looked way too interested in the guy.

And Dex didn't like it one bit.

With difficulty, he wrenched his gaze from that looming fiasco and pivoted to confront this latest difficulty.

"What kind of trouble, Marcus?"

Through the flickering emerald hologram of the gin joint's jungle motif, his *optio*'s grizzled face reflected unease.

"We, uh, can't seem to hail 'em on Quorum. Been trying nonstop since thirteen hundred. Not the quartermaster at the spaceport. Not General Hadrian at the Mogadon base. Which means—"

"Solar storms?" Damn it to hell, what the devil was Nero doing? Was he *flirting*—with the bruiser Dex's men called the Butcher of Beta Prime? "What about the Imperator's secure channel?"

"No joy. It's farking odd."

"Odd? It's more than odd. It's unprecedented." Frowning, Dex gave the problem his full attention. "Even with solar storms or electromagnetic pulse, that secure channel's engineered and reinforced to function."

"Oh, it's functioning right as rockets. It's just no one's answering at the other end."

"Are you telling me," Dex said carefully, "we can't *reach* the Imperator? Or any blooming one of his twenty-five aides?"

Marcus pitched his voice low. "Yup. That's what I'm telling you. Turns out no one back on Mogadon home world's heard a peep from His Imperiousness neither. Not since yesterday. Even missed his morning vid call with the magistrates. I embargoed that intel—figured you'd want it kept quiet."

Suddenly, unmistakably, Dex's infallible battle sense was tingling.

"Good man." A barrage of imperatives scrolling through his alarmed brain, Dex spared him a crisp nod. "Here's what I want. Keep pinging all channels to Quorum. Meanwhile, you contact the Kryll and confirm the Patriarch's docked and ready for our arrival day after tomorrow at eleven hundred sharp."

"On it." Marcus hammered out a quick note on his tablet. "'Course you know our ETA's oh-six-hundred."

"You tell the Kryll it's eleven. Because that's an open line." Dex slanted a cautious glance around the Blind Tiger and leaned in close. "Scan for any Mogadon vessels in the quadrant—and do it *quietly*. Any vessel you find that's closer than we are does a fly-by and reports right back."

His *optio*'s grizzled face turned cautious. "What if I can't find eyes in the quadrant? I mean eyes we can trust?"

"Then you send a scout ship ahead—at once. The last thing I intend to do is fly the maharani and her top ten straight into a Swarm ambush. Or a Syndax raid."

Together, they pivoted to eye the Syndax leader, formidable in his gleaming titanium mask, sprawled casually in a back booth with his rogues' gallery of disreputables cluttering up the space and Kaia perched on his knee, booted legs crossed and leather skirt riding high on her thighs. Despite this latest worrying development, Dex was distracted all over again by the unsubtle possession of Zorin's powerful arm slung around her waist.

*Right in the thick of this bloody Tombola, he's telling every man in the galaxy whose cock she'll be riding tonight.*

Because no one in the galaxy who saw the two of them together—courtesy of those infernal cameras broadcasting the whole gig on interstellar news—would believe for a heartbeat they weren't already lovers. No matter what kind of puritanical restraint the Tombola ritual required. Clearly the Apocrypha hadn't been written with the unquenchable sexual needs of a fertile half-Valyrian maharani in mind.

*Don't be paranoid. Zorin's the last man standing—except for you and Ben. He's already all but won. He'd have zero motive to stage a raid on Quorum.*

"Nevertheless," Dex heard himself murmur. "Let's keep a close eye on our notorious Syndax." *As if I weren't already having the devil of a time keeping my eyes off the man.* "I want full-scope sensors riveted on the *Relentless*. And her accursed torpedo tubes. Make it happen."

"Gonna be one helluva night." Marcus threw him a casual salute and hustled off to execute his orders.

Dex ordered up a Mogadon whiskey for fortitude and watched Zorin wind a lazy hand through Kaia's curls. Clearly looking for a little attention. She turned her cheek absently into his big palm—a gesture of such tenderness it made Dex's chest ache. But her anxious eyes stayed fixed on Nero and the Butcher of Beta Prime the whole time.

She'd ditched her mask clicks ago. Now a worried line creased her copper brows.

Dex focused his uneasy brain on the immediate imperative and chatted up a few disconsolate suitors. Prodded them a bit too pointedly toward the option of withdrawal. But he too was having trouble keeping his gaze away from the bar.

Nero was definitely flirting with that brute.

Mask or no mask, Dex would recognize anywhere that slow smoldering stare, that secret smile that promised soft surrender to a man's every sordid whim. Because until that afternoon when he'd blown it so spectacularly, Nero had been aiming all that sensual smolder at *him*.

And the Butcher looked more than ready to shove the Valyrian facedown over the bar and bury his cock balls-deep in the guy right here and now.

If he laid one bloody finger on Nero, Dex was going to destroy something. Right after he ripped the Butcher's marauding balls off and rammed them down his throat.

*Because the only bed Ben Nero's warming tonight—and every night—is mine.*

An apologetic prefect claimed his attention with a tablet full of orders for his biometric signature. By the time Dex finished dealing with that and glanced up, Nero and the Butcher had vanished.

He must have wasted two ticks staring like a fool at the empty space before he spun toward the exit.

Just in time to see Nero sauntering through it with a backward look under his lashes that pulled the Butcher after him like a tractor beam.

Just like that, the two of them were gone.

Dex felt the staggering blow of that rejection—the irrevocable moment Nero deliberately turned away from him and chose someone else—sear through his chest like a blaster bolt.

A blow so crippling he couldn't think.

Couldn't move.

Could barely even breathe.

He might have been standing there a tick, a click, or a lifetime when Zorin's hand landed on his shoulder from behind and squeezed.

"Punked it up big time, didn't ya, kid?" the pirate murmured in his ear.

Dex unclenched his jaw and bit out the words. "Ben and I have thoroughly discussed this topic. I felt I'd made my position abundantly clear. That he understood the paramount need for discretion." Zorin's patient silence dragged the difficult admission from his lips. "Nevertheless, I… may have been a bit… abrupt."

Which had to be the understatement of the millennium.

"You think?" Zorin's wry chuckle brushed his ear and shot goose bumps down his spine. "He's on his way out the door to another guy's bed. You just gonna stand there and let him walk?"

He'd always had a positive talent for getting under Dex's skin.

"What does it matter to you?" Dex muttered, sounding far too surly to his own ears.

"Come on, kid." Zorin pushed out a sigh. "Kaia's pretty upset. Far as she's concerned? Even though we haven't talked it through, the four of us are a done deal. Ben's not thinking straight since you stomped on his heart—not to mention his pride. And I didn't much like the look of that brute he picked up. Did you?"

*Like it? He's the farking Butcher of Beta Prime. After the battle, I watched the bugger cut a man's heart from his chest while the poor sod was still twitching—and eat it raw. I don't want him anywhere near Ben.*

And that was the guy Ben had just chosen.

Over Dex.

Stung by the lash of pride, he clenched his fists and stayed stubbornly silent.

"Here's the deal," Zorin said flatly. "If you don't go after him, I'm gonna have to do it myself. But the guy Ben needs going after him right now is you."

"Pluto's coldest hell," Dex clipped out. "I can't go anywhere. In case you haven't noticed, I've a Tombola to run."

"In case *you* haven't noticed, this hootenanny's over. I just won it," Zorin drawled. "And you and me and gorgeous, we're gonna get the girl. But only if you go after our boy, apologize for being a certified ass—and *tell him how you feel about him, Dex.*"

*Our boy.*

A contraband pulse of pleasure made him stagger. To hear the incendiary truth he'd been so desperately avoiding acknowledged out loud, so matter-of-factly, by this rival and nemesis he'd spent the past eight years despising.

That it wasn't just Kaia. It was all three of them he'd be taking as consorts.

It would be the four of them together—all night, every night—sleeping naked and sated with pleasure in the First Indomitable's oversized bed.

Whom precisely did he fancy he was fooling, pushing Nero away like that? Every Mogadon in the galaxy would very shortly learn it wasn't just the Kryll maharani who made Dex Draven climax so hard he couldn't see straight.

It was going to be Nero and Zorin.

And every Mogadon in the galaxy could bloody well get used to it. Because his accursed father and his infernal interdict were ancient history.

Because Dex called the shots.

And because he simply wouldn't give the galaxy any other choice.

Dex's heart was hammering against his ribs. His chest was heaving like he'd run a blooming marathon. But an alien sense of elation, infused with daredevil courage and consequence be damned, made him feel like he was floating.

His gaze shot through the haze of sweet-smelling incense and the shimmer of holographic light to find Kaia, masked once more, doling out dutiful consolation dances to her sullen suitors.

Of whom there were still far too many.

"I *need* to stay," he ground out. "I need to protect Kaia. The same way Ben should bloody well be protecting her."

Zorin's hands landed on his shoulders and eased him back against the pirate's colossal bulk. Dex wasn't used to feeling overpowered by anyone—much less liking it. Especially this Syndax rival he'd just given orders to place under surveillance.

Yet he breathed in the gamy musk of hunting wolf and felt all that overwhelming power shoot straight to his shaft. Making him remember just how much he'd liked kissing the guy over Kaia's writhing body.

Zorin had definitely been in the pilot's seat.

And Dex hadn't… exactly… minded.

His skin rippled with a shudder of naked need. But he didn't pull away. On his shoulders, the pirate's hands tightened.

"Kid," Zorin murmured, voice husky in his ear, "either you trust me or you don't. Tell me now. Which one's it gonna be?"

He swallowed hard against the sudden blind craving that pounded through every pore. "Trust doesn't come easily to a man like me. And you haven't exactly made it any easier. But I am… trying."

*Yet I'm still keeping an eye on your torpedo tubes, Syndax.*

"I know you are." With a sigh, Zorin gave him a steadying squeeze and stepped back. And for the life of him, Dex couldn't discern if the guy had just read his mind or not.

"I got her. I got all three of you—if you'll let me. So you go on." Zorin gave him a friendly shove. "Go on out there and get our guy."

# CHAPTER TWELVE
## The Confession

Nero strolled through the entry portal to his quarters without looking back. Because he knew his prey was back there. Following him. It hadn't taken much to reel him in. Nothing at all, really. For him, it never did.

Except where Dex was concerned. Seducing Dex was like scaling a mountain. Barefoot, in the dark.

But he was done with Dex.

Leaving the door open behind him, he walked straight to the liquor cabinet. He was halfway there when he felt the Mogadon praetorian slide into the room behind him. Without saying a word.

Silent as a killer.

Some fantasy scrolling through the murky darkness of his mind about stalking Nero. Pushing him facedown over the table. Shackling his wrists behind his back. Ripping Nero's fancy-boy clothes to ribbons when he stripped him naked. Shoving Nero's face roughly into the polymer steel while he rammed himself home inside him…

Good. That was what Nero wanted too. No time wasted on pointless preliminaries.

And if this guy whose name he hadn't bothered to learn wanted to give it to him, that suited him just fine.

The door hissed shut in his wake. Soft blip as the praetorian engaged the lock. Making damn sure there'd be no interruption while whatever-his-name-was indulged at leisure the assault-rape-degradation fantasy that had the guy's cock rigid and straining behind his fighting leathers.

Without looking back, Nero unhooked his gleaming raven's wing cloak and dropped it to the floor. "You want a drink? Because all the gods know I'm having one."

The praetorian cleared his throat. "Yeah."

*I can't believe my farking luck. I'm alone with Ben Nero. Thought he was Commander's boy toy. He's got Draven's scent all over him—*

Nero shut down the channel. Just like he shut down the sharp stab of pain that seared through him at this vivid reminder of the way he'd been linked with Dex last night—body, mind, and soul. All that Mogadon drive and domination softened by tenderness and wonder.

Dex didn't want Nero anywhere near him where anyone could see. Didn't want to share with Nero the deepest, most meaningful act of intimacy he knew. Didn't care enough to give Nero what he needed most.

But when Nero moved on to someone else who would, Dex hadn't liked it one bit.

*Good. I hope it drives him demented.*

Without warning, the staccato rhythm of space thrash ripped from his sound console, loud enough to make the walls vibrate. Nero grimaced at the unholy racket but didn't protest. The guy hadn't asked before he touched—but that was why Nero had chosen this particular piece of meat, wasn't it?

And the fringe benefit of all those decibels? He and Butch back there could make all the noise they wanted, and no one would hear a peep.

Carelessly he splashed a generous slug of Kryllian firewater into a pair of glasses. No sense pouring his good Solarian red for a bruiser like that—

With his barriers jacked up and the music blasting, the brush of hot breath against the back of his neck actually gave him a start. A shot of adrenaline spurted through him, spiked with anticipation and apprehension.

He braced to feel hands, mouth, a dick that wasn't Dex's. Even though that was what he wanted.

Still, the guy hesitated.

*Juno's flaming tits, he smells like Draven. Am I really ready to challenge the top dog over this pretty piece of ass? Yeah, that was always the plan, if that Syndax doesn't space him for me. Zorin might still whack him over the girl, that bitch they're all hot for, even pretty boy here—*

Nero slammed down his barriers and slid away, pushing the guy's glass toward him without looking. It wasn't exactly a revelation to discover another of Dex's supposed bodyguards harbored homicidal tendencies toward his leader.

Still, he supposed he'd let Dex know about it.

After.

He'd liked the look of his latest diversion well enough back at the bar, all thick neck and rough tongue and thighs solid with muscle, the threat of violence lurking in his clever eyes. Dark and earthy and coarse enough not to remind him of Dex.

Yet now, for some reason, he couldn't stand the sight of the guy.

*You won't have to look at him when he's pounding into you from behind.*

Nero had reached the long table that featured in his houseguest's violent fantasies. He tossed back his firewater and welcomed the harsh burn searing down his throat.

Again the hot meaty whisper of breath against his neck. The guy thought he was stalking Nero. Thought he was the predator and Nero was the prey. But Nero knew how to handle him. He'd always known how to handle them. How to play his dangerous games with these coarse and brutal but relentlessly virile men without losing control.

How could he not, when he could make blood pour from a man's ears with a thought?

"You know what I'm here for, pretty boy," the brute growled in his ear. "Make it snappy. Gotta get back to my post before centurion sees I'm MIA."

Moving on autopilot, Nero peeled his tunic over his head and let it drop. He worked open the laces of his breeches and heard the other's breath quicken even over the thrashing beat.

"Faster," the guy said hoarsely. "You been teasing me all gods-damned day. Now I wanna see you scramble. You play games with me, pretty boy, and I'll beat the living shit out of you. Bet you'd like that, though, wouldn't you?" His voice thickened. "Bet we both would."

Rough hands gripped Nero's hips and ground his ass into the guy's straining cock.

Nero waited for the familiar tingle and jolt of arousal to get him hard. For some damn reason, it wasn't happening.

"Jupiter's balls, can't believe I'm actually touching you." Now the whisper in his ear sounded almost reverent. The guy rubbed his rough-shaven face into Nero's neck. "A real looker like you. Dex Draven's guy—"

"Do me a favor and don't talk about Dex," Nero said roughly. "In fact, I'd prefer if you didn't talk at all."

"Suits me fine." The other's voice turned ugly. "Bend over."

Gods knew why Nero hesitated. This was what he wanted.

Wasn't it?

"Want it that way, do you? Suit yourself."

The fist came out of nowhere. Like Vulcan's hammer from Mogadon myth, slamming straight into the side of his head. Hard enough to knock Nero sprawling across the table, legs turning to rubber, thoughts running from his head like water.

Dimly he cursed himself for a fool. He hadn't even seen it coming. Because he'd had his barriers locked down so tight he might as well be blind. Now, too late, he tried to pull his head together. Sparks sputtered at his fingers—

"None of that, pretty boy." A harsh fist lifted him by the hair and slammed his head against the table. Nero tasted the salty tang of blood and watched the world darken.

Fighting to stay conscious, he got his arms under him, tried to push himself up. A hard hand shoved him flat against the table and dragged his breeches down around his thighs. A jumble of shouted words scrolled across his scrambled brain. Words like *No not like this never wanted stop no STOP.* He thought maybe he was even yelling it out loud. But the music.

He knew now the guy had jacked it up so no one would hear him scream.

For a breath he was free as the brute behind him unbuckled his belt and dealt with his leathers. But he couldn't seem to clear his head.

He heard the guy hawk and spit, a few wet-sounding strokes as he used his saliva to lube his own cock. Which wouldn't be nearly enough in the foreplay department.

Meaning this was really going to hurt.

A sick fury churned through his gut. Nero bared his teeth and snapped his booted leg back, burning to kick the bastard's balls through the farking wall. His heel slammed into the solid muscle of the guy's thigh.

Eliciting a pained grunt—but no real damage.

"You like it rough?" Again the brute dragged him up by the hair.

Clearing his head, Nero reached deep inside and coiled a fistful of psi fire like a whip—

The brute gave his head a brutal shake and groped roughly between his legs for a hard-on he still wasn't sporting. His concentration shattered. A gasp of frustration slipped out. Teeth rattling, head swimming, scalp burning like fire, Nero cursed and flailed and clawed for the guy's blaster.

"How about I bring out my cargo knife and work you over? That what it takes to get you hard? Won't be so pretty after that, will you? I bet Draven won't want you anymore. Then you'll be all mine. I'll have you begging me to let you take my cock—"

At the edge of vision, Nero glimpsed a dark blur of motion. Desperately he braced against the blade.

Then something large and solid and lightning fast drove snarling into the monster behind him and knocked him halfway across the room.

Gasping for breath, Nero dragged his breeches around his hips and flung his hair out of his eyes.

To find his aspiring rapist sprawled on his ass against the far wall, leathers loose around his knees and his thick, still furiously erect hardware on full display. Red hatred mottled his swarthy face and red murder glittered in his cunning eyes. Hatred for the man who towered over him, bristling with violence and burning with rage.

Nero staggered against an onslaught of emotion that poured through him like an electric current.

Humiliation to be found powerless and hip-deep in such an out-of-control, undignified disaster.

Gratitude to be found when he was, before the brute went to work with his cargo knife.

And a devastating flood of tenderness to be found by the only man he could bear to see him like this. Tenderness so soul-shattering it made him want to weep.

*"Ben."* Firm hands steadied him on his feet. Cobalt eyes searched his face for damage. "Are you hurt? Talk to me."

"I'm… fine." Nero felt gingerly at his throbbing head. "Except for my pride. Dex, I…"

"Hold that thought for me." The ghost of a smile flickering in his eyes, Dex squeezed his arms and stepped back.

He strode to the praetorian, now trying clumsily to get his legs beneath him, a wary slant to his brutish eyes.

"On your feet, man," Dex bit out, looming over the guy with fists clenched and face livid. "I'll allow you that much. I'll even let you throw the first punch. Then I'm going to bloody take you apart. And you can't begin to imagine how much I'm going to make it hurt."

#

Dex followed up his right hook with a vicious undercut to the Butcher's jaw and put all his weight behind it. Cartilage crunched and teeth snapped under the blow. The impact slammed up his arm to his shoulder, so hard it knocked his own teeth together. His knuckles throbbed red with fiery pain. But Dex didn't give a single shit how much he hurt.

His driving imperative was paramount.

To make his enemy *bleed*.

Swinging his big fists blindly, wheezing through his damaged throat, his opponent spat out a broken tooth and staggered under the punishing rain of blows.

Still, Dex didn't make the mistake of underestimating him. He'd trained the guy himself. He knew when the Butcher was backed in a corner, he was at his most lethal. Dex had already disarmed the bastard with a sweeping crescent kick when he'd pulled his blaster. He was comfortably certain he'd at least fractured something with that move.

Judging by the bestial way he'd howled.

Still, Dex was keeping a wary eye on the wicked-looking cargo knife—a machete as long as his forearm—strapped to his opponent's belt.

Finding his back against the mirrored wall of Nero's slate-and-silver bathroom, the Butcher spread his meaty hands.

"Okay, boss." He hawked out a mouthful of red blood to spatter the white tiles. "Pax. You got me."

"Not even close," Dex bit out. "You tried to take what's mine. We're done when I say we're done. Hands up, soldier!"

A pure cold rage had been burning like liquid nitrogen in his blood since the singular moment he overrode the lock on the door and burst through to find that bastard with his leathers around his knees forcing a struggling and frenzied Nero over that bloody table.

And feeling the psychic impact of his lover's terror and fury and despair battering and howling like a chained titan inside his head had nearly driven him mad.

"Uh-uh. I've had—enough." The Butcher braced hands on knees and panted. Through blackened and swollen eyes, he slanted an ugly look at Nero, lurking fully clad and remorseless in the doorway. "That fancy-pants bitch you're boning? He ain't worth it."

A red haze darkened Dex's vision. Fueled by white-hot fury, he snapped his booted leg out in a knife-edge kick that connected with the Butcher's sternum. The crackle and crunch of breaking ribs punctuated the thrashing racket still pouring through the console.

With a wheeze, the bastard flew back four cubits and slammed into the full-length mirror.

Glass shattered and rained down around his sprawled and gasping form.

Dex loomed over his fallen foe, fists clenched and throbbing, and barely reined in the impulse to drive his foot through a few more ribs.

Without looking away, he grated to Nero, "Had enough? Or would you like me to keep going?"

"Enough," the Butcher wheezed, every breath an obvious agony. "Commander—please—enough. I'm beggin' you."

"We're done here," Nero said, eloquent with disgust. "Just get this space trash out of my quarters."

Dex dragged in a ragged breath and fought to tamp down the inferno of Mogadon bloodlust still raging through his veins. He wanted to kill. He wanted to feel flesh yield and bone break under his bare hands. He wanted to tear out his rival's throat with his teeth.

*Mine,* he wanted to snarl.

*Mine!* he wanted to roar.

The genetically bred possessiveness of the Mogadon male unleashed at full throttle. And knowing what it was didn't help him control it.

But he wasn't a mindless beast. He wasn't his stark raving father. With his responsibilities, he couldn't afford to be.

At last he managed a nod.

"You heard the man," he said tightly to the human wreckage panting on the floor. "Get the hell out of here. I'll dispatch a med squad to collect you in the corridor. Which is far more mercy than you deserve. You can expect your centurion to impose severe discipline for deserting your post. If for some reason he doesn't, rest assured I'll see to it personally."

*And that conduct violation should be sufficient to get you kicked off my elite roster. So I never have to look at your sneering face again.*

"Fair enough," the Butcher panted.

Dex pivoted away, knowing if he had to stare at the wretch a breath longer he'd finish the job and kill him.

He was halfway to the door, where an uncharacteristically disheveled Nero had watched the beating with a face white and cold as death—when a frisson of alarm spiked through him.

His battle sense…

*Screaming.*

Nero's eyes flew wide. Raw fear invaded his face.

"Dex!" he roared. "Down."

Dex dove to the floor like a falling meteor. Something hissed past his head, close enough to clip his ear.

To embed itself quivering in the wall.

Grimly Dex touched his stinging ear and saw blood on his fingers. This time his own.

*That bloody cargo knife.*

*Another breath and it would have been sticking out of my back.*

Nero's chest rumbled with a subterranean growl. His chiseled face hardened to a mask of pure malevolence. In an instant, his purple eyes flashed a blinding platinum. An icy gust of wind lashed his hair and garments and tore through the bathroom.

Dex wasn't easily alarmed, but the look of Ben Nero in this particular moment scared the spit out of him.

Nero's arm swept up to pinpoint the fallen praetorian. To fix him with a single remorseless finger.

No more than that.

With his eyes, Dex could see nothing. But he felt the raw malignant force of psychic power pour through Nero's rigid body and howl over his own head in a silent hurricane.

The ungodly racket of space thrash mingled with a soul-shredding scream.

Heart jackhammering, Dex rolled swiftly to his feet and spun. Powerless to do anything but watch torrents of dark blood pour from the ears and nose of the Butcher of Beta Prime where he lay thrashing on the floor. Eyes rolling and rimmed in panic, the brute coughed. Gouts of black blood exploded from his mouth and ran down his chin.

Nero stood in stony silence and watched with a face like a gorgon's.

While his attacker gurgled and hacked through a wet-sounding throat. While the whites of his eyes went ruby-red like dying embers and rivulets of blood poured down his cheeks. While his broken body hunched and vomited up the bloody contents of his own pulverized guts.

"Sweet bleeding Jupiter," Dex whispered.

The Butcher's breeches darkened with rapidly spreading blood. He was bleeding out from every orifice, limbs thrashing with violent convulsions in a widening pool of crimson. Bleeding out as his brain turned to pulp in his skull.

"Please," he croaked between spasms, fingers outstretched in a futile plea for mercy. *"Pleesh."*

But Nero in that moment knew nothing of mercy. And neither did Dex.

Eons passed before the last flicker of intellect drained from that ravaged face. A ragged breath rattled from his liquefied lungs.

The Butcher of Beta Prime never drew another.

"Gods of Olympus," Dex managed, his own voice thin and strangled. "Remind me never to get on your bad side."

"I think you've earned… a little leeway," Nero said faintly. "Dex… can you just… come here for a tick?"

Looking sick, Nero staggered and gripped the doorframe.

Dex was feeling more than a little sick himself. Gods knew he was more than accustomed to violent death, but he'd never seen a death quite like this one.

Not that the bastard hadn't earned it.

He never knew quite how he managed, but somehow he lurched across the floor faster than he thought possible, shards of mirror crunching under his boots, and got his arms around Nero before his legs gave out.

Nero's arms closed around him in a desperate clutch, all his usual grace and mastery stripped away. His lean frame trembled under Dex's frantic grip.

In truth, Dex was trembling himself. He could barely bring himself to contemplate what would have happened if—

"No," Nero said hoarsely. "He would have lost control when

he…" He swallowed hard. "And then I would have killed him. Still, I'm… glad you came… before that."

Dex needed to get both of them away from this abattoir. But he found himself swaying and more than a bit unbalanced. He turned his face into Nero's neck, shook with adrenaline, and filled his lungs with the familiar dark sweetness of his boyhood best friend's musk and sandalwood fragrance.

Spiked with his own feral scent.

Animal instinct hit him low and hard with a sudden savage lust. The fierce, desperate, nearly unstoppable urge to push Nero into the wall, grapple down both their breeches, and rut into him hard and fast until they both climaxed with the explosive force of megaton warheads.

He'd be lucky if Nero ever wanted that with him again after everything that had happened. He certainly wouldn't want it now.

Which meant Dex needed to master the frenzy of need clawing through his cock to possess him, claim him, ride him until they were both mindless and gasping with pleasure…

He closed his eyes and voiced a low groan.

"Let's get out of this room," Nero mumbled.

Somehow Dex dragged some semblance of wits together and did what needed doing. Covering the Butcher's still-oozing body in a blanket and closing the bathroom door firmly on that ungodly mess. Mercifully silencing that barbaric music. Persuading Nero finally to stop pacing like a caged panther and sit on the couch with an analgesic compress from the med kit pressed to the side of his head.

Finally Dex seized a badly needed moment to splash a goodly quantity of Mogadon whiskey into a snifter. He bolted a bracing swallow of the smoky liquor to steady the post-combat tremor in his bruised hands.

Then he keyed open his wrist unit. "Marcus."

"It's Titus, sir," a thin voice came back. "Marcus is in the hangar bay packing off more of the maharani's suitors. That lot are puking drunk, sir. It's a right mess down there."

"Titus." Dex imposed order on his weary brain. "Dispatch a cleanup crew to the Precursor's quarters and alert the morgue to expect one of my former praetorians. I want a dishonorable discharge drawn up and posted for public notice. I want deep-space jettison of this trash with no military honors. And I want half this ship to witness. Just in case anyone else is contemplating felony assault and high treason."

"Right away, sir." A pause. "Sir, are you—?"

"Make it happen, Titus."

Dex closed the link on his aide's startled questions and sank down to the couch with a groan.

"You do realize, of course," Nero murmured, "that this whole unsavory mess won't do your Indomitable reputation any favors. Once that cleanup crew turns up and starts nosing it around that you killed one of your own men in a jealous rage over my affections—"

"Do you honestly think I care about that now? Hells, Ben. I was a Prime Class *idiot*. I could have bloody lost you."

Dex still burned with the brutal need to drag Ben Nero into his arms, haul him to the nearest bed or just pull him to the floor, and ride him until the guy uttered all the promises and reassurances and commitments Dex needed to hear from him right now.

Instead, keeping all that primal instinct tightly in check, Dex slid closer on the couch and leaned over him. "Let me see your head, love. How many fingers am I holding up?"

"Three." Nero eyed him dryly, and Dex was more relieved than he could express to see some of the Valyrian's customary self-possession seeping back. "Except for a pounding headache and a severely bruised ego, I assure you I'm going to be fine. Telepaths can monitor their own vitals, Dex. Looks like your ear's stopped bleeding. What about your hands?"

Graceful fingers grazed his throbbing knuckles.

"It's nothing. You should have seen the other guy." Dex's thin attempt at humor fell flat. Because he'd never been much of a comic. And he certainly didn't feel much like laughing.

Nero's eloquent eyes looked right through him. Gently he lifted Dex's battered hand to the warm silk of his lips.

A shaft of need knifed through Dex. Need laced with desperate contrition.

"Damnation, Ben," he breathed. "We really need to talk. I need to tell you—"

The cheery blip of the entry portal cut him short. Cursing, he let in the cleanup crew and subsided grimly to the couch, where he reached again for Nero's hand. When the guy glanced warily at their viewing audience and started to slide away with a sigh, Dex tightened his grip and kept their hands laced.

Kept Nero right next to him.

Right where he belonged.

Which was all that got him through the next ten ticks, chafing with impatience while the cleanup crew did its unsavory work, carting out Nero's would-be rapist and tidying up the mess.

He was sharply alert to the curious looks this spectacle was attracting—scrutiny that in his father's time would have gotten him crucified—but it seemed insane to care now what anyone thought. If he thought Nero would've tolerated it, he would have pulled the guy right into his lap the way he did Kaia. Because right now Dex needed a little comforting himself.

But his best friend was the Valyrian Precursor. He possessed his own stiff-necked pride.

*Less of that right now than you might think,* Nero's wry tenor whispered in his head. *Which is why I don't exactly mind the way you're looming over me.*

Dex shot him a bemused look. *Am I looming?*

*Little bit.* A smile lurked at the corners of Nero's mouth. *You look like if any hapless soul strays within ten cubits of our defensive perimeter, you'll incinerate him with your eyes.*

*Too blooming right.* Dex scowled at an advancing prefect so fiercely the poor kid paled and beat a speedy retreat.

Still gripping Nero's hand, Dex spoke into his comm link. "Titus. I want an escort under your personal command to take the maharani to my quarters. Use those paroled felons from the brig. The praetorians are hopelessly compromised." He hesitated, still resistant, then took the plunge. "Send Zorin and those Syndax jackals of his with Kaia. Then secure all remaining candidates in their quarters under guard until the midnight broadcast."

"Will do, sir. We shan't let you down."

To Nero's startled look, Dex said grimly, "I fully intend to have that conversation you and I should have had days ago. And I bloody well intend to have it without one more gods-damned interruption."

Nero shifted uneasily. "Ah, do you really think Kaia—"

"Zorin has her. She trusts him. That means we're going to." Dex's minatory look dared him to object. "You keep applying that compress."

It felt like decades before the cleanup crew finally finished. Dex all but shoved the last stragglers out the door and locked the portal behind them.

At last, he had Nero to himself. His ally. His best friend. His lover. *Safe.*

Slowly the battle-ready hum of testosterone and aggression drained away. Dex leaned his brow against the closed door and released a long exhale.

"Now," he said softly. "We talk."

Booted footfalls whispered behind him. He tingled with awareness of Nero's electrifying nearness.

"Dex," Nero breathed at his shoulder.

He lifted his head and turned. "Listen—"

The silken heat of Nero's mouth found his in an openmouthed kiss, tongue meeting tongue. The burn of Kryllian firewater seared through him, sweet with cloves and laced with desperation. Urgent hands pinned his shoulders to the portal and lean hips crashed into his. The jutting shaft of Nero's arousal thrust against him.

A bolt of raw lust shot straight to his cock.

Apparently, in the wake of that near-death experience, Dex wasn't the only one battling a few elemental urges.

He fought to clear his head. "Wait—"

"No more waiting."

Nero was kissing him like he wanted to crawl down his throat— way more aggressive than Dex was used to. And this unexpected flash of dominance and aggression instead of Nero's usual soft submission was intoxicating as the devil. Desperate hands grappled to unbuckle his belt.

And Dex was pure animal instinct when Nero was desperate.

He barely managed to keep hold of his head.

"Look," he panted as demanding hands dragged his zipper down. "We need to talk—"

"No more talking."

Skillful fingers closed around his cock, and Dex thought he would lose his mind. This desperate, sexually aggressive Nero roused all his most primitive instincts. He wanted to wrestle Nero to the floor, pin him down, tie his hands. And just rutting against him wouldn't do the trick.

Not even close.

He needed to brand his mark of ownership so deep in the guy's very soul he'd never break free.

But Nero wouldn't want that, would he? Not after what just happened—

"No, don't be gentle," Nero gasped between kisses so hot, steam practically rose where their lips met. "Don't hold back. I need you."

Nero had one hand locked around his throat, holding him still for his searing kisses, while his other hand jacked Dex's desperately aching cock until he lost all control and thrust into his knowing fist. Dimly, through the haze of lust, Dex barely grasped that Nero was deliberately pushing all his Mogadon buttons. Almost as if he…

"Ben, wait. Do you… not *want* to talk about this?"

"Give the man a prize," Nero growled, nipping Dex's lower lip in warning. The sting of those sharp feral teeth, coupled with the swipe of Nero's thumb over the head of his shaft, just about launched him into orbit.

Dex gasped and gripped Nero's shoulders to subdue him. "Would you care to enlighten me as to precisely why not?"

Nero's heliotrope eyes were glowing with passion and hazy with lust. But his barely contained panic battered at Dex's brain.

"Because I already know everything you're going to say," Nero muttered, still working him. "Believe me, there's no need. I'm leaving as soon as we hit Quorum—"

The force of that revelation slammed through Dex like Jupiter hurling a lightning bolt. He locked a hand around Nero's wrist to hold him riveted.

"You're *leaving*? Again? Seven bloody hells! You're leaving me—us—the three of us, damn it—over my dead and disintegrated body. I mean it."

Before Nero's obdurate face, looking positively mutinous with determination, Dex's eyes narrowed. "Out of curiosity, what precisely is it you fancy I'm about to say?"

Nero rolled his eyes toward heaven and heaved an impatient sigh. "You're going to lay out the terms of our tidy arrangement in a classic Draven diktat. You and Zorin both take Kaia as consort—while you both busily keep pretending you don't want the hell out of each other. And I'm your dirty little secret on the side."

"Great flaming comets!" Astounded and offended in equal measure, Dex gripped the guy's sulky face between his palms and nailed his angry gaze with his own blazing stare. "I've been trying like the devil for days to beg you to be my consort. Don't you know I'm out of my head in love with you?"

Ben's mouth went slack with shock.

And just the sight of his blank-faced astonishment fanned the flame of Dex's fury.

"For Juno's sake, Ben! I've loved you half my life. Ever since that summer at the ashram. How in blazes could you possibly not know?"

Carefully Ben eased his hand from Dex's trousers. In his tone, annoyance struggled with disbelief. "Well, how the hells would I know?"

"Because you're a bloody *telepath*! The strongest in the galaxy, I might add."

Ben shook back his disheveled hair and started pacing. "Did you or did you not tell me in no uncertain terms to stay out of your head? I've tried my damnedest to honor that demand. As a matter of telepath ethics."

Dex snorted and jerked up his zipper. "You're so bloody ethical you'd rather leave me—leave Kaia—than talk this thing through? Because we all want you—need you—to be part of this union. It's the four of us! None of it works without you. Why the hells do you always have to run away?"

Eyes wild, Ben whirled to face him. "Because I'm tired of being hurt, all right? Because I want everything from you—everything, Dex! And you've made it crystal clear you can't—"

"Can't *what*? Tell the universe I love you so much my life doesn't make sense anymore, that it's never made sense without you in it?" Dex felt like tearing out his own hair with frustration. "I do believe I've just done that, haven't I? And I'll do it again in spades when I swear to you as my consort on the interstellar broadcast."

Ben's sculpted face burned with shame and anger. "But you can't... you won't..."

"What? What can't I do?"

"Oh, Dex." His proud shoulders slumped. "I can't be with you the way you want."

"The devil you can't."

"And you can't be with me the way I need. That's why I'm leaving." In despair, Ben spun away and stalked toward the bedroom.

"Like flaming hell you're leaving!"

Desperation lashed through him and drove Dex right after him.

Anything—he'd do anything to stop Ben from leaving. Nothing else mattered right now—nothing. Not the hateful echo of his father's sneering slurs, not the certain knowledge of his race's ingrained prejudices, not the chafing itch of his tired old hang-ups. Nothing mattered except proving he could be what Ben needed.

*Everything* Ben needed.

Hearing—maybe sensing—Dex closing the distance behind him, Ben slanted him a wrathful look of warning.

"Don't come after me. I'm serious. You've seen what I can do."

He punched the button to seal the portal between them. Dex got in the way and shouldered it back open.

"You can hurl me through a wall or liquefy my organs to a pulp," he said fiercely. "But you can't make me stop loving you."

*And knowing what you can do—that you're my equal in combat but you submit to me anyway? That you're so bloody perfect when you do it? That damn well obliterates me far more completely than having you blast me into the next star system.*

Catching the thought Dex lobbed at him like a photon grenade, Ben pushed out a choked sound. His eyes were glowing, psychic winds stirring the ends of his hair.

But he was backing away. Not attacking. Just running.

Same as always.

"Don't come any closer, Dex." He flung out a warding hand edged in purple fire. "I want you to leave."

Dex advanced on him relentlessly, stalking him toward the oversized bed spread with Valyrian furs where he'd lost his mind and his heart forever last night. A clutter of packed baggage stood piled at the foot. Seeing that incontrovertible physical evidence of Ben's imminent departure pushed him past the brink.

Like fueling a rocket with flammable chemicals and igniting the fuse.

With a growl, he caught Ben's angry hand and dragged him into his arms. Ben's lean sinewed frame was fire and rain and lightning, crackling with psychic force and fierce as a raging cyclone under Dex's urgent touch.

But when their bodies locked together, Ben was violently aroused.

The same way Dex was himself. Ben gasped his name as their mouths came together.

"Don't tell me you're leaving," Dex muttered between scorching kisses that tasted of fire and despair. "And stop running away. Drives me out of my mind. You're staying right here with me and Kaia and Zorin."

"Meteors," Ben moaned, gripping Dex's shoulders in some misguided effort to push him away. But the friction sparking down both their cocks was making them both pant. "Will you just be reasonable for once! I've seen inside your head, remember? You *know* you can't—"

"Do me a favor, gorgeous. Don't tell me what I can't do."

Ruthlessly appropriating Zorin's nickname for Ben, because he knew Ben liked it—and right now he was all about doing anything Ben liked—Dex pushed him back hard onto the bed and crawled right in after him. Into that decadent pile of sleek gleaming furs that already reeked of his own mating scent. His palms slid under Ben's tunic to find hot bare skin stretched over smooth rippling muscle.

"Take this off for me," Dex ordered, guttural with need. "Take everything off. I'm going to make you climax hard enough to shift the orbit of a mid-sized planet."

Ben laughed a little angrily under his breath. "You can make me come hard enough to shift the orbit of a gas giant. But you won't change my mind about leaving."

Suddenly Dex found himself grinning. "You know how I love a proper challenge."

Ben looked maddeningly defiant. Still, he was obeying, uncharacteristically clumsy with anger and urgency, wrestling his tunic over his head.

Right now that was all that mattered.

Dex eyed his own infernal boots. He'd be damned if he called in a prefect now. "Help me with these, will you?"

Ben slid him a sidelong look under his lashes that heated Dex's blood to the boiling point, then slithered out of his breeches, his gorgeously erect cock springing free, flushed with passion and dripping with need. And Dex Draven, who'd never done such a thing in his life, gave serious thought to abandoning his own frantic efforts to disrobe, along with the last of his Mogadon inhibitions, and just swiping his tongue down that quivering shaft and working him with his mouth until Ben Nero lost his mind.

"Comets, Dex," Ben whispered, low and throaty with desire.

Naked and perfect in the dusky twilight that seeped from the ceiling panels, muscle flexing under silky skin, Ben slid out of bed and knelt between Dex's knees. Gleaming black hair curtained his face as he eased Dex out of his boots. An image blazed through Dex of Kaia doing the same—right before he first kissed her. So sleek and soft and sultry she'd driven him straight to bedlam.

A shudder of hot craving arced through him.

"That would have been something to see," Ben whispered, head still bowed, clever hands peeling Dex out of his trousers.

"What I can't wait to see is the two of you down there together," Dex said hoarsely. "Kneeling at my feet."

*While Zorin loomed behind him, growling demands in Dex's ear. Describing in scorching detail precisely what he wanted all three of them to do...*

His eager cock swelled and jerked at the visual. Ben knelt, barely breathing, at his feet.

"Dex." Deft fingers seared his naked thighs. "Do you want me to—"

"No. Tonight's all about you. Kneel on the bed for me."

Graceful as a serpent, Ben uncoiled to his feet and crawled onto the fur-piled mattress. Dex pushed him forward until his forehead touched the furs, rose to tower over him, and breathed in his ear, "Hands behind your back, gorgeous."

A low moan rumbled from his throat, but Ben submitted. Same as always. Dex snared from the bedside table a swath of fabric—a scarf or something, crimson so deep it was nearly black—and bound Ben's wrists together snugly at the small of his back.

Then he stepped back to admire the visual.

He swore he'd never in his life seen anything so arousing as the galaxy's most powerful telepath, skin pale against the dark sweep of sangoire silk, hair a shining ebony banner unraveling across the dappled Valyrian fur. His back and shoulders gorgeously muscled, strength honed by the brutal demands of the feudal ice world where he'd grown to manhood. His luscious ass tight and bulging with muscle…

But quivering with nerves.

So helplessly exposed. So singularly focused on Dex's slightest word or deed. Yielding to him so completely, needing him so completely, trusting him so completely—despite the horror and abomination Ben had just barely avoided.

Dex gasped under a shuddering surge of love.

So intense it was agonizing.

If Ben left him, Dex was going to self-destruct. And take the whole farking galaxy with him.

Dex crawled over him and pressed his lips to one sinewed shoulder, glittering with a fine sheen of sweat. Ben trembled under his kiss. Tasting salt on his lips, Dex nuzzled and licked his way down his beautifully arched back. Ben panted and shivered beneath his touch.

When his lips grazed the small of his back, at last Dex spread his palms across the smooth hot skin of his ass. Ben whimpered and undulated beneath him, clearly craving friction against his straining cock.

Dex's heart was cartwheeling like it would vault right out of his chest. He saw his hands, bronze against Ben's pale skin, spreading him wide and exposed to his gaze. He had the sweetest pucker—sweet as a girl's. Dex heard his own labored breath, loud and harsh in the fraught silence.

"Tell me—" He had to stop and clear his throat. "Tell me what you want."

"You." The words were soft explosions in the purple dusk. "Inside me. Gods, Dex! Do you want me to beg?"

"Yes." His own voice sounded thick and strange. "That's what I want. Let me hear you beg."

A soft sob slipped from Ben's lips. He was trembling so violently the entire bed was quivering. Dex needed to see him react. Needed to push him over the edge. He leaned in to drag the flat of his tongue across Ben's pretty pink pucker and watched him just fall apart, gasping *please oh gods Dex please* and straining to thrust his aching cock into the mattress.

Dex gripped his hips to hold him good and steady and probed him with his tongue, pushing into that tight needy hole, and savored the sound and sight and feel of Ben losing his mind, desperate cries and gasps alternating with just about the sweetest pleas he'd ever heard. If he'd had any earthly idea a rim job would make Ben Nero come to pieces like this for him, he would have mastered his own absurd apprehension and done this to him years ago, way back when, that summer at the ashram…

"Yes, gods, I wanted you to!" Ben moaned, his channel softening and opening just beautifully to the insistent thrust of Dex's tongue. "Tried everything I could think of—to seduce you—oh *please*—"

"And I thought you were just teasing." Dex alternated sharp thrusts with long slow strokes, savoring every gasped plea that fell from Ben's lips. "You teased me all summer. You know you did. Now I want to hear you beg me."

Ben's cries were growing louder, more desperate, like he didn't care if they heard him in the hall—just the way Dex liked him. He thrashed against his bonds, tried rutting into the mattress. When Dex thrust a finger into his mouth to get it good and wet, then eased it into his hot tight passage, a long throaty moan spilled out.

A moan so deep with yearning Dex nearly came himself.

"You're ready for me, aren't you?" he breathed.

Gods on the mountain, he'd be lucky not to have a heart attack. He didn't think he'd ever been so terrified yet simultaneously so desperately aroused by anything in his entire life.

"Please, Dex, please—I—need you inside me—oh *gods*—"

With a haste fueled by urgency, Dex rummaged in the bedside drawer and found the reliable stash of supplies no Mogadon bedroom came equipped without. Clumsy with nerves, he dumped oil into his palm and lubed up his own throbbing, aching, pulsing cock.

When he lined himself up against Ben's hole, shiny with his own saliva, watched him cant his hips and undulate and try to back onto his shaft, a moment of blazing realization seared through him.

*Great gods of Olympus. I'm actually doing this.*

"Please," Ben repeated, raw with need. "I'm begging you—need you so much—"

"Ben," Dex whispered, voice shaking with restraint, "I've never—loved anyone like this. I'm afraid of—hurting you."

"Don't be afraid. I'm so—so ready for you. Now, please, please do it now."

Dex gripped Ben's hips, squeezed his eyes closed, and buried himself inside him with one smooth deep thrust. They both cried out, voices mingling in the night. The incredibly tight heat of Ben's channel gripped him, all the way down his shaft, his passage already pulsing with pleasure that milked Dex like a fist.

Then Dex forgot everything except the mind-blowing bliss of riding Ben Nero. His best friend. His ally. His lover. His everything.

Dex gripped his hips and slammed into him, finding a rhythm that drove both of them to madness. Ben writhed against his bonds and sobbed with frenzy. Dex reached around him to find Ben's cock, slick with need and precum, and worked him in time with his punishing thrusts.

With every stroke he asserted his dominance and possession. His inalienable right to have a voice in Ben's erratic and alarming choices. His right to keep Ben with him—with all of them—forever.

Bringing the four of them together against the forces of war and prejudice that kept them apart was Kaia's job. Holding them there with a steadying grip strong enough to anchor their volatile energy was Zorin's.

But convincing Ben to stay was Dex's.

"Want to give you everything you need. Always," Dex panted and pistoned into him. "Ben—oh Ben—you're so perfect for me."

"Gods—the way you—fill me—" Beyond pride or restraint, Ben thrust hard and fast into his hand. "I can't—can't wait."

Dex quickened his pace and rutted into him harder. Inflamed to madness by the sight of his own thick cock, shiny with lube, sliding in and out of Ben's drum-tight pucker.

"You're so tight and hot for me, aren't you?" he praised. "So desperate and needy." Ben moaned in agreement. "You're going to make me come for you—love you so much—"

Ben's channel clenched around him and contracted still tighter with the fluttering pulses of climax. Dex's shaft swelled and stretched him further. A hoarse shout tore through Ben and the rhythmic hot spurt of spunk splashed Dex's hand. Dex flung his head back as blinding pleasure thundered through him. For what felt like forever, his own climax roared over him, emptying wave after wave of his own release deep into Ben.

Not only giving Ben Nero his body and his seed and his passion.

But every atom of his soul.

Streaming with sweat and gasping like he'd just run a fifty-mile marathon, Dex collapsed on top of him. Barely conscious enough to fumble the knot open and release Ben's hands. Ben squirmed like an eel to align their sweat-slick bodies, sticky with semen, and wrapped himself tight around Dex.

*Why in blazes did I waste so much infernal angst and energy all these years resisting this… this transcendent connection?*

"Because of your father," Ben answered.

"But I hated my father. He was a hateful person." Dex chuffed out a wry breath. "Do you know, it's taken me twenty-eight blooming years to be able to say that out loud?"

Ben murmured something drowsy and snuggled deeper into his arms.

"Talk to me, love." Dex turned his face into Ben's neck, drenched with his own mating scent—a circumstance he found deeply satisfying. "Did I shift any planets for you?"

"Maybe not a gas giant," Ben mumbled sleepily. "But perhaps… a small moon."

"No doubt I'll improve with practice. Lots… and lots… of practice." Dex tightened his grip and plastered their bodies together. "Which, as a practical matter, will only be possible if you *don't bloody leave.*"

Ben heaved a sigh and said nothing.

Sharply Dex lifted his head and locked onto his wary face.

"No leaving this time. I mean it," Dex growled. "This thing with the four of us? You're all in. And so am I."

Brow furrowed, Ben studied him, gaze intent as he searched his face. At last Dex felt that deft probing touch sort through his deepest secrets. He let it happen. Because he had nothing to hide.

Which meant he had everything to lose.

"All right, Dex," he sighed. "I warn you, the Senate of Psychics won't much like it. In fact, they're likely to cause real trouble. But I'll stay."

Tension eased from the powerful body pressed tight against him. A smile of drowsy satisfaction slipped across Ben's lips as his lids drifted closed.

Dex released a shuddering breath and pulled him still closer. He'd have to get up in a tick and get them both cleaned up. Then deal with the latest of Kaia's spurned and increasingly surly suitors. But right now he didn't think he was ever going to let Ben go.

"It would help," Ben breathed, words slurring with sleep, "if Kaia conceives. Especially if I can tell them… he's mine."

# CHAPTER THIRTEEN
### The Snatch

Kaia cried out and writhed with abandon in the disastrous tangle she and Zorin had made of Dex's sheets.

When Zorin first climbed in there with her, she'd been desperately focused on keeping the volume dialed down. At least for the sake of the pack of Syndax guard dogs hunkered in Dex's living room while Dex was off doing whatever it took to make Ben happy.

Which he was still off somewhere doing.

Now, with Kaia and Zorin naked and gasping and streaming with sweat, thighs slick with her own craving after he'd rung her bell so many times she lost count, her entire body humming at his slightest touch the way the *Angel* hummed after a stem-to-stern tune-up, she was way beyond caring how much noise they were making.

Mindless with the pounding rush of pleasure, she arched her back, undulated into the mattress that reeked of Dex and Zorin's potent scents, and screamed as an avalanche of orgasm poured through her.

When she finally lay spent and gasping in the sheets, Zorin's head lifted from between her thighs, his sand-and-salt hair tousled from her desperate grip. Lazy satisfaction gleamed in his aquamarine eyes, rimmed with the hard glitter of driving arousal.

He'd already climaxed twice inside her. But as he nuzzled and licked and crawled his way up her body, pale starlight seeping through the viewport to bathe their naked skin in blue, the jutting shaft of his cock nudged between her thighs.

Telling her he was more than ready for Round Three.

"No more," she panted, hoarse from all the noise he'd wrung out of her. "I can't… can't come anymore."

But her body was saying something else. And their minds were linked and synced so tightly now he had to know it.

His tongue lapped her taut nipples, exquisitely sensitive from all the attention they'd already gotten. Tingling pleasure streaked through her and sparked a breathless moan.

"Like that, don'tcha?" His teeth grazed her nipples just to feel her shiver. "This too?"

"I can't," she gasped again, hands spanning his big shoulders, half pushing him away.

But not really meaning it.

The weight of his powerful body, sweat glittering on the tribal tattoos wrapped around his bulging biceps and inked across his broad back, felt way too good on top of her.

"Sure you can, sweetheart," he rasped, a little husky himself. "And, just in case you're curious, you still taste like Dex. Just how hard did you make him come today?"

Heat bloomed in her face and made her squirm. He'd already enticed her to describe the whole scorching encounter in graphic detail while he teased both of them to a frenzy rubbing his cock against her clit. Until her breathless recital in response to his explicit questions dissolved in a symphony of desperate pleas for him to take her.

That was how they'd both come the first time.

"It's driving you crazy, isn't it?" she breathed. "Being in Dex's bed. Breathing in Dex's scent. Coming in Dex's woman. I'm the closest to him you can get right now."

His cavernous chest rumbled with a growl of warning. "He mighta been your first, sweetheart. But you're my girl too, Dex or no Dex. If he wants you—and judging by the way he's scenting and how hard he came inside you, I think we both know how much he wants you—he's gonna have to share you with me. Isn't he?"

He rubbed the swollen head of his cock along her slick and pulsing slit. Helpless with pleasure, she rocked against him and a deeper moan spilled out.

Triumph sparked in his eyes, hot and blue as neutron stars.

But it wasn't only the way she responded to him that was flipping his switch. It was tasting Dex's passion spilling out of her every time Zorin went down on her that was driving her Syndax lover with such tender, relentless purpose.

A drive she didn't think would be sated tonight until this space pirate she'd chosen for a consort got everything he needed.

Tonight he needed more than her submission.

He needed… whatever he needed… with Dex.

The same way she did. Both of them ached with needing Dex.

Angels and asteroids, the blazing image of Zorin tumbling both of them in the First Indomitable's oversized bed. Pulling her down on top of him, working his prodigious length inside her one finger at a time, spreading her bottom with his big hands and growling for Dex to take her from behind…

A powerful pulse of anticipation rolled her hips beneath Zorin's questing cock and lodged his tip against her soaked and eager channel. She couldn't bite back a needy cry.

"Have I mentioned," Zorin murmured, leaning in to kiss her, "how hard I'm gonna get off on having a telepath for a consort? Especially one with your inventive imagination?"

"Just wait till there's two of us, big guy. Ben's twice the telepath I am. And just as inventive."

Their tongues came together, and she tasted the musk of Dex and Zorin's passion inside her, salted with her own desire. She twined her hands in his hair and deepened the kiss.

*Gods, he tastes like all of us. Imagine how it'll be when it's Ben too.*

His voice thickened with intent. "You're ready for me again, ain'tcha?"

*"Zorin,"* she gasped. Even as her hips tilted up to welcome him and her hands slid down his back and gripped the hard muscled globes of his ass to pull him closer. "The way I come for you… every single time… especially when you… ride me. I swear I can't."

"Sure you can." His mouth lifted from hers and his eyes, gleaming mercury with passion, nailed her with a look that seared through her like a sulfur fire. "You need this to conceive. You need it from Dex and you need it from Ben and you need it from me. Put me inside you, sweetheart."

She gave way to a soft sob of anticipation. Even as her hands wrapped around his spectacular shaft, swollen and jerking with need at her touch, and fitted him where she needed him.

Already slick and stretched from his recent incursions, her body welcomed him with an eagerness that belied the pleas and protests she was still gasping.

Breathing harsh and audible in the sex-drenched darkness, he pushed inside her slowly—the way he always did—giving her every chance in the world to push him away. Instead her legs wrapped around him, pulling him in tight, hips already moving against his, eyes never leaving his. He gripped her arms and pinned them overhead.

Fierce satisfaction hardened his face as he drove into her.

"Show me how much you want me," he demanded. "I want my boys in the next room to hear how ready you are for me. Want 'em all to hear how hard you make me come."

Why in the seven devils that turned her on, she really couldn't say.

All she knew was her legs, wrapped tight around his hips, followed a soul-deep instinct. Never letting him pull out of her more than a little before he thrust home inside her again.

All she heard was the slap of flesh against flesh and the wet friction of his cock. Riding her. Already dripping with his earlier release, Dex's need and the ample evidence of her own utter surrender to both men who'd had her today.

And all she felt were the sharp spasms of pleasure that tightened her channel around his swollen shaft and wrung urgent cries from her throat. Cries that rang in rhythm with his own deep groans and increasingly desperate thrusts.

His incendiary eyes stayed locked on her the whole time. She knew he liked watching her face when she came. And with him pinning her arms overhead and pistoning into her hard and fast and urgent as need spiraled sharp and high between them, she *was…*

Definitely…

*Coming.*

"Gods, Kaia—just like that," he groaned. "Do you even know— oh gods!—know good you feel wrapped around my cock? Loving you like this—loving you—you're unreal."

With all the promises and threats and reassurances he whispered or growled while he was inside her, this was the first time he'd used the L word. She wondered if he meant it.

*Don't get excited, samurai. It's probably just a euphemism.*

"This feel like a euphemism to you?" Pinning her wrists with one hand, he tilted her hips, eased her leg over his shoulder, and electrified her with the angle of his driving thrusts. "Use your telepathic brain, samurai. How could I not love you? You and me—we're the same.

Rebels, rule-breakers, hellraisers, the both of us. You were made for me. Made for the Syndax. I'm so much in love with you I can't see straight."

Her toes curled in helpless pleasure. Helpless even to move as he pinned her in place and pounded into her. It was that sense of being helpless, forced to take him and loving it, spread wide and eager for every punishing stroke, powerless to resist what was coming as his tempo turned jerky and desperate, that pushed her over the edge. Her channel milked his length and her exhilarated cry of climax rang out, echoed by his exuberant shout of release.

His whisper chased her down into darkness. The same words he always said when he spurted deep inside her.

*"Give me a son, Kaia. You know I'm the one."*

When her swirling head cleared and her racing heart slowed, she lay sprawled across his massive body, cheek pressed to his shoulder, the texture of his old blaster scar rough against her skin, his calloused palm soothing as he rubbed her back. Beyond the viewport pulsed the double glint of the Kryllian system's twin suns—no bigger than diamonds in the cosmic night, but gleaming with distant menace.

The familiar confines of Dex's bedroom wrapped them in shadow, waiting to be fired with its owner's invigorating presence.

Still no Dex.

And maybe there'd be no Dex until he announced on the midnight broadcast the names of the lucky candidates who'd survived this latest culling. The suitors who'd fight to the death through an even more brutal culling twelve clicks from now to make the final ten. Every man of them steeled to slaughter a sexual rival to claim his place in her bed. Or else be slaughtered himself.

The way this brutal, barbaric, bloodthirsty butchery of a ritual demanded.

She could barely bring herself even to approve the list. A list with Zorin's name blazoned on top and Cato's spot—since his defection had been promptly classified and kept under wraps by Dex—ready for his brother to fill fighting in his place. For both of them, she was terrified.

*Angels of Anaxos, protect them. All three of them.*

*And protect us from my father. Because we'll see him in the divine and wrathful flesh in less than two days.*

A fresh twinge of worry plucked at her nerves and made them sing.

But fear of her father was a familiar demon. He didn't own her.

Not tonight.

Not with every neuron and synapse in her telepathic body still heavy and sated with sexual satisfaction. And she didn't think she'd feel that way, with her lifemate on board the same ship, unless Ben too felt sated.

She hoped that meant she'd see them both soon. Together.

Because she needed them. And so did Zorin.

"I didn't know you loved me," she whispered to him—this Syndax pirate, scourge of the galaxy, who'd soldered his ruthless reputation and brutal strength into a formidable armor for the sterling decency of the man beneath.

The last thing she'd expected to find in an outlaw was integrity.

She'd never dared dream of finding love.

His big hand rubbed the back of her neck. "Loving comes easy for me. Always has."

"Then you're lucky," she said softly. *And so am I.*

He pushed out a snort. "The real deal? The stuff all those poets obsess over? Not so lucky. Not when you're flying solo because that special someone doesn't love you back."

*Like Dex all those years?*

*And maybe like me?*

A squirm of guilt wiggled through her. She couldn't deny her play for Zorin had been purely opportunistic. At least when they'd first met.

Dex had just declared interstellar war. And she'd been more than ready to trade her body and her bed in a cold-blooded bargain to bribe her Syndax suitor to stop him.

Zorin had known. But he still hadn't walked.

"Zorin, listen. I…"

"Hey. It's okay." He pushed out a chuckle and pressed his lips to her forehead. "You've known me less than a week, sweetheart. And no girl looks at a guy the way you look at me when I'm buried deep inside you if she isn't falling in love with him. Does she, Kaia?"

Whoa. Now she was definitely swimming out of her depth.

Feeling way too awkward, she turned her face into his shoulder and twined her arms around his neck. Her curls tumbled over them and his feral scent of wolf and steel wound through her.

"I've got you and Dex and Ben to figure out," she whispered. "You and Dex risking your necks for me. Ben and me still grappling with what happened all those years ago. Not to mention a galactic peace to forge, a vengeful god to placate, and a prophecy son to conceive. It's a lot for a runaway circus acrobat to process. I'm not a god myself, you know."

He eased a comforting hand over her hair. "Now don't get all spun up. It's been a doozy of a week for all of us, hasn't it. Especially you. Your hormones are out of whack and your dad's on the warpath. No big surprise you're still wrapping that clever samurai head of yours around the way you feel."

A blade of contrition knifed through her. "I know I'm a cosmic mess. I'm sorry."

"Don't be. I'm not in any hurry here." His lips nuzzled her hair. "Our problem's your Pops, ain't it? He's jonesing for you to conceive and perpetuate the dynasty. And I got a hunch you need to be in love… maybe in love with all three of us… maybe sharing this bed with all three of us… in order for that to happen. So the sooner we can make that scene go down? The sooner we solve our problem."

His words hung heavy on her heart. Because she'd figured out she loved Dex days ago. And she'd loved Ben forever. Why couldn't she say the words to Zorin?

*Because I've been playing him since the day I met him. Playing him against Dex. And he knows it. That's why I don't want to say the words. Until I'm sure I mean them.*

"That's what I want too, sweetheart," he breathed into her hair. "And I'm willing to wait as long as it takes. For all three of you."

The scuff of knuckles against the door pierced her chest with a javelin of anticipation. She was jittery tonight and she didn't know why. Because it couldn't be Dex. He definitely wouldn't knock before invading his own bedroom. He'd stride right in and own the place.

And she'd know if it was Ben.

"Uh, chief?" An apologetic voice seeped through the door. "You and the missus decent in there?"

The edges of her anxiety softened, but the blade of her tension lingered.

"The missus?" Kaia rolled away from Zorin and tucked the silver thermal blanket beneath her armpits. "Ugh. Whatever happened to 'queen of the Syndax horde'?"

"Aw, shoot." Zorin sighed and pushed up to sit, the sheet pooling around his hips. "C'mon in, Tick Tock."

Wryly Kaia eyed her spectacularly naked lover as the door slid open to reveal the living room littered with armed and boozing pirates. She couldn't imagine Dex blithely receiving casual callers and taking military briefings from his subordinates while lying spent and naked in their bed, with her barely decent beside him.

Apparently for Zorin, this was SOP.

*Suck it up, samurai. Just one more difference between a Syndax pirate and a First Indomitable. Gods know how the four of us will manage to rub along as roommates.*

*To say nothing of bedmates.*

The space pirate slouched in, waist-length dreadlocks glittering with beads and bits of bone, a pitcher and two glasses incongruously gripped in his tattooed hands. His eyes veered studiously away from Kaia's well-tumbled form.

"Figured you'd want to wet your whistle after, uh, *after*." Under his scruffy beard, Tick Tock's skin darkened. "Draven sent up some grub and plenty of space ale. Says he'll be right up after the midnight broadcast."

"You're a real pal, Tick Tock." Zorin pushed a hand through the tousled spikes of his hair and shot him a rueful look. "Sorry about all the racket in here. You boys post a guard out there and get yourselves some shut-eye. You able to get Praxis on the horn?"

"Nope." Carefully the pirate deposited his burdens on the bedside table. "No one's home at the Syndax digs on Quorum. *Relentless* keeps pinging 'em though, chief."

Midway through pouring their ale, Zorin's head swiveled sharply toward him. Sudden vigilance invaded his craggy features.

"We still can't reach 'em? Praxis is always reachable. I gave those orders six clicks ago." When the other guy shook his head and looked troubled, Zorin pushed out a breath. "You tell *Relentless* to keep trying. If you can't get Praxis, ping our guy at the miners' guild out there. And you have Remus fly a couple fighters up ahead to scope out the sitch. If something's up on Quorum, a miners' strike or something, we don't wanna fly right into it."

"Aye, aye, Cap'n." The pirate thumped a fist to his chest in casual salute and backed out.

When the door closed behind him, Kaia popped up—blanket falling to her waist—and reached eagerly for her ale. "Who's Praxis?"

"Syndax rep on the Quorum of Four." Eyes running over her with an appreciative gleam, Zorin tipped back his glass and drained half its contents. "Steady and reliable as an orbiting moon, which is why I gave him the gig. One of the boys who sprang me from the slammer and lit out with me from Mogadon. That means he's someone I trust."

*Which marks another fundamental difference between Zorin and Dex. Zorin trusts and Dex doesn't. But Dex is learning. At least, he's learning to trust the three of us.*

*I think.*

"If something's wrong at the Syndax outpost on Quorum, we need to tell Dex and Ben. They have their own presence on Quorum." Kaia paused to savor a swallow of ale, letting the dry hoppy crispness— laced with the mineral tang of star iron—foam over her thirsty tongue. "Especially if you think we could be flying into trouble."

"If someone's kicking up a ruckus out there, Dex's first instinct's gonna be to blame me." Zorin drained his glass slowly and thought about it. When his glass was empty, he spoke again, syllables blurred with drowsiness. "But yeah, I'll tell him. Soon's he shows up. Wonder what he's hearing from his guys."

Kaia was feeling more than a little sleepy herself, after the various stresses and stimuli of her Tombola day, then being teased and tongued and ridden until even her fertile body was heavy and humming and replete.

Replete enough that a few swallows of ultra-proof space ale was enough to send her straight to dreamland.

And plainly the ale was having the same effect on Zorin's big body.

Some instinct was tugging at her brain for attention. But she was already too far gone to follow it.

Still sitting up, Zorin was already dozing. Sliding her half-empty glass to the bedside table, she pulled him down beside her in the blue twilight and snuggled up against his warm solid bulk.

An eruption of good-natured brawling seeped through the closed door, but quickly dwindled. The pirates too seemed to be winding down for the night.

"I don't know how I'll face them in the morning," she murmured into Zorin's shoulder. "You and I, um, weren't exactly discreet."

"Doesn't do us any harm for them to know I make you happy, does it?" Sleepily his muscled arm pulled her across his chest. "Want to make Dex happy too. 'S all I ever wanted. Sleeping in his bed, breathing in his scent… hard being so close to him… without being close to him."

"He needs you too. Even if he's only starting to admit it. I can feel it. You both… need each other so much."

"Hope he shows up soon. All these years…" His whisper ended on a soft exhale.

Then he was gone, and she was going, floating through space in a capsule of dreams.

#

Dex felt like he was floating in zero gravity a good six cubits above the floor.

For this remarkable condition, he blamed the excess of feel-good endorphins still flooding his system after the supremely satisfying encounter he'd just enjoyed in Ben Nero's bed.

Along with the intense relief of kicking off his ship fifty more of his bloody rivals for Kaia's bed. His just-concluded midnight broadcast, with a thoroughly claimed and bedded Ben standing at his side, would thankfully be one of his last as Tombola master.

Soon when he stood before the glaring eye of the interstellar cameras, he'd stand revealed and proclaimed—along with Ben and Zorin—as the maharani's chosen consorts.

Marcus assured him the galactic betting pool was going wild, with Zorin the odds-on favorite. In contrast, Ben was a dark-horse candidate. Anyone who'd put their creds on him was going to make a killing.

And he'd been oddly touched to hear a growing faction of Mogadon bidders were placing their hard-earned money on Dex.

Despite the fact that, as master of ceremonies and neutral referee, he'd supposedly removed himself from the running.

Well, he made his own rules. All the gods knew he'd made his intentions regarding Kaia abundantly clear. When he exercised a brother's privilege and took Cato's spot at the blood games tomorrow—even in the absence of a formal declaration—his intentions would become clearer still.

And his own race knew him well enough never to bet against him.

When he finally announced she was mating all three of them, the betting pool would probably explode.

Striding through the *Inevitable*'s shining corridors, with uniformed men at every juncture snapping to salute, Ben a graceful shadow gliding at his side, and a tingle of anticipation coursing through his blood at the intoxicating prospect of both Kaia and Zorin waiting in his bed, Dex felt so good it was practically godlike.

The sight of two unfamiliar men guarding his door, wearing brand-new Mogadon uniforms without the titanium insignia of his elite guard, slowed his stride. They looked vigilant and capable enough—albeit a bit scruffy—these convinced felons Marcus had dredged up from his brig.

And Ben at his side seemed entirely unconcerned by whatever he was getting from their heads.

"Gentlemen." Dex swept the pair a narrow look. "I trust you find your altered prospects satisfactory?"

They hastened to assure him they did, with earnest assurances of loyalty and valor. One was a solid-looking seasoned veteran he liked the look of. The other was younger, skinny and gawky but wiry and quick. Dex would have liked the look of him too.

If not for the irritating expression of moon-faced adoration the lad was sporting and the way he kept stealing smitten glances at Ben.

"Very good, soldiers." Dex worked to keep annoyance from crackling through his words, with mixed results. "Discharge your duties as promised, and you'll not see the inside of my brig again. I've always a place in my army for brave and loyal men."

He pressed his palm to the biometric plate and the newly repaired portal shot open. Dex ushered Ben before him with a proprietary hand at his waist and kept it there, just to make a point. As he strode past the young miscreant who was mooning over Ben, he sliced the kid a scowl that made the youngster pale and lower his eyes in a sign of submission that placated him.

Somewhat.

The door whooshed shut and enclosed them in the starlit twilight of his living room, littered with the shadowy bulk of snoring pirates.

"Are you really going to be this possessive?" Ben murmured, sliding deftly between sleeping men as he angled for the bedroom door.

"I am," Dex said flatly. "Get used to it."

Thankfully, Ben's soft exhale sounded more amused than annoyed.

By the silver glow of the vid screen, Dex was displeased to note this disreputable rabble hadn't even bothered to post a guard. Which comprised a rather staggering lapse in military discipline he hadn't thought Zorin would tolerate.

He eased past the screen, flickering a silent replay of the midnight broadcast. There they stood before the whole galaxy—the Valyrian Precursor and the First Indomitable, the formidable apex of both their races—shoulder to shoulder behind the podium, announcing the penultimate tranche of candidates for Kaia's bed.

*We look good together,* Dex realized with a rush of gratified pleasure. His icy imperial authority, underscored by burnished hair and flashing epaulets, stood in striking contrast to the dark glitter of Ben's barbaric finery and brooding beauty.

*We look right together.*

Theirs would be a union not only of men, but of two warring races. The first Mogadon—Valyrian alliance in galactic history.

His madman of a father must be spinning in his grave.

As they wove between snoring Syndax, Ben led the way, because he'd always been better than Dex at maneuvering in the dark, relying on senses beyond his physical eyes.

When Dex trod on a sleeping Syndax by mistake, evoking a thick mutter and a curse, Ben's slim fingers wound through Dex's to guide him.

There were convicted felons guarding Dex's front door. His living quarters were littered with passed-out pirates. The woman he burned for relentlessly and his boyhood mentor-turned-nemesis were making love like marsh rabbits in his own bed. And half his ship already suspected their First Indomitable fully intended to buck centuries of Mogadon prejudice and his own father's draconian taboo by taking a male consort.

They hadn't yet tumbled to the fact he'd actually be taking *two* of them. Assuming he and Zorin could work things out.

Not that he fancied for a heartbeat Kaia would give them much choice in the matter.

Somehow his previously well-ordered and painfully proper life had devolved into a sloppy, scandalous, unmitigated mess.

But, for nearly the first time he could remember since his introverted, isolated, overachieving childhood, Dex Draven actually felt...

*Happy.*

Before him glowed the crimson square of a biometric panel. The lock to his bedroom door. Dex palmed it open and they both slipped in. A deeper darkness, tinged with starfire, enveloped them.

Along with a potent whiff of Zorin's mating scent that hit him in the chest like a hammer.

A sudden curl of lust coiled hot fingers around his cock. Mingled with a sense of savage possession that was pure animal instinct. Another Mogadon… mating with *his* woman. And in his own infernal bed.

His lips curled back from his teeth. His chest rumbled with an audible snarl.

"Easy," Ben whispered, so soft he barely heard. "It's the four of us now. And half of what he's longing for is you."

Deliberately Dex unknotted his jaw and unclenched his fists.

As his eyes adjusted to the darkness, he discerned the powerful bulk of Zorin's body wrapped in a riotous tangle of sheets and bedding. Kaia's slight frame was lost somewhere in the mound of thermal blankets behind him. The slow rhythmic buzz of breath told him the Syndax was sleeping—and deeply.

Which struck him as a trifle odd.

He'd just invaded the guy's lair. If Dex were an actual intruder, he could pose a threat to Kaia. The Zorin he knew, sleeping or not, would have catapulted out of bed in a heartbeat and had a knife at his throat.

Warily Dex released Ben's hand and approached the bed. Zorin was evidently an unruly sleeper, sprawled facedown with one muscled arm flung overhead, barely a corner of the sheet still wrapped around his sinewed hips—

And all too clearly naked underneath.

His vantage gave Dex a privileged view of the black bird of prey inked across the pirate's mighty shoulders and spread down his powerful back. Another Syndax tribal tattoo wound around bulging biceps. Under a thatch of tousled hair, Zorin's rugged features were furrowed in a sleeping frown.

Familiar enough, even after all these years, to make Dex's chest ache.

The crooked nose he'd broken years ago in a training mishap. The pale scar slashing through one sandy brow he'd picked up at the Battle of Epsilon.

The full-lipped mouth, parted in sleep, that promised such devastating skill when it came to kissing…

Beneath one slitted lid, he glimpsed a glitter of silver.

Ben warned, "Dex, he's not sleeping—"

Before Dex could wrap his head around that discovery, the Syndax exploded into motion. A hand like hot steel clamped around his wrist. One deft twist he never saw coming—and somehow the First Indomitable of the Mogadon Empire found himself lying flat on his back in his own tumbled bed. With two hundredweight-plus of relentlessly naked pirate sprawled solidly on top of him.

Pressed searingly against him from chest to thigh. With Dex's right hand gripping the hot smooth skin of one muscled shoulder. And his left still sitting right where it landed while he'd grappled with Zorin.

Clutching the hard-muscled bulge of the guy's ass.

"Thought you'd never get back," Zorin growled. "I'm losing my ever-loving mind lying naked in your bed."

Dex sucked in a startled breath to say gods knew what. Zorin dove in to silence him with a scorchingly dominant kiss.

Openmouthed and hungry, their lips crashed together, tongue meeting tongue with a desperate heat that left him frankly breathless. The crisp tang of space ale filled his mouth, laced with the sizzle of sex and something far more potent that made his senses spin.

*Something's not right here,* his battle sense whispered. First the passed-out pirates and the lack of a posted guard, then Zorin's uncharacteristically heavy slumber on the Tombola's most dangerous night, and now this odd, almost medicinal aftertaste…

The rigid blade of Zorin's cock, awe-inspiring in its proportions, nudged against his, barely separated by the trousers stretched over his own straining length.

Dex couldn't bite back a low groan.

Long-buried memories exploded through his senses. Incendiary memories of training together, fighting together, serving together. Ignited by the combustible charge of the constant bombardment of wet dreams and erotic fantasies featuring his unattainable hero the young Dex had so ruthlessly suppressed and denied.

A dynamic made all the more combustible by Zorin's unwavering refusal to act on Dex's boyhood infatuation.

But he wasn't a boy anymore.

And Zorin was definitely acting now.

Dex tried to get a breath between these mind-blowing kisses that were making it so infernally difficult to string two thoughts together. But, with every gasp, his head filled with the predatory musk of Zorin's mating scent.

With both of them hard and scenting, it was bloody impossible not to run his hands over all that naked, tattooed real estate. Actually, he *was* running his hands all over it. Gods on the mountain, the guy was massive.

In *every* way—

"You got about two ticks to get out of that uniform, kid," Zorin breathed against his mouth. "Then I'm gonna get you out of it myself. And I'm not gonna play nice with all those shiny buttons. Don't keep me waiting. I've been imagining for years how good your mouth's gonna feel wrapped around my cock."

He gave Dex a little leeway to do what he was told. Which got him his first good look into Zorin's eyes.

Glassy. Dilated. Clouded with whatever the hell he'd been drinking.

*Sol's flaming chariot! He's farking stoned.*

Ben's blade-sharp voice sliced through the entangling web of confusion and lust.

And felled him like an axe.

"Not that I'm opposed to the two of you going at it. But where in the seven *hells* is Kaia?"

Dex twisted free of Zorin and rolled to his feet. With a single violent snap, he flung the bulky coil of blankets to the floor.

The bare mattress stared up at them in silent condemnation.

Dex felt like someone had just poured a bucket of liquid nitrogen down his back. Every nerve and neuron in his body shrilled the alarm.

*Battle stations.*

"Bloody hell, Syndax." He barely recognized his own throaty growl. "Where the devil is our girl?"

"Our girl moseyed out of here clicks ago with *you*, space cadet," Zorin growled right back, nailing Dex with a look that vaporized his blood. "Fact is, you had to carry her, cuz after that high-octane space ale you sent up, she was too bombed to walk. That brew even knocked my boys on their backsides."

Dex's heart thundered with apprehension. "I didn't send up a bloody damn thing—"

"And I was way too out of it myself to go with." Zorin's brow furrowed and he scrubbed a rough hand over his face, plainly fighting to clear his head. "Figured it was okay, cuz she was with you…"

"And the real Dex was with me all night," Ben finished grimly. "Which means Kaia walked out of here with Proteus."

# THE *ASTRAL HEAT* ADVENTURE CONTINUES WITH *ATOMIC ANGEL: AN ASTRAL HEAT ROMANCE #3*

Fully written, edited, and releasing on February 8, 2022

Preorder your copy here:
https://books2read.com/AtomicAngel/

For a sneak peek at the first two chapters available immediately—and to find out how Kaia deals with Proteus!--sign up for my newsletter here.
https://dl.bookfunnel.com/4bvs7j26aq

Want to share your thoughts on *Renegade Angel*? You don't have to write a lot. Even a few words helps! Reviews persuade readers like you to give writers like me a chance. To post a review with your favorite retailer, here are the links:

https://books2read.com/RenegadeAngel

Prefer to review on Goodreads? You can do that in a flash here:
https://bit.ly/2S09H6D

# OTHER STEAMY ROMANCE READS BY LAURA NAVARRE:

**Fantasy Historical Romance: The *Magick* Trilogy**
*Magick by Moonrise*
https://books2read.com/MagickByMoonrise/
*Midsummer Magick*
https://books2read.com/MidsummerMagick
*Mistress by Magick*
https://books2read.com/MistressByMagick/

**Steamy Historical Romance Standalones**
*By Royal Command*
https: //books2read.com/ByRoyalCommand

# ACKNOWLEDGMENTS

They say writing and publishing a book takes a village. When you're a debut reverse harem sci fi romance author with three back-to-back releases, it takes a starbase. I could never have written the *Astral Heat Romance* series without the encouragement and insight of my cosmic mate and hubby Steven—my first writing mentor, alpha reader, business partner, and CEO at Ascendant Press. And I can't rave enough about my editor, Deb Nemeth, who first acquired me for a traditional press way back when I was starting out, and works with me again now. She makes my prose sparkle and my stories sing. Also high on my eternal-gratitude list are my writing guru Angela James, my awesome cover artist Kim Killion, my diligent copy editor Elizabeth Flynn, my miracle-working formatter and uploader and hand-holder Judi Fennell, my friend and indie inspiration Dana Delamar, my marketer Heather Roberts at Elle Woods PR, and every single one of my wonderful ARC reviewers and readers! I appreciate you all to the moon and back.

# ABOUT THE AUTHOR

A long time ago in a galaxy far away, Laura Navarre was an award-winning dark historical romance author for Harlequin, while her diabolical twin Nikki Navarre wrote sexy spy romance. In a daring bid to escape a global pandemic, armed only with an MFA in Writing Popular Fiction, Laura voyaged through a wormhole to an alternate universe where she crafts turbocharged, hyper-sexy reverse harem sci fi romance starring three super-sexy heroes, one seriously kickass heroine and plenty of sleek, sizzling outer space action.

Laura's intergalactic adventures are trackable by humans and aliens alike on social media here:

Facebook: www.facebook.com/LauraNavarreInterstellarRomance
Twitter: www.twitter.com/LauraNavarre
Goodreads: www.goodreads.com/LauraNavarre
TikTok: https://www.tiktok.com/@LauraNavarreAuthor
BookBub: https://www.bookbub.com/authors/Laura-Navarre
Amazon Author Page: https://amzn.to/3AU7Ssk
Website: www.LauraNavarreSciFi.com

www.ingramcontent.com/pod-product-compliance
Lightning Source LLC
Chambersburg PA
CBHW070937190726
48292CB00004B/1224